Patrick McGrath is the author of two short story collections and nine novels, including *Asylum*, the international bestseller; *Trauma* and a ... for the Costa Novel Award; and *Spider*, filmed by David Cronenberg. He lives in Manhattan and London.

Praise for *The Wardrobe Mistress*

'A brilliant evocation of the theatrical world's seedy glamour, *The Wardrobe Mistress* is also a moving portrait of a woman struggling to make sense of her past and imagine a future for herself.'

Sunday Times

'*The Wardrobe Mistress* isn't just an entertaining ghost story, assembled by a master-manipulator to be full of narrative trapdoors, tantalising at one moment and agreeably grotesque the next: it's also an exploration of the deep mythology of theatre.'

Guardian

'[A] terrific tale of intrigue and heartbreak . . . absolutely superb.'

Saga Magazine

'A portrait of a strong woman, written in a distinctive voice.'

Good Housekeeping

ALSO BY PATRICK McGRATH

The Wardrobe Mistress

Mistress

PATRICK McGRATH

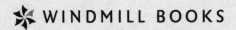

WINDMILL BOOKS

1 3 5 7 9 10 8 6 4 2

Windmill Books
20 Vauxhall Bridge Road
London SW1V 2SA

Windmill Books is part of the Penguin Random House group of companies
whose addresses can be found at global.penguinrandomhouse.com.

Penguin
Random House
UK

First published by Hutchinson in 2017
First published in paperback by Windmill Books in 2018

www.penguin.co.uk

A CIP catalogue record for this book is available from the British Library.

ISBN 9781786090003

Typeset in 12.38/15.86 pt Baskerville MT Std by Jouve (UK), Milton Keynes
Printed and bound in Great Britain by Clays Ltd, Elcograf S.p.A.

MIX
Paper from
responsible sources
FSC
www.fsc.org   FSC® C018179

Penguin Random House is committed to a
sustainable future for our business, our readers
and our planet. This book is made from Forest
Stewardship Council® certified paper.

FOR MARIA

1

THE ACTOR CHARLIE Grice was dead. It was a shock, and that good society, the men and women of the London theatre, had come together for the funeral. It was January 1947 and a bitterly cold day in Golders Green. We gathered in the forecourt, and there were so many of us, once we got into the big chapel, that late-comers had to stand outside. A full house; well, Gricey deserved no less. Although whether he'd have chosen Golders Green, we rather doubt *that*. His daughter Vera was in dark glasses and a black fur coat. Herself an actress, she looked fragile, and clung to her mother's arm throughout. Joan Grice was the mother, also in black and wearing a veil. Not well liked, Joan, but it was hard not to feel sorry for her that day. The marriage had apparently been a good one.

We've heard Joan Grice called a beautiful woman. A striking-looking woman, certainly, and a formidable one.

Her hair was black and without a thread of silver. She wore it pulled back with some severity from her face, the better, it was said, to come at the world like a scythe. As tall as her late husband and a slim woman, her face was pale and sculpted, with the chin carried high, the whole seeming forged from some hard white stone; the effect could be dramatic. But oh dear – we hate to say it – her teeth were horrible! Discoloured, black at the roots and with gaps between. And as is the case with so many of the English, it may have accounted for the sourness of her personality, that is, her profound reluctance to smile. But if her tongue could be vicious her mind was clear, even in drink. And she was one of the best wardrobe mistresses in London.

For herself she liked good black cloth, an old-fashioned cut perhaps set off with a touch of silver at throat or wrist. With a needle she was more adroit than most, when she had to be, and fast too. With a little padding, a trim, a pleat, a pin, a stitch – a scrap of lace – she could turn the most unpromising garment into a thing of elegance and distinction. Under the coat she wore a boxy jacket, broad in the shoulder with a narrow skirt. Legs in sheer silk.

Joan took pride in her work and expected those who worked under her to observe her own high standards. She'd always tried to spare her husband the devastation she could visit on other, lesser mortals, not always successfully. But where their daughter was concerned – that is, when it came to Vera – she was a lion. Most of those present were known to her but there were a few – we

2

knew who they were, oh yes – she'd never seen before, and they weren't theatrical types, but then Gricey had mixed with all sorts, criminals not excepted. Sir John Brogue was there, and in good order, she'd often looked after his costumes, and there was Dame Anna Flitch, all in white, a vague smile on her badly powdered face as she handed out lilies, and where in god's name did she get lilies in this winter of austerity? Ed Colefax was present, and Jimmy Urquhart, looking none the worse for a spell in the nick, her old friends Hattie Waterstone and Delphie Dix – that old hoofer in a wheelchair now – and Rupert, of course, skint, they said, but yes, so many of the old crowd, the ones who'd survived the war – and to think that Gricey missed it. He'd have loved it.

Vera meanwhile was still in her dark glasses, gripping tight her mother's arm as they moved towards the chapel, and it was clear the poor girl was in some distress. So tall and lovely, a more statuesque woman than her mother and yet so delicate today, heartbreaking really, we thought so.

Vera's husband was Julius Glass, the former impresario, a thin, sallow-skinned man some twenty years her senior, and he was on her left flank, and beside him was Gustl Herzfeld, a Jewish refugee he'd apparently saved from the Nazis, and a most interesting creature. She'd told Hattie she was Julius' sister but we had our doubts. It seemed improbable, frankly. Julius meanwhile was sombre and watchful and loomed close over his women like a kind of yellow marsh heron. How Joan felt about *him* that day was anybody's guess, but we'd heard talk that

3

Julius and Gricey were not on the best of terms – put it mildly – and it was even said that Julius was there, on the steps, when he fell.

But this was the family, and together they were ushered to the front of the chapel and there took their pew. Joan could hear from behind her a murmur of chatter, and now and then some laughter. We'd all loved Gricey; some of us had, anyway. Then came the coffin. Oh, the hardest moment of all, surely. It entered stage left with six strong men carrying it. One convulsive sob from Vera, and Julius slid an arm around her. Joan thought she'd shake him off but instead she leaned into him as though she might otherwise crumple legless to the cold stone floor, poor girl. And cold it was in there all right, bloody freezing, we saw the speakers' breath turn to smoke in the chill damp of that packed and steamy chapel. Snow was forecast for later in the day. We're in for it, we thought, another foul bloody winter.

Then up they came to the podium to talk about the man. There were anecdotes. His war work as a special constable in the West End. The stories he'd told. He'd been there after that dreadful bomb came down the ventilation shaft of the Café de Paris, no laughing matter. It blew Snakehips Johnson to pieces. A hundred and eighty-six people died in London that night. Acts of kindness were remembered, support he'd given to others both moral and monetary at times of crisis or loss. *Monetary,* thought Joan, and where did that come from? There'd never been that much to spare.

Waves of sympathy flowed from the back of the chapel

to those who'd been closest to him, she could feel it now, and much of it was for Vera, whose own story was familiar to this company. Such promise, a luminous stage presence; everyone said so. Absolutely distraught. She'd been very close to her father, of course. Everything she knew she'd learned from him, and just look at her now. Shattered.

When the service was over we watched old Gricey going out the back way, through the curtains, in his coffin – *in his coffin! – and how are we supposed to live without him now?* must have been their common thought, mother and daughter – then the danger of collapse was most real. But upright they stood, Vera's dark glasses having come off, damp red eyes revealed in the wan, tragic face, lovely even in grief. Her arm was in her mother's now as slowly they moved down the aisle, and not a dry eye in the house, every one of them fixed on these two tall, slow women in black, the mother upright and slender, the daughter swaying ever so slightly, seeming almost to totter in her sorrow. Like royalty they turned this way and that, nodding, offering the pressed-lip stoic half-smile to faces both sympathetic and tearful, but above all familiar from a thousand dressing rooms and curtain calls, opening-night parties and chilly rehearsals in cold church halls with frost on the windows. This was our world. We were saying goodbye to one of our own.

Then we were milling about in the courtyard again. Julius had offered his house for the wake, even laid on transport for those who had none. Joan wasn't too happy about it, that was clear, but she didn't have the energy to

5

protest, poor thing. It's a long way to Tipperary and it's even longer from Golders Green to Pimlico but off we went, dozens of us, and when the family joined us later, after seeing Gricey laid to rest, or his ashes anyway, the party was going strong.

> *Under the wide and starry sky,*
> *Dig the grave and let me lie.*

Actors are like priests, or perhaps undertakers, we've heard it said, for we live with death in a rather intimate kind of a way. We've all died a thousand deaths on a public stage and we don't take it lightly. We don't take it too seriously either. What we do take seriously is the suffering of the bereaved, and we'd turned out en masse for old Gricey, and when Joan and Vera entered Julius' house it was packed, people in every room – in the backyard even, despite the cold and despite the long journey, but Vera had insisted. She wanted her dad's wake in her husband's house, as she'd wanted him cremated in Golders Green, and who could deny her? She had her reasons, and her mother knew better than to argue with her when Vera's mind was made up. Even if it did mean having the wake in *that man's* house.

It was just as the front door closed behind them, and the great wave of voices was upon them and they had to go forward and be part of it all, in fact play leading roles, that Joan first heard it – quiet, amused, oh, *unmistakably* him – her husband's voice.

– *Now just pull yourself together, dear. You're on.*

*

6

When she reached the kitchen she was given a large gin but she was bewildered, almost undone at hearing Gricey's voice, and she wanted more. She wanted to hear him again, what she actually wanted was *conversation*, so she left the kitchen and went upstairs to Julius and Vera's bedroom. She sat on the bed but there was nothing. Silence. She pleaded with him to speak again. She heard the cries and laughter of the several dozen people gathered below, but no Gricey. For the first time since his death she felt herself starting to crack, like a dead twig in winter, she told us later. She was weeping now, in frustration as much as sorrow. She didn't notice she was shivering until the door started slowly to open. She turned, frozen – rooted to the bed – expecting she knew not what – then a head came round the door. It was Vera.

– Here you are. Oh god, Mum, you're freezing.

A sorry sight she made, she supposed, shivering and weeping on the bed, and she hated Vera seeing her like this. Vera in fact had very rarely seen her mother cry before, and she watched her now with some curiosity. She sat on the bed beside her and gently put her arms around her. Joan told her what had happened, hearing Gricey's voice, and Vera didn't say she'd heard him too, for she hadn't. She just held her mother, murmuring words of comfort. Then she said they should go down to the party, and this Joan hadn't expected, Vera having earlier given her to understand that a party was the last thing she needed but it *was* her father's wake, after all. She now told her mother she had to get back in the swim. Or as Gricey would have said – as he *did* say – *just pull yourself together, dear. You're on.*

7

So they went downstairs, where in the kitchen some old girl told Joan that she knew how she felt because she'd lost her husband too.

– When? said Joan.

– Seventeen years, love, this last Christmas.

– I'll never last that long, said Joan. Then she asked the woman if she missed him still.

– Yes, dear, oh I do.

Drawing close she said: I haven't told him he can go yet.

She clutched Joan's elbow, all talcum powder and cackle and mothballs and gin, and said she hadn't finished with him.

Joan thought, *finished* with him? There'd be no finishing for her either, not until she too was dead and the pair of them, she and Gricey, just dots of light in the minds of whoever remembered them. Yes, and then fading with each passing year until they grew so dim as to be practically invisible, and then blinked out. There'd be nothing left of them after that, she thought, just darkness. That's *finishing*, she thought.

Yes, January it was, 17 January 1947. Coldest day of the year so far. Never forget it, well how could you?

> *Glad did I live, and gladly die,*
> *And I laid me down with a will.*

Later that night, as the snow started to come down, she sat at the kitchen table in the flat in Archibald Street where they'd lived for almost thirty years. Mile End. Just up from the cemetery and St Clement's. Her head was in her hands and there was a nauseous feeling in the pit of her stomach. Grief comes in waves, this she was learning and it also happens in stages. She was at last starting to make an account of what had happened and it was hard not to place blame. Of course it was her fault, she was quite well aware of *that*, she should have been able to save him, although Christ alone knows, she thought, he was a diffi-cult man at the best of times and these days, unless he ran them every morning he had trouble remembering his lines. He was at the Irving Theatre in St Martin's giving his Malvolio at the time and yes, he'd been drinking, he was angry, and this she knew for a fact, that it would never have happened if he hadn't been in a rage with Julius Glass, though what was said between the two men she had no way of knowing other than that it probably concerned Vera and, given what she knew about Julius, anyone would have got furious with him, stormed out the back door, oh dear – poor Joan – and fallen down the steps—

A week later she felt no better. Worse, in fact. Things hadn't been so good between them for a while, well, years, if she were honest, but it made no difference to what she felt. She'd given her heart to that man, if he'd drifted away from her, she thought, that's just what men did. He still came home to her every night. Now she was convinced he hadn't died at all. No, he'd been *buried alive*. She'd let them *bury him alive*. Actually she'd had him cremated, but of course she wasn't thinking straight. Again it was late, again she couldn't sleep, and she'd gone into the kitchen to get a splash more gin. They were two parts of a whole, she thought, she and Gricey, indivisible. Or no, *inseparable,* even when apart. Even when he was in an out-of-town production they were inseparable; in spirit. And they were inseparable still. It was an idea she tried not to dwell upon but at times it arose with such clamour that against her will she was forced to attend to it. It had happened once already while she was coming home on her bicycle. A sudden cry in the darkness that seemed to leap from her throat like a fish, and of course it was for Gricey, who was *dead,* or so they claimed, who had left her to deal with it all, life ongoing, their daughter's troubles, everything. They'd cremated him, she'd started to grieve, and now for what seemed the first time she was yet again faced not only with his absence, and a silence that once had been filled by that incomparable man, oh yes, tender, funny, faithful, in his way – he was an *actor,* dear, she'd had no illusions on that score – but loyal to a fault – was there no end to the qualities she discovered in him now he was dead? What'd it matter if he was short with her at times, if he had a temper, if he waxed hot then cold – he was the man she'd lived with for twenty-seven years, and herself not the easiest of women. And it wasn't even just himself she missed. It was his sure, clear instinct as to what needed saying to Vera, how seriously her crises were to be taken; above all, how to bring the girl down when she started to climb the walls, which seemed to be happening more frequently these days, these bleak, desolate days of cold and want and loss—

No, Joan's problem was, he wasn't there to advise her, and she was angry about it, and frightened too. So when was he coming home? *When?*

She'd got back to the flat exhausted, fed the cat and poured herself a nice drink. She'd gone into his room, where he kept his clothes in the wardrobe, and he'd sometimes slept there – often he'd slept there, if she were honest – and she stood at the window and looked down at the street. Lamp post, railings, cobblestones, the cemetery walls down the way, and it was snowing again. She sat on his bed for a while. She finished her drink and decided she'd have another. Why not? On her way back to the kitchen she realised there were tears streaming down her face. All she wanted was to hear his bloody voice again.

When she awoke the next morning she was at once aware of the two large gins she'd had before bed. In the old days they'd have a cocktail, sometimes they'd go down the pub, or up west when they were flush. Drinking alone had always seemed a pitiful business to Joan, for it smacked of despair. Who you going to talk to, yourself? Those first days she was tempted to drink herself into a stupor every night, but that way madness lay, or if not madness then a kind of *dissipated languor* that would soon sap the light from her eye and the fire from her brain, and then where would she be? Not running the wardrobe of the Beaumont Theatre, that's where. And that job, it was her task in life. Give that up, you might just as well turn your face to the wall.

But she'd made an exception last night and now she regretted it. She knew exactly what had happened. It was being in his room. She'd made a fatal error. She'd gone into his wardrobe.

Yes, we know. Ridiculous. Most unwise. Move along, dearie, how mawkish can an old girl get? She hadn't told Vera, she could imagine what she'd say. She'd told herself she'd get rid of them but it was almost two weeks now and they were all still there, all his suits, shirts, shoes, underwear, everything. So much he had, even despite the years of austerity, the rationing of cloth. What was so very, *very* destructive was that she could still raise a faint residue of the man if she pressed her nose to a collar or a cuff and it always finished her off. That hair oil – why such almost *imperceptible* traces of a stale fragrance should summon the essence of a man whose earthly remains had now apparently been reduced to a small heap of ashes and put in a pot she kept under her bed, this she didn't understand. But all it took was a large gin or sometimes two and she was at them again, oh yes, and oh, she *hauled* them out, she laid them out as though she were his valet, or his dresser, spread them across the bed all the while in her mind's eye admiring him as they went out the front door together, or even as he emerged from this same room to ask her if he looked all right. For he was a dandy, old Gricey, he liked a sharp crease and a clean line, he was a Tottenham boy of course but he did enjoy carrying himself like a gent – a proper man of the theatre – and in another second she was on top of them on the bed with the fabric clutched in her fists and her nose buried deep in collars and cuffs, in armpits, in crotches—

Funny, isn't it, we said, how it's so often the strong women who give themselves to these tricky men who don't really seem worth the trouble?

She sat at the kitchen table in her overcoat and cut half a banana into small slices (it wasn't often you got a banana) and drank her tea. She'd have the other half later. A grey, windy day, very cold already. In five minutes she'd go in and put them back on their hangers, tidy the place up. Like looking in on the scene of an orgy the morning after. The hint of dawn in the sky when the revels have come to an end and the revellers all gone home. That's depravity, she thought. That's excess. They wanted her to come to some kind of a benefit performance at the Irving, for Gricey, see his *Twelfth Night* again. No, she wouldn't be doing that. She wasn't up to that.

But she did have to go to work. We see her now as we often did that winter, all in black, coat, gloves, hat, stockings, on her high black ladies' model Raleigh with a basket fastened to the handlebars and a silver bell, and a reflector on the back mudguard, the lower part of which was painted white. She rode in stately fashion with her back very straight and her eyes on the road ahead. Mile End, Whitechapel, Aldgate, then the City, Holborn to Shaftesbury Avenue then the freewheel down to Piccadilly Circus and a little sweep round the corner to the Beaumont. Her hand signals were meticulous in their precision, the propriety of her dismount a joy to behold.

– Morning, Mrs Grice, murmured one or two tired voices when she walked into the costume shop, the steam irons hissing, sewing machines whirring away. *Whirr–pause–whirr–pause,* they went. *Thunk-a-thunk-a-thunk.* The windows were steamed up but they only looked out on a wall, here in the basement at the very bottom of the building. The dawn chorus, she called it. Why was it always so gloomy in here? She'd asked for brighter bulbs, but no, even light was rationed in this dark new world, and sometimes they hardly had any light at all, no wonder they were all going blind, bent over their Singers, hands, eyes, shoulders knackered by the end of the day.

– Morning, ladies. Esther, you finished Miss Conville's bodice yet?

They were getting ready for a show. *Heartbreak House.* Lots of corsets and gowns. Steel bones and horsehair, tricky work. Tweed suits, merchant seaman's kit, and one man in full Arab. And the wigs! But she ran a good shop, best in London, some said.

– Almost there, Mrs Grice.

– Hurry it up, dear, I shall be wanting you on the trousers. Eunice?

– Yes, Mrs Grice.

– That a scrap of *fabric* I see on the floor?

– Oops, sorry, Mrs Grice.

– Death fabric, that is. Slip on that, bang your head, curtains.

– Yes, Mrs Grice.

She had a little alcove from which she could keep an eye on things. She'd sit at her desk and get her spectacles out of their case to look at the budgets and what-have-you. But today she removes her spectacles almost at once, and instead gazes out across the busy room. She barely sees the toiling women, the heaps of muslin, the shelves spilling out their grommets and needles and buttons and zips,

14

the steam presses, the long table where her draper cuts the patterns. And there's Esther, foolish young Esther, a clutch of pins between her teeth as she flattens a length of thin black silk on a table, folding it down one side to make a hem then rapidly pinning it. Oh, and Joan sees herself all those years ago at the Watford Palace when she was Esther's age, working for a wardrobe mistress no less exacting than she is now, and as she hemmed and sewed her mind was elsewhere, as Esther's is now, yes, for that night, that distant night, she was meeting Gricey Grice, who was playing the lead in the new touring show just come in and he was taking her out for a drink after.

Yes, and later, in the men's stockroom, in amongst the military uniforms, against the wall, in the dark, the smell of stale sweat and old wool serge strong in their nostrils, and him still with his slap on, she was in his arms, one leg up, clinging to him tight, kissing him with her mouth open and her tongue out and her fingers in his thick wavy chestnut hair all clogged with oil, the pair of them panting, gasping, loudly striving for a more perfect union—

Dear god it was good then to be alive, and heaven itself – how did it go? Heaven itself a quick shag in the men's stockroom.

– Where you want these, missus?

A youth in shirtsleeves and braces stood in the doorway clutching an armful of trousers. The older women in the room paid no attention but the girls flicked their eyes at him, exchanged glances, and him trying not to grin.

– Those my trousers? Hang them up over there, Jimmy. Esther, get them sorted, will you, dear, soon as you've finished you and Eunice can start with the fittings. We've got Mangan at twelve and then the Captain. Thank you, Jimmy, you can go now.

– Yes, Mrs Grice.

– Jimmy. You can go now.

Jimmy left. A bit later, as the girls laid out the trousers fetched in from the stockroom, Joan's mind was again elsewhere. But this time she wasn't thinking about hot nights in Watford with Gricey, but about that last conversation with Julius, about what was said between the two men before he fell down the back steps into the yard. She wasn't a woman comfortable with vagueness and imprecision, Joan. She was never one to be satisfied with the *misty outline* of a thing. It mattered, for it was at her insistence that he'd gone to talk to the bloody man in the first place.

She'd been round there a few days before, in fact, having a cup of tea with Vera in the kitchen when in he came.

– Ah, Joan. Joan, he said, taking his gloves off, and then his wire-framed spectacles, so as to polish them. How are you, my dear?

– Getting by, said Joan.

No smile, of course. It was only Gricey ever got her smile. The teeth, of course. But how calm he was, she thought, how composed, how bloody regal, as he settled at his kitchen table, with his heavy-lidded eyes and his long yellow hands, as though he were a gentleman butcher, or the son of one. Butchers were important men in London then what with the meat ration. Here's a man

16

might sell you a nice bit of tenderloin out the back of the shop if you treated him right, she thought. He'd produced instead what he called a nice drop of claret from under the sink and offered the women a glass. Where'd he get that then? On the fiddle. On the black. He'd crossed his legs and allowed one beige suede slipper to dangle from a silk-socked foot. The trouser leg had risen above the sock to reveal a hairless white calf. Vera once told her mother that Julius had three nipples, he'd shown them to her the night of the *Doll's House* party. Joan had noticed something else that was strange about this awful man her daughter had married. At times in the late afternoon that winter, with the fading of the day, a faint shimmer of sunlight would seem to gather around his pale blond head. It created a halo, of sorts. As though he wore a crown of light.

But a bloody halo, thought Joan, when the last of the sun came drifting through the kitchen window of the house in Pimlico, the three of them drinking claret, talking for all the world as though nothing had happened, nothing had changed, Gricey was just – elsewhere. Later, when Joan was leaving, Vera reminded her she wanted to see the play again. Joan was reluctant, to say the least of it, but Vera wanted her to come. And what Vera wanted, Vera generally got.

– Esther! Pay attention to what you're doing, please.

– Yes, Mrs Grice.

Joan was standing in the door of her office, face white as chalk and her eyes like hot coals, red at the rims.

– I don't know where they find you girls these days. Where do they find you, Esther?

– Don't know, I'm sure, Mrs Grice.

– Don't know much, do you, child?

Esther flushed puce, poor thing, and stared at her fingers as she fed thin silk under a flickering needle. Joan went back to her desk, thinking, how am I to find out what he said, the cunt? And poor Gricey – to die in a rage. What kind of a way to go is that? She'd go round and see him again, that Julius Glass, break his bloody windows for him.

2

IT HAD BEEN a bad year anyway. Oh, an awful year, even if it was barely three weeks old. Still not enough to eat, and last summer, that was 1946, of course, the year of the big march, they'd put bread on the ration, and the war already over! Magnificent in victory, oh yes – and bankrupt. Morally magnificent and economically broke. Exhausted. Oh, England. Smog, ruins, drab clothes, bad food, bomb craters and rats. There was work to be had – in demolition. Someone said, some writer whose name we can never remember, that England was made of coal and surrounded by fish so why were we always so cold and hungry? And it's not to mention the electric going off all the time so the blackouts were worse than in the Blitzkrieg, though at least you didn't smell gas in the streets like after a bomb when it came up from the broken pipes. No more bloody bombs anyway. But after all that, oh, the endless sacrifices and all the rest – were we rid of the fascists?

We were not. Oh no. The Blackshirts that got banged up during the war under Regulation 18b – sympathy for enemy powers – they were back out on the streets. Joan used to see them on her way home and was glad her parents weren't alive to witness it. They marched through the East End three abreast, they held public meetings, they papered walls with swastikas, spewing hatred like they'd never been gone, like there hadn't even *been* a war, *which they'd lost.* Of course there was trouble. Fights broke out and people got hurt, hardly surprising. No, these were *active fascists*, selling their newspapers outside Tube stations, and of course it was worst in the East End, that's where the Jews lived, Joan being one of them, her father a tailor who'd settled in London end of the last century, from eastern Europe, and raised his family in Stepney. Poverty, overcrowding, violence and political dissent, this is what we knew Stepney for, and Jews. And that's where the fascists held their meetings. All over the East End in fact, men on platforms with bullhorns shouting for the expulsion of what they now had to call 'aliens'. Telling us Hitler didn't go far enough, didn't finish the job. If you can believe it. In 1946.

The Sunday previous Joan had once again summoned her resolve and gone to see Julius but he was out with Gustl Herzfeld, or *Auntie* Gustl as some of us knew her, lord knows why. Julius' house was a thin one with pointed gables and trees in front, late Victorian, built of yellow London brick stained black with coal dust. It was just a few steps from Sutherland Terrace, or what was left of it.

It was on the corner of a short block of mews houses, Lupus Mews that was, not far from the Victoria railway yards. But Vera was home, and when they were settled in the kitchen Joan asked her how she was getting on, and that's when Vera told her she'd moved up to the attic.

– No!

– Oh yes.

They were in the kitchen having a cup of tea, it was the warmest room, of course. Like so many London houses near where the bombs once fell it couldn't be kept clean, for the soot would pour down the chimney and the carpets weren't bright and the brasses didn't shine, and it was dark, so many boards in the windows where the panes were smashed. And draughty. Joan kept her coat on but Vera seemed not to notice the cold. She was in a black sweater that nicely showed off her bosom, and what with her milky skin and long black shiny hair, which she usually wore up, she was turning into really a very lovely young woman, more so every day, that's what her mother thought, apart from the rings under her eyes. Nice teeth too, unlike some. But yes, she'd moved out of the marital bedroom, and a bit soon for that, thought Joan, though she didn't say it, of course. Vera nodded, rueful, amused. There was a bathroom up there with a bathtub and a toilet, what else did a girl need?

– You need a proper husband, that's what you need, said Joan.

Vera looked at her teacup and said quietly that Julius thought she might be having a relapse.

– You think I am?

21

– No, dear, you've lost your father, that's all. And you need a job. What you up for?

– Not much out there, Mum.

– Not what I heard.

She was highly strung, Vera herself admitted that much. There'd been that touch of hysteria a couple of years ago but she'd been fine for a while now, until she lost her father. Joan felt badly about it. She knew it was all her fault because when Julius phoned her, and told her Gricey had had a heart attack and was in an ambulance on his way to Edward VII, she told him she didn't want Vera at the hospital, she couldn't cope with her and Gricey too. So when Vera came home and he told her that her father had had a heart attack and was in Edward VII, of course she wanted to go to him at once. That's when Julius locked the front door and pleaded with her not to go. So she tried to climb out the window and he stopped her, and that's when she lost her temper and threw a glass at him and only just missed his head. Joan thought, I should have taught her to throw straight.

Julius was still worried about her, Vera then said, staring at her hands, turning her fingers over to examine her nails, which she'd painted scarlet. Joan said nothing, but oh, this gifted girl of mine, she thought, up in the *attic*? What would Gricey have said about that? So she offered her the empty room in the flat, the one that used to be her father's. She felt she had to.

– No, I can't, said Vera.

– I don't see why not, love.

– I just can't. It's Daddy's room. Anyway—

– Anyway what?

– I want to live in this house.

That was all she'd say. What sense was her mother to make of it? Presumably she wanted to be near Julius because she loved him. But didn't she see it as a humiliation?

– Mum, you must understand, she said. He's my husband.

– Yes, said Joan, I suppose he is *that*.

– Anyway I want to sleep in the attic.

Just like your dad, Joan thought, rather sleep alone. She was actually relieved. Better this way, she thought. She needed to be by herself in the flat for when he came home.

After they'd had a cup of tea Vera took her mother upstairs and showed her the room. You could hear the trains late at night, she said, the clanking and shunting as the railwaymen uncoupled the wagons. Intimacy could be suffocating, Joan thought, when what a woman wanted was distance from a husband, specially a husband like bloody Julius Glass. There'd never been an intimacy problem for her and Gricey, she then thought, whatever the sleeping arrangements. Oh no, nothing like that.

But upstairs in that tall, thin, ugly yellow house, down the end of a gloomy mews, in an attic, that's where my daughter wants to live now? This was her thought. There was an old bathroom up there, with an ancient lavatory with a wooden seat, a deafening flush, wake the house, it would – poor Auntie Gustl – and a bathtub with claw

23

feet and a plughole, the porcelain surround stained ochre. That's where she washed her smalls now. The water came out rusty from the tap and lukewarm at best for the boiler was in the cellar, a very long way down, and who had the coal for a good hot bath these days? It was a small bathtub and Vera was a big girl. She told her mother it was like getting into a child's coffin.

– Don't say *that*, love.

The last coffin Joan had seen was Gricey's, of course. Vera laid a hand on her arm and said, Mum, don't be silly.

– But where do you hang your frocks?

– In here.

There was a door between the beams and when Joan opened it there was only darkness. Vera switched the light on, a single dim bulb hanging off a rafter. It was not much help. This was the attic proper, a narrow slanting space that ran the length of the house under the eaves. Joan stepped in, sniffing, her head bowed. In the gloom she saw piled up cabin trunks and suitcases with shipping labels, and cobwebs glistening in whatever wintry light got in through the dormers, and everywhere dust. There was also a stack of paintings in the back there, stretchered and with a sheet thrown over them. These would be Gustl's, self-portraits mostly. It wasn't insulated and the air was chill and a little bad; dead rat somewhere. From nails in the rafters between the roof beams Vera's frocks rustled slightly on their wooden hangers. Joan was horrified. Had she learned nothing?

– What about the moths, dear? And the damp? There'll be mould before you know it. And sunlight, oh it'll bleach the colour out of these things in no time. Oh dear no, you can't ruin them like this.

– Not much sunlight these days, Mum.

– I'll have to get you some muslin bags. Oh dear.

She was genuinely distressed. But the point was, Vera chose to stay in her husband's house even though she now apparently preferred to live in the attic like a servant and put her entire wardrobe at risk. And he allowed it. He must have thought she was mad, this was Joan's conclusion, that's why he let her go up there, that's where you put the madwomen. But oh, no, not mad, let her not be mad, she thought, sweet heaven, poor Vera—

But confused, yes, divided, uncertain who she was when she wasn't onstage, and of course it had all come to a crisis when her father lay dying and Julius tried to stop her going to the hospital. And that, thought Joan, was entirely my doing, selfish bloody woman I am.

3

W HEN SHE GOT home she didn't have another drink, nor did she go to bed. Instead she started in on a piece of work she'd been meaning to finish for weeks now. She wanted to make some alterations to Gricey's coat. The fit of it displeased her. She'd bought it in the Ridley Street market for next to nothing, first year of the war. It had fitted him nice and snug but she didn't like that it was too big for her, not the length of it but in the chest and shoulders. She felt he was close to her, and she could smell him in the lining. But she wanted to wear it as though it were her own, so nobody would guess how close to her he really was.

Poor Joan. Because as she sewed and picked and bit off the thread with her teeth, her eyes lifted and she wondered if he was angry with her that she'd allowed all this to happen. His death. She was tormented by the thought. But what could she have done? She wasn't there! Oh but she worried at it often, and made endless reconstructions of the events that led up to the – what? – the *tragedy*, if that's what it was, although she was starting to think it was something other than that, for *tragedy*, the idea of *tragedy*, as she understood it, lacked an element of *agency* – tragedy *happened*, it wasn't done to you, was it? – unless by fate, or destiny – and it was *agency* that she now glimpsed in the slowly clarifying outline of the thing.

She remembered a day in December, just a few weeks before, and the weather already very cold. There was an area of high pressure somewhere over Archangel, moving across Scandinavia – so we heard on the wireless – heading for England and sucking Siberian air in with it as it came. Londoners could talk of little else. In fact we could talk of much else, but we started with the weather – it broke the ice. That was the joke going round. Because that's all we did that winter, break the ice. Or slip on the ice, break an arm or a leg, and put up with the blackouts and the slow trams, the bad coal, and an east wind that blew nonstop for a month. Worst weather in living memory.

Joan remembered a tall and rather stylish couple, the man in his sixties in a black coat with leather at the cuffs and lapels, and fur on the collar, the woman some years younger and more soberly dressed – it was them, of course, Mr and Mrs Charlie Grice, walking down the Charing Cross Road one cold grey Saturday afternoon. How handsome, how smart they were! As they turned along the Strand Joan murmured, as though talking to herself – it's a thing that happens to long-married couples, speaking without preamble, on the assumption that the other has followed their train of thought – that Vera might be having a bit of trouble with her nerves again.

– Yes, Gricey said.

He too had been far away. Joan turned to him as though awoken from her own distant reverie of their daughter.

– You think so?

– I'm worried about her.

– You're always worried about her.

– It's different this time.

– I wish you'd say something.

This is how she wanted to remember it. But she knew this wasn't what she'd said, that her tone had been harsher by far, for she could be a sharp-tongued woman. For Christ's sake, Gricey, what's the matter with you? Just *tell him*! Or do I have to do it for you?

They'd walked on in silence. Now she thought, if only I could say to him I never meant to be so cold. She'd slipped her arm in his. But it was a concern they'd expressed to each other for years, that they were worried about Vera, although this time it *was* different because so much more was at stake, because she was doing so well. It was in her bones, of course, acting, but where did her bones come from? From them, from what they'd given her, the exposure she'd had all her life to actors, to theatres and to costumes, and Gricey had encouraged her, they both had. And then the inculcation of taste, without which of course there's nothing.

How the mind will drift. Thinking about Vera got her thinking about Julius Glass, and she remembered the night Vera opened in *A Doll's House*. The reviews were excellent, really. The best of her generation, one of them said. A luminous stage presence. Then for a while it seemed there'd been nothing she couldn't do. She played Nina in *The Seagull*. People were hungry for theatre during the war, well, it raised morale. The theatres were only dark for a few weeks, that's when it properly started, the Blitz, late 1940, then they were up again, first show at lunchtime, the second at five so they could let out before dark when the bombers came back. Entire audience in uniform. What's it look like out there? an actor might ask the stage manager, and *khaki* came the answer. Sea of khaki.

Julius was the man who'd lost Swinburne's. The building across the street got flattened by a big one and his place was hit by the blast. He was no less shattered than his theatre, poor man. Always he'd kept his seats cheap, and there was no white tie or low-backed evening gowns at Swinburne's, it was the people's theatre. He put on Shakespeare, Sheridan, the Jacobeans, the Restoration comedies. Good actors came so they could play the classic roles. It wasn't the Old Vic, but it was in the tradition. And then in the space of one night it was gone. He'd never forget what it looked like. Ground-floor façade more or less intact but nothing above it except bits of walls and charred rafters. What was left of the stage was covered with broken scenery and blackened wreckage fallen from above. He remembered, too, finding a fluttering envelope, and on the back of it, in pencil, in block capitals: MAD TOM, NEW PANTS FOR THE FIGHT. GLOUCESTER BOOTS NOT COMFY. And he thought, Mad Tom and Gloucester would never tread these boards again. A month later he went to the opening of *A Doll's House* and met Vera Grice. It was the worst month of his life, but then – suddenly – from out of nowhere, so it seemed – here was this glorious girl, and life was not over yet.

Joan said, although not in her daughter's hearing, that it wouldn't be the first time a man fell in love with an actress from a good seat in the stalls, or from a cheap seat in the gods, for that matter. She was with a few of our friends, Hattie and Delphie, one or two others, in the snug parlour of a pub in Greek Street. She didn't trust it, she said. She didn't trust *him*. He gave Vera expensive gifts, she said, for he'd been in the money before the Luftwaffe put him out of business, and he always seemed to have enough still. Of course he invested shrewdly in other men's plays. And he did like to see Vera wearing the clothes he bought her, the fancy frocks and such.

Once when the four of them were out together – and this was long before things soured between the two men – Joan remarked on what Vera was wearing. It was a black cocktail dress with a tight bodice that lifted her bosom, made a lovely cleavage, then blossomed from the waist like a parachute. They were in the Ladies, mother and daughter, powdering their noses. It seems Julius had already proposed marriage but Vera was taking her sweet time deciding. He was a lot older than her, of course. Some of us thought that a good thing.

– I *hate* it, said Vera, leaning into the mirror over the

sink to do her lipstick. I'm bound to spill something down it and Christ alone knows what he paid for it.

– Arm and a bloody leg, you ask me, said Joan. Unless he got it on the fiddle. Or in *Paris*.

That was a laugh. Paris was full of Nazis.

– Which he undoubtedly did.

– Which he undoubtedly did.

Because it was whispered that Julius had been over there more than once. *On government business*, it was darkly hinted. And that from one of these trips he'd returned with Gustl Herzfeld: snatched from under the noses of the Gestapo, we heard.

Joan was reminded of this as she sat on a chair by the door of the Ladies and watched her daughter gaze at herself in the mirror, frowning, pushing her tits about.

– I'll give it away. I'll let some fucking charity have it.

That was Vera. Then several women came in and Joan and Vera left, and were shortly back at their table where they couldn't pursue the conversation. Later Julius told them about a party they'd attended, and how Vera, wearing that same frock, was applauded when they walked through the door.

– Why were you applauded, love? said Joan.

– Oh, who knows. It was ridiculous.

Fame, how very tiresome it was. Joan glanced at Gricey, who mildly snorted. Julius threw up his yellow hands.

– Because she's a star! he cried.

The Irving Theatre was under the management of Edwin Herbert, a corpulent man. The building had suffered a

31

bit of bomb damage but it stayed open all through the war, with the posters out front proudly proclaiming the fact: OPEN FOR BUSINESS STILL! The foyer was given over to the selling of tickets and packets of potato crisps, but it wasn't the point. Nor was the point of the Irving the auditorium. It was shabby. Worse than shabby, it was a risk to public safety. The seating was rickety, the arms broken, unloosed springs, ragged upholstery, and the curtain sagged. But Edwin Herbert said the curtain was not the point either. It was what was behind the curtain that mattered. Usually it was Shakespeare.

To Joan's dismay everyone who'd been at Gricey's funeral seemed to be there for the memorial perform-ance. The old friends were out in force, Hattie, Delphie, Rupert and Co., old Mabel Hatch was there, and the Chorus, of course, our own good selves. No sign of the grandees but enough citizens of the London Theatre to make it a family sort of affair, and Joan was glad now that she had Vera with her, although less glad of Julius. Auntie Gustl had come in a floor-length green velvet frock with a parrot on the front. There was some milling about in the foyer but nothing to drink, only crisps. Joan was in black but Vera was wearing a cream blouse under her burgundy jacket, and black slacks, and her hair was washed and set. She was heavily made up, and Joan understood why: weeping. She was relieved to get into her seat. Then the lights went down.

It happened almost at once, his first entrance. Act I, scene v. What's happened so far? Duke Orsino, played by Ed Colefax, an old friend of Gricey's, opens with the

32

music-food-of-love speech – such cadences! – and how deftly he avoided the various acoustic dead spots in Edwin Herbert's notorious auditorium – *That strain again, it had a dying fall . . . Enough, no more/'Tis not so sweet now as it was before.*

No, thought Joan, it certainly bloody is not so sweet now as it was before. In a state of angry misery she dug herself deeper into her raddled seat in the balcony stalls, front row centre, with Vera beside her, as on came the shipwrecked sailors and the lovely Viola, and rapidly the plot was laid out before us. There's a beautiful widow living nearby, one Olivia, and oh, irony, thinks Joan, who has never considered for a second that she'd be in the same boat as Olivia, although without the wealth, of course, or the youth. A few short scenes later we meet the lady in question, along with her steward, Malvolio. Himself. Gricey's part, but now played by an actor who had previously been a lord with two lines, but had taken the trouble to learn the part of Malvolio and let this be known the day Gricey died. He'd gone on that night. His name was Daniel Francis. He'd been playing Malvolio ever since.

Attending upon the lovely Olivia (the leggy Miriam Atkins, poorly cast, thought Joan), the new Malvolio stepped onto the stage with the same curiously delicate footstep Gricey had invented, spoke his first lines – *Infirmity, that decays the wise, doth ever make the better fool* – and got Gricey's laugh! Vera sat up, frowning, evidently disturbed. He was as tall as her father, this one, although much younger, but he lifted his shaggy head, extended a languid arm, inflected the line *exactly the same*. So yes, Vera was disturbed. But Joan, no, Joan wasn't disturbed: the reverse. She was leaning forward barely able to believe it. For it was her Gricey, somehow made – visible – as Malvolio. For she could see him! Gricey was there, he was in there! He was in there *behind the eyes*.

She gazed at the stage below, saw the back canvas flapping a bit when anyone entered downstage left, and there, strutting about was this Malvolio, with his Olivia, and Joan was rapt with astonishment. She didn't want to believe what she was seeing; and then she did. Then she was drinking him up, but because Vera was distressed she kept it to herself. Not easy, when what she really wanted was to clap her hands over her head and do a little dance, shouting out her joy. Could it be? *Was he back?*

She calmed down and for the rest of the play remained demure, her shining eyes alone betraying the emotion the production aroused in her. Even in the high comedy, the absurd yellow cross-gartered stockings, and the forged love letters and the rest, he was Gricey's Malvolio every second, so very much in love with Olivia (who is quite unaware of it) that he plays it with a kind of rapturous erectile tenderness, just as Gricey had: he was a walking penis. Oh, but when later he's flung into the dark room, incarcerated as a lunatic, and pleads his cause so very pitifully – *Good Sir Topas, do not think I am mad. They have laid me here in hideous darkness* – he managed to arouse precisely the mixture of laughter and unease that Gricey had, reckoning shrewdly on his listeners' cruel mockery being not uninflected with compassion for a sane man unjustly condemned as a lunatic.

For who among us hasn't worried about *that?* But yes, he pulled it off without losing the laugh, and as for his final dramatic exit – *I'll be revenged on the whole pack of you* – chills up the spine. Oh, an inspired performance, we all thought so, and when the curtain fell, then swept up again for the players to come forward, Joan was not the first on her feet but she wasn't slow.

Afterwards the director took Joan and Vera round to the stage door and down a flight of stairs to the green room. All the usual detritus back there, flats and ropes, malodorous corridors with sweaty brick walls, coils of electrical cord hung on nails, and glimpses of dressers clutching heaps of sweaty costumes, hastening for the wardrobe sinks. The actors knew they were in, of course, and soon they started to appear, in twos and threes, having wiped off their slap, more or less, some of them, others greasy-faced and still in costume, or partially. They all knew each other and it was heartbreaking. They missed him, they loved him. Everybody loved Gricey. Ed Colefax was in tears.

Then came Malvolio.

Joan had been watching for him. Daniel Francis. His entrance was diffident. Gone, the measured step, the arrogance, the simper, the languor. He was thinner than Gricey, his long jaw blue with shadow, and he had a cliff of pale forehead over sad, deep-set eyes from which he had not as yet removed the mascara, and there was a little something of the *décadent* about him. His hair was very black and lacked the oiled amber density of Gricey's mane, rather it flopped, and he pushed it off his forehead with nervous fingers. There was a touch of the antic in him, you'd need it for Malvolio, but he was keeping it under control now, for he understood the peculiar significance of his situation as he shook their hands and muttered his condolences – *sorry for your loss, Mrs Grice*. To Joan he appeared – at first, at least – a little *resentful*, somehow, or just touchy perhaps, as though it were onerous for him to have to show sorrow for their loss, as though they might think it was his fault (because in fact it was his good fortune) although that wasn't his fault *either*; and he wished it were otherwise.

All this Joan read in his hesitant, frowning approach. Of course he was in an awkward position, being as it were the embodiment of a dead man for whom these women actively grieved, while at the same time very much alive, but masked and costumed in an alien persona that had until very recently been assumed by Gricey himself. Joan had never met him, but understanding his discomfort she felt a distinct sympathy. Quietly she told him how much she'd liked his performance.

She saw the hint of a flush briefly sweep across the man's cheeks.

– Thank you.

He made a slight bow and smiled a little, but still frowning. It must have been preying on his mind, she thought, the reaction he'd get from Gricey's widow, even more so the daughter, Vera Grice being a much-admired actress and on her way to becoming a star, so we all thought. He was still holding Joan's hand.

– Yes, I did, said Joan. Really and truly, love.

She clasped his hand in both of hers and we think some kind of understanding must have passed between them. She imagined perhaps that this man understood what she felt, since he too lived in Gricey's shadow. She knew how closely he must have studied her husband's performance. He'd have stood in the wings every night with the other actors, all watching the master at work. And he must have wondered when – or *if*, more like – he'd ever go on in the role, since he'd taken the trouble to learn the part through slavish imitation of Gricey's exact timing and inflection – his every entrance and exit, every gesture, every pause, every preen, sneer, reproach—

Do ye make an alehouse of my lady's house, that you squeak out your coziers' catches without any mitigation or remorse of voice? Is there no respect of place, persons, nor time in you?

That comes in Act II, scene iii, when Toby Belch and his friends are making too much noise in the kitchen late at night. His indignation, that his beloved, his Olivia, whom he serves as her steward, should have her hospitality abused in this way, oh, it was every bit as nicely judged as Gricey's, a pleasure to hear, and there was much laughter in the auditorium.

But the broken heart, the pain breaking the surface like a dying dolphin when in the last act he says: *Madam, you have done me wrong/Notorious wrong* – this alone was worth the price of admission.

Gricey invented that, thought Joan, and this man

knows its value. He knows what treasure he's been given and for that if nothing else she now continued to clasp his hand in both her own.

Then Miriam Atkins, with the tears standing in her eyes, was asking her how she was getting on, and Joan became aware, as though awakening from a trance, of familiar movement backstage. The collecting of props, of costumes flung on hangers and racks, goodnights cried out as the cast dispersed, eager now to get home, or to the pub or wherever it was they had to be. Vera kissed her mother and went off with Miriam, and only Daniel Francis remained.

– Go on now, said Joan, having blown her nose into a little hanky she kept in her handbag. Someone will be wanting those wet things.

The wardrobe mistress, she meant. He'd been sweating into them all night.

– It was all right, Mrs Grice? Not too much for you?

– It was very good. Now off you go, dear.

– Thank you.

He turned on his heel and left her there, not pausing in the doorway to fling a look at her over his shoulder, as she rather thought he might. Small thing, she thought, this flicker of feeling between widow and cover, but all the same she carried the warmth of it with her as she left through the stage door and round the front to St Martin's Lane.

Later, standing at the window of her empty flat, watching the falling snow, she decided she would see it again. Watch it more carefully this time, with a cooler eye, properly extract from it what she'd merely glimpsed in Daniel Francis' performance. Savour it more deliberately than she had tonight, for she hadn't anticipated seeing Gricey there, it hadn't occurred to her. But of course he was there, onstage at least if not back in his own home. Just like him, show up in a theatre first. But of course she hadn't told him he could go yet.

She went into her sewing room, turning the light off as she left the kitchen. She'd always had a sewing room where she could close the door and not be disturbed, but who'd disturb her now? she thought. She was alone. Alone in a small dark room, like poor Malvolio in Act IV, yes, and a very cold dark room it was, with a sewing machine and all her fabrics and scissors, bobbins and thimbles and spools of thread. Her shrunken world. She sat at the machine and with a listless toe she touched the treadle and heard the familiar staccato motif, the empty needle tapping at the plate, *tap-tap-tap-tap-tap*. A frantic fingernail inside a coffin, she thought. An icy draught entered the room. The flat had ceased to be her home. It was a crypt, she thought, although Gricey – Gricey! – seemed now to have come back from the dead. Yes, back to life, by way of Malvolio, and wasn't that just like him?

She heard the hour chiming, faint in the distance. It would be another two weeks before the old clock's cogs and gears all froze solid and it ceased to move. Ah, Gricey, she thought. Who could forget you at the Watford Palace? Most of the world could, and had, was the answer, for you only played there three weeks to scant unfriendly houses, and not surprising, awful play, whatever it was, dull as Chekhov – except for you. Joan was working in the wardrobe, her first job, and she knew she'd never forget his performance.

She told him so, and of course one thing led to another.

She didn't want to think about it now.

But Malvolio, victim of small minds. Driven half mad and shut up in a dark room by drunken fools abusing the hospitality of the poor grieving woman to whom he is devoted in every way. Whose pens he straightens on her desk, whose every care he attends to, believing that only he can protect her, a young widow alone in the world, and all this with no thought of recompense. She would tell that actor what Gricey had said about Malvolio's love for Olivia when they talked, just the two of them, over a drink or two after the show—

Ah no. No, what she wanted – *all* she wanted – was to help Gricey come through. It was as simple as that.

She sat in her chair at the sewing machine through the hours of the night, laughing and sobbing, remembering the man she'd lost.

4

S HE WENT BACK. She bought a cheap ticket in the balcony stalls and slipped into the theatre unseen, this time wearing one of Gricey's overcoats with the collar turned up and his hat pulled low on her forehead, the soft homburg she'd got him in Lock's of St James. She didn't want to be recognised. She wanted to watch this Daniel Francis undisturbed. She remembered from the earlier visit that each time she recognised Gricey in his performance she'd felt a spike of emotion for which she had no name. She wanted more of that feeling.

And she got it. Yes. It was there when he first stepped onto the stage and was so tartly put down by Olivia, being told he's sick with self-love, and *tastes with a distempered appetite* – and doesn't care, being blind and deaf with love. Joan remembered that in the face of these insults Gricey had arrived at an expression of the fondest simpering indulgence towards his mistress, and it aroused laughter. Miriam Atkins was in part responsible for this. With a large household to run, of course she needs a steward. Malvolio is indispensable to her. Not so miscast after all, perhaps. He'd always be a pompous ass, but Gricey thought he was something more, representative perhaps of an older order. He was a great one for tradition, Gricey. So proud of being an Englishman, always.

By the time she heard Feste's last song Joan was in tears. She sat very still, with her head down, the hat pulled low, and she let the audience stream out around her. Then she was alone in the auditorium. The usher came down the aisle, a cleaner appeared, the curtain was up and a stage-hand was sweeping the floor. She rose to her feet and made her way down the stairs just as the theatre went dark.

She stepped out into St Martin's Lane.

– Mrs Grice?

She turned. Malvolio! Or no – Gricey! Or no – it was Daniel Francis.

She was taken aback. She responded with unfeigned surprise.

– Oh here you are, she said, Mr Francis.

– Back again, then, Mrs Grice?

Oh, just tell him, she thought.

– It was you I came to see, Mr Francis.

She saw the sudden flare of the eye, the wolfish pleasure and surprise. His coat was unbuttoned and a ratty scarf was wrapped around his neck. The coal-black hair had scarcely glimpsed a comb. A smear of powder still on his temple, and again the mascara, this time with a suggestion of the silent screen about it, ghost of Valentino. She wanted to spit in her hanky and wipe it off, as she would have done if it were Gricey. He was a lean, lanky, intense, untidy man in mascara and a darned sweater and baggy corduroy trousers worn through at the knees as though he spent half his life knelt down in prayer, and god knows, she thought, most of them did, praying for work.

His shoes were of good quality, or they once had been, but they were worn out now, needed new uppers, needed new soles, there'd be holes where the snow came through and she could imagine the state of his socks. If he had any socks. Poor as a church mouse but a kind of actor she knew well, and she felt both a little uneasy with him, given who he was, or who he *contained,* rather, and at the same time curious. He had of course that fierce bright fire in his eyes, it was always there when they came off stage at the end of the night, when they were full of life and of themselves.

Oh, and she remembered Gricey, how he'd sit in the pub after, start telling a story, and after a few seconds the people at the next table would be listening, so he'd bring them in, and then the people at the bar, they'd be turning to listen, and he'd bring them in too, and soon the whole pub was listening to Gricey tell his story, and how they'd roar and clap when he finished—

– How was it tonight, Mrs Grice?

– You were very fine, she said.

She touched his sleeve and yes, the coat was as cheap as she thought. But how careful she must be – this delicate vessel!

– Mrs Grice, may I buy you a drink?

What a bold fellow. Could he buy her a drink? She'd buttoned her coat, turned the collar up and had planned to ride her bicycle back to Mile End and have a drink at home, but she knew what would happen if she drank alone after watching *Twelfth Night*. But a drink with this threadbare actor in whom dwelled like a dybbuk the spirit of her dead husband?

– Why not, Mr Francis?

So they went into the pub on the corner there, and Joan sat at a table near the fire while Daniel Francis went up to the counter. The room was far from quiet. Three beer pumps and a group of men and women at one end, and a larger group at a table, many of whom worked in theatres nearby. A few overhead lamps, the room gloomy and not warm. It was an old pub, all glass and brass, seen better days. The group at the table hailed her new friend and she was pleased to see Malvolio complimented on his perform-ance while he was paying for the drinks. She'd have liked to give him money but she didn't know him well enough yet.

He returned to the table with a small gin and a glass of mild. He didn't talk at once, and seemed not to dislike a silence, as most actors do. So she watched him, the *vessel*, as she now thought of him, and wondered why Gricey had chosen him. It was their shared Malvolio, of course. He now appeared a serious man, grave, self-possessed, inward, one of those solitary actors perhaps, she thought. They do exist. He lifted his glass and inclined his head. She was aware that the people at the table were talking about him. One of them had turned in his chair and was

44

staring at him. He seemed less friendly than the others, perhaps it was the mascara. But he was far from the most exotic man in the room.

– What did you do before? said Joan.

– Before *Twelfth Night?*

– No.

She accepted a Woodbine and leaned forward to the match.

– Before you started acting, she said.

– I was in rep, you see, and before that a theatre orchestra in Hampstead, third violin. Straight from school, Mrs Grice.

– Knew what you wanted, Mr Francis.

– I suppose I did, yes.

– What's your real name, love?

– Frank Stone.

He looked down. He fell silent once more. One of those. All he wanted was to work in the theatre, god help him, poor deluded bugger. That's why Gricey chose him. *Empty* vessel.

– Married?

– No. I used to live with my mother, Mrs Grice.

Not queer, though, she thought. There was a very slight something about his accent she couldn't place.

– But not any more. She didn't like seeing you up on the stage. That it, Mr Stone?

– No, it wasn't that. She died.

Of course. She recognised it now. It was obvious. It had been there in the handshake in the green room. Her own grief was too fresh, it made her blind. She didn't see

45

the suffering of others. But of course she wasn't alone now, and a kind of relief swept through her.

– You miss her, Mr Stone?

– Oh yes.

His eyes were on her. Dear innocent man, she could never tell him, of course.

– See her in the street, do you?

Now he laughed. He liked the idea. It brought her to life in his mind.

– No, Mrs Grice, I haven't seen her in the street. You've seen Gricey, have you?

– I've heard his voice.

Watching him close now she lifted the gin to her lips. She felt the familiar pain, for Gricey hadn't spoken to her since the day of the funeral. Why would he not speak to her again? *Or was this it now?*

– Yes, I have too. Not Gricey's, I mean.

– What was her name?

– Rosa.

– Rossa?

– Rose-ah.

– You have brothers and sisters?

– No, he said, and frowned for some reason. Where was he from? She still couldn't place it. Hadn't been there onstage.

– Just as well.

– I don't know.

– Make the theatre your family, Mr Stone.

– There is that, Mrs Grice, he said, and produced that grin again, the one that split his cheeks like two thin flaps

46

of leather, oh, he could charm the birds out of the trees, this one, she thought.

Then the landlord was calling time and Joan said she'd better be getting home. Her heart was full. She wanted to be alone. They stood outside the pub and shook hands on the cold pavement. A gust of wind came up from Trafalgar Square and she shivered. A dog was barking and high clouds blustered across the pale night sky. More snow on the way, said Joan. They'd reached her bicycle, parked beside a dustbin down the alley by the theatre. Someone had thrown out a bucket of water earlier and it had frozen and was now a little glacier in miniature, gleaming there in the moonlight.

– Do your coat up, Mr Stone, you'll catch your death.

– I haven't far to go.

She'd pulled on her gloves and turned up the collar of her coat. She mounted her bicycle.

– I do. Mile End.

She almost said, but you know that, of course.

– Goodnight, then.

He wanted to say something more, seeing her on the saddle.

– Wait, Mrs Grice—

But Joan had lifted her head, looked both ways, pushed off and sailed away down the empty street, with him gazing after with his hand lifted.

Joan rode home as though her bicycle wasn't on the road but several inches above it, winged at the axles. Nor did she feel the cold despite the dropping temperature and the wind freshening as it came up off the river. It was often like this, flying by bicycle, in the weeks that followed, in what she would come to regard as the opening act in a comedy of errors, the first of those errors being in the minds of those who believed that Gricey was dead.

It's certainly what we thought, and to think otherwise was mad, frankly, and heartbreaking too, poor Joan. But it seemed she could think both things at once, that he was dead, and alive too, in the body of another man.

5

A FEW DAYS later she went to see Vera again. As she cycled across the city in the late afternoon she grew disconsolate. Her daughter's continued occupation of Julius Glass' attic depressed her, and it also distracted her from the quiet wonder of this man who'd entered her life, and who by some miracle carried her late husband's spirit into the world and who, if not driven off, or otherwise estranged, could yet be persuaded to allow him to *come through*. Quite what that would look like Joan had as yet no idea. But she felt sure she'd know it when she saw it. And thinking this, she knocked on the front door of the thin house in Pimlico.

Not far from Julius' house there was a small public square. Elms and ashes had been planted in the last century, and an old synagogue stood on the far side, which some fascist had defaced with a swastika. The graveyard with its scattering of headstones was of more ancient provenance still. Nearby there was a narrow terrace of houses and a high brick wall with the railway yards behind, and a small pub on the corner called the Builders Arms. All but one of the houses had escaped the bombs and in summer it was pleasant enough, although at this time of year it was bleak. Children didn't go in even though there was a stand of swings hung from a rusty structure, like a gibbet with chains. The Jewish graveyard was said to be haunted by a German soldier. Perhaps that was why.

Joan and Vera had gone out for a walk. Vera said she was desperate for fresh air. More desperate, thought Joan, to get out of that house for a bit. She and Julius had had a late night, she said, but whether that meant carousing or what, Joan didn't ask. Mother and daughter had found their way to the little square. They'd brought a few slices of the horrible grey bread we got that winter and were tossing crumbs to the pigeons. A few flakes of snow were drifting down.

It was too cold to sit on a bench so the two women walked around the square arm-in-arm. Vera was bundled up in her black fur coat and was telling her mother how a few nights earlier she'd been out to the theatre and got home late. Joan was at once disturbed. Here it comes, she thought. It wasn't so much what Vera was saying as her manner. The tone was feverish. Her eyes were too bright, and she was clinging too tightly to her mother's arm. She'd come into the kitchen, she said, and saw at once that there'd been people round. Chairs pushed back from the long kitchen table. Empty teacups, a few beer bottles, and oh, a lot of cigarette smoke, it was like a fog in there. She was about to open the back door, let some air in, when she heard someone coming downstairs. It was an old house and the stairs creaked, and she said she felt at bay for some reason. He hadn't told her he was having people in.

– Go on, dear, said Joan, a feeling of weary dread gathering in her breast now.

Well, suddenly the door was thrown open, said Vera, and with a click of the switch the kitchen was illuminated, but only dimly, just the single bulb in the yellow shade. Vera shrieked, she couldn't help it. But it was only Julius, and he didn't seem to hear her shriek. Oh it *is* you, he said, yawning. Why didn't you answer? What are you doing down here in the dark, love?

Vera, still clutching her mother, fell silent.

– What did you say? said Joan.

– I told him to go away. I thought it was someone else!

– Who?

– I don't know.

Apparently he sat down at the table anyway and pressed his hands to his face. Don't make so much noise, he said, Gustl's asleep. He'd been asleep himself, he said, and Vera said she was sorry if she'd woken him, she was trying to be quiet, but please would he just go away? He then said she hadn't woken him, he'd been having a dream. The dream had woken him.

– Did he say what he was dreaming about?

– The Blitz. Swinburne's.

– Then what?

Then he yawned again. Vera had stood there with her back to the back door, still in her coat. Terrified of him for reasons she couldn't explain.

Vera was becoming more upset now. Why she was in high heels was a mystery to Joan, for even with her mother for support she was tottering on the gravel. But that wasn't important.

– Now be calm, dear, said Joan, I want to understand this.

She thought it was just the girl's nerves playing up again.

– Julius, please go back to bed!

– I can see I'm not welcome down here, he said.

She heard him going back upstairs. Then the clouds parted, and she saw through the kitchen window the moon come out. For some minutes she was still, she said, because she was trying to understand a thought that had occurred to her with a quite startling flash of clarity when she'd first heard him call her name. He'd been expecting someone else. And then she thought – and she turned, and gripped her mother's arm more tightly still – I know that's daft.

– Oh no, said Joan, who wasn't surprised.

Vera stared at her.

– There's more, she said.

Vera had been standing in the kitchen in the dark. She opened the back door and went out and stood at the top of the steps. At the far end of Julius' narrow garden the branches of a weeping willow in the alley beyond fell bare and thin over the back wall like ropes, swaying a little, said Vera, and the ground beneath was patched with shifting moonlight. Vera was slipping. She wasn't strong, at times, particularly when she wasn't working. And of course she'd lost her father. Her eyes came up, wide with astonishment. I saw something move, she whispered, over by the fence. It was like a crouching shadow, that's what it looked like, then it was creeping along the fence!

– Slowly, sweetheart. Where was this?

– Near the back wall under the tree. Then it disappeared.

– What was it, a cat?

Vera was still clutching tight to her mother's arm as they struggled on through the empty square, Vera staggering, almost, in her big fur coat, on her high heels, as though a little drunk, but with her mind clearly still fixed in horror on what it was she'd seen that night. No, she said, not a cat, it was too big. Or a dog. It was a *man*.

– A *man*?

– *Yes*.

Vera stopped. Again she turned to her mother. Her eyes were wild now and her face was pale as a bone.

– Mum, who'd be out in the garden that time of night?

– What did you do? said Joan.

– I went down the steps, very quietly, she said, then I went down the garden until I was in among the branches of the tree, and I didn't move, Mum, I just stood there, not moving, and all I could hear was the snow dripping and there weren't any footsteps from down the alley, nothing. Quick and stealthy he'd run off, whoever he was, when he saw me come out of the kitchen!

– Did you go into the alley?

– He'd gone.

– Vera.

– What, Mum?

– You're sure it was a man.

– You think it was a woman?

– No, dear, I wasn't there! It could have been a dog.

– I thought that too, that it was a woman.

She sounded frightened. Not often Joan had heard that, not from Vera. There was a bench by the swings. They sat down. Joan was shivering. She couldn't stay out in this cold much longer. Next to the pub stood the one house in the square that had been hit by a bomb. Much of the front was blown off and the roof sagged but it hadn't collapsed, so it was half a roof supported by half a wall, and all through the war that broken house had stood there like that, but an effort was being made to shore it up now. Metal pipes and planked walkways and ladders enclosed the structure so it appeared only in dim outline as though seen through a scrim, prisoned in its own scaffolding. Joan thought if that scaffolding came down it wouldn't take long for the house to come down after.

It was getting dark, and the gloom crept like a kind of fog into the spaces between the bare trees and the lamp posts and the hanging swings. It brought a deeper chill, and Joan felt it at once. She stood up from the bench. Vera looked up, those luminous eyes still wide with fearful bewilderment and filled now with tears. There was a sudden movement of warm sorrow in her mother's heart, and she sat down again and took her daughter's hands.

– Now stop it, my love, she whispered. You're all right. Listen to me, listen, Vera, you're all right. Look at me, Vera. Sweetheart—

Gazing at her, stroking her trembling hands, doing what she'd done so very often when Vera was a child, telling her that whatever pain she had, a grazed knee, a bad dream – usually it was a bad dream – she was all right now, it was nothing, and so she would comfort her in her child's distress, by saying it was nothing. It still worked, up to a point. Vera was in her arms now, sobbing, and what a rare pleasure this was, thought Joan, to sink her face into all that thick warm fur. Then she saw over the girl's heaving shoulder, across the square, in the dusk, lights coming on in the Builders Arms.

– We'll go and have a little drink, shall we, dear, she murmured. The pub's open.

Then they were sitting by a coal fire in the small saloon bar. It was empty but for them. They each had a large gin. It helped, Joan knew it would. She thought, dear Uncle Alcohol, why are you so good to us? Vera got her fags out. A clock ticked. There was a small black cat purring and snoring on the rug in front of the fire. Vera was still in her fur, Joan in her black coat. She leaned down and rubbed the cat's cheek just below the ear. But for the clock and the purring of the cat there was silence. Their mood was subdued now; peaceful, almost. Then Vera was talking again.

– I came in from the garden, she said quietly. I wasn't so upset as I had been and I took my shoes off in the kitchen and turned off the light. I went upstairs in my stocking feet but slowly, and I stopped every time it creaked. I had to know, you see.

– Know what? said Joan.

She didn't want to look at Vera now. With every step up those creaky stairs she saw her moving further into some place from which she might not easily come down again.

Vera stopped at the bedroom door and opened it a crack. Very dark in there, the merest catch of moonlight in a long slit where the blackout curtain failed to meet the wall. Quiet snoring. She made out the form of the bed, and the humped mass of the man in it. Himself alone. But she could smell it!

– Mum, I could smell it!

– What, dear?

– The perfume.

– From the person in the garden?

– Yes.

Joan had one thought only. This girl had to get back to work. Leave her to her own devices and idle hands, idle mind, trapped in an attic and a cold husband two floors below – this is what happens. She imagines women in the garden. Or was it Joan herself who put that thought in her head?

– I'm so sorry, my love, and I do hope you're wrong.

– It stank in there. I'm not wrong, Mum.

– Stank of what?

– Perfume. Jicky.

56

Her tone now was one of quiet certainty. There was no point arguing with her. That creeping man was a woman and she'd been in Julius' bed. She'd been there when Vera got home earlier that night, and had got into the garden through the cellar. It explained everything. Or at least Vera thought so.

They left the pub soon after. Vera had forgotten her keys so they had to ring the doorbell. It was Auntie Gustl who answered it.

– You are frozen, she cried. Come into the kitchen where there is more warm!

But Joan didn't want to come in. Whatever it was that was happening in Julius' house, she couldn't be certain, but it made Vera unhappy. She must wait. She had a nice bit of tongue put by for her supper, and a little cabbage. She liked a bit of cabbage, when she could get it.

6

TWELFTH NIGHT HAD only seven performances more, and Joan had started to anticipate yet another death: the end of Malvolio. She couldn't stay away. The following night she purchased a ticket, yet again in the balcony stalls, and again she wore the soft black homburg pulled low, and the black coat that fitted her nice and snug now and still carried Gricey's scent in the lining.

We see her leaning forward, gazing like a child at the players below, one in particular, of course. She stayed in her seat through the interval and prepared herself for the horror of Act IV. For it's then we see a sane man incarcerated as a lunatic, that sane man being Malvolio. How quickly Gricey used to draw his audience into this nightmare predicament, locked in an asylum, your every protestation of sanity serving only to convince your gaolers that you are indeed mad – no surprise then that on his release he's furious at the cruel trick played on him, and flings out, oh, in *such* a rage, promising revenge. Gricey struck a dark shock into his audience in this scene, and at the same time made them laugh. Extraordinary.

And so it ends. A brother and sister, twins, separated by shipwreck, each presumed dead by the other, are re-united. And each finds his or her true love. Who cares for old *Malvol*? It's Viola and Orsino who matter, and Olivia and Sebastian. Are they not the lovers? Does not all the world love lovers?

> *When birds do sing, hey ding a ding, ding,*
> *Sweet lovers love the spring.*

Now it was dead of winter but Joan waited in her seat until the audience had shuffled out and only then did she make her way downstairs. She turned up her collar. Another cold night. Frank Stone was leaning against the brick wall by the stage door. He was concealed, deep in shadow with his head down, as before. Seeing her, he stepped out into the pool of light under the street lamp.

– Mrs Grice.

She'd hoped he'd be there. And how well he'd found his light.

– Hello, love. Now tonight I'll be paying, no argument.

He joined her and she slipped her arm in his. Later he said he liked that she became at once familiar with him, for at that time he was of course still very unsure of her. But there will always be those rare men who see in a woman like Joan Grice that to which most others are blind. He couldn't care less that there were more than a few years between them, nor did he find her sour, or cold. He knew she was grieving and would never show it, and he suspected, too, that she was far from lacking in the humour and, oh yes, the passion that others of more limited imagination never guessed at.

They talked until last orders were called. She asked him how it was to play Malvolio after watching Gricey do it. It was bold of her to do this, considering what she thought she knew about him, but she was curious. He surprised her, he told her he had no thought of Malvolio, no, all that was required of him was that he do exactly what Gricey did. It began with his posture, how he stood – at times like a quivering poker. So he stood as Gricey stood, he moved as Gricey moved, and slowly, or perhaps not so slowly, a curious thing began to happen. He began to acquire his *body memory*. Yes. He began to know, without having to think about it, not how to play Malvolio, but how to play Charlie Grice playing Malvolio.

– Is that so?

– Yes. But when I talked about it backstage I was told I should have known. It happens all the time.

He tipped his head to the side and lifted his beer glass. What was it in his voice? Then she had it. The faintest suggestion of an *eff* at the end of *have* – German! He was grinning at her, a bit of the wolf in his face again. She didn't know what to say. She lifted an eyebrow and shook her head. She felt confused, and a little aflutter.

– Yes. So I stepped in and I played it exactly as he had. The others appreciated it.

– They did? The actors?

She'd regained her composure.

– I didn't upset their performance, you see.

– No?

– It was still Gricey.

– You make it sound easy, Mr Stone.

– People came to see it again. They wanted to see if the new man could do it. Get all the laughs Gricey used to.

– And of course you could.

He said nothing for a few seconds and then quite solemnly he nodded his head.

They parted as before on the pavement outside the pub. They made no arrangement to meet again. But it was understood that Joan would see the play once more before it came down. They shook hands and went their separate ways. Each was quietly satisfied that, whatever was going on here, it was at least becoming a friendship.

Joan's improved temper did not go unnoticed in the costume shop the next day. The girls called her Saint Joan. They lived in fear of her displeasure.

– Morning, Mrs Grice, they trilled, although not the two older women, who had more complicated relations with her.

– Morning, girls. Esther!

– Yes, Mrs Grice.

– Where did you find that skirt?

– I made it myself, Mrs Grice, it came from an old curtain.

– Well, dear, you're showing a little taste at last.

This counted as high good humour in the costume shop. The older women glanced one to another, as though to say, well, fancy. But she'd slept well, and the gin bottle on the high shelf in the kitchen cupboard had not been disturbed.

7

S HE CHOSE TO attend not the last night of the run but
the night before last. And again she waited until the
theatre had emptied out before she made her way downstairs and into the street. It was snowing that night. It
was a heavy downfall with strong wind behind it and she
struggled with her umbrella, for it was a large one and
not easy to handle in the conditions.

Then the strong, sure fingers of a man were on the
shaft. The flapping canopy was brought under control. It
will happen in friendships like this, is our observation,
that a few days after the second or third meeting, when
it's become clear to both parties that something's afoot –
in the time spent apart, changes will have occurred
within the imagination of each, and a new level of famil-
iarity, or even intimacy, will have been achieved. It was
the case here. He offered his arm and she took it and,
clutching tight to one another under the shelter of the big

umbrella, and with their heads down, they hurried the few steps through the driving snow to the warmth and light of the pub on the corner of the street.

With what relief did she again in his company sit quiet over her gin. Again she wouldn't let him pay. He said it was surely his turn, and anyway it was for the man to buy the drinks, and she told him not to be so foolish, as she fetched out a half-crown from her purse, and gave it to him, and it said as much about their relationship, this transaction, as any frank exchange of feelings would. In fact their traffic was hardly verbal at all, rather it was a growing recognition of an ease in each other's company which felt very much like the beginnings of trust. They sat side by side at their little table, backs to the wall, herself upright as ever and himself with his hands thrust in his trouser pockets, his long legs outstretched and crossed at the ankles. His coat was swept back and fell almost to the floor, and a cigarette dangled from his lips. Untidy hair, and his hat on the chair beside him. To the casual glance a bohemian, perhaps a painter or even a musician, but what was he doing with that smart, rather attractive woman with the chilly demeanour who never smiled?

Thus did they view the world from the same prospect. Joan needed this; she needed *him*. As for him, now he sat with Joan Grice and was enchanted by the woman he watched emerge with quiet humour from within her carapace of grief.

– You were very good tonight, Mr Stone, she said. We may make an actor of you yet. Now I have a suggestion.

64

– Oh you do, he said.

He turned towards her, sat up straight and got his hands out of his pockets.

– Yes I do. I would like to give you supper in my flat. Tomorrow night. I want to put some flesh on those bones of yours.

He gazed at her. He was not at a loss for words, but he was aware of a slow joy rising in him.

– But we don't come down until after ten.

– I know that.

– Then thank you, Mrs Grice, I would like that very much.

This was the bold advance Joan made, seeing no reason why she should not. She saw her new friendship as a delicate flame and knew it must be nursed. Not so it would grow, necessarily, but so it could continue to exist.

They parted soon after. She rode home on her bicycle. She lay awake for an hour thinking about one thing and another, Vera mostly, then she fell asleep. The next day she was aware, as she bicycled to work – it was cold, but dry at least, and the drifted snow was not as deep as she'd expected – and she'd worn a good black scarf knitted by herself that fluttered about her as she pedalled through the busy streets, Holborn, Aldgate, Shaftesbury Avenue, then sweeping, *soaring* into Piccadilly Circus and past the Statue of Eros – she was aware that, despite everything, despite her anxiety about Vera's collapsing marriage, and the poor girl's state of mind, she herself was in better spirits than she'd known since Gricey's death.

It was the prospect of her late supper, of course. She'd

planned the menu in some detail, to the inclusion even of that precious long-cherished tin of pork sausages that had entered her larder before the war. Her ration card would be clipped all to hell for this feast but she would put flesh on those bones all right, she thought. A simple supper but one that Gricey always appreciated when he came in from the theatre. An actor's supper, he'd say, as he set to with exclamations of delight. Dear Gricey. Again came the pangs, but tempered now by the thought that he wasn't so very far away after all.

It was after eleven when she heard the doorbell and went downstairs to let him in. Daniel Francis – or Frank Stone, let us call him, this was how Joan thought of him now – Frank Stone stood in the street rubbing his mittened hands together and blowing cold steam into the night.

– Come in, please.

He followed her up the narrow ill-lit stairs. He was relieved of his coat and his hat and scarf, which Joan hung in the cupboard in the passage by the front door. He saw that the flat was austere and shabby and in need of repairs, but clean and tidy. Joan's sewing room was behind the kitchen, and across the hall was Gricey's room with the big wardrobe. At the end of a short passage was the master bedroom, sadly of course without a master, for Joan slept in the old broad bed alone now. And next to it was the sitting room. But the kitchen being the warmest room in the flat, it was there Joan mostly lived.

Near the cupboard by the front door was a small table and on it various pieces of mail which Frank saw were all addressed to Charles Grice. There was a pair of men's shoes under that table, which he assumed correctly were also Gricey's. Joan took him into the kitchen. No man had been in that kitchen for more than a month. The table had been laid with a starched white cloth and two settings. Joan wore a string of pearls that once had been her mother's. She offered him a drink and he asked her if she had any beer. Of course she did. She took the bottle of pale ale down from the shelf and poured him a glass. He was silent. He felt a strong intimation of the presence of the man who until recently had been the master there, and whose personality was still palpable.

– How was it tonight, love?

– Ah, he said, everyone was sad.

She didn't reply. She was at the stove with her back to him. She knew why they were sad. It was more than the end of the run, when every actor feels the loss as he hangs up his costume for the last time and says farewell to his character. Like saying goodbye to a ghost, Gricey used to say, but who's the ghost, eh? Me or him?

– I walk away, Gricey said, and the clothes get packed up, and he's the ghost. But when *I'm* dead, old Malvol will still be here.

She thought of the stockroom where all the men's costumes hung thick like headless horsemen, a ghost every one. As she added salt to the soup she could see him standing in the kitchen door, rolling a cigarette and enjoying his own joke. Oh, and it was a question of some peculiar significance that night, for in Joan's mind, at least, Gricey's ghost was present. She was leaning over the stove, her back to the table, and she experienced a small convulsion of grief. She heard her guest push his chair back, and as a teardrop fell into the soup there was a hand on her shoulder.

– We remembered him, Mrs Grice.

She lifted her head and turned to face him.

– We were all in the green room. Mr Gordon said a few words.

Albert Gordon was the company manager.

– Albert would know what to say, said Joan.

She wiped her eyes on her apron and became brisk.

– Now sit down, please, Mr Stone – she paused – *Frank*, she said – and you can tell me what you'll be doing next.

– What will I be doing next? he said, with lifted eyebrows and half a grin, once more seated at the little table under the clothes pulley. The kitchen window was still curtained for blackout. His position in the company was not secure, as Joan well knew, and he had no idea what he'd be doing next. More work as a messenger, or the carrier of a spear. For actors like him the end of a job could mean a gap in life signifying nothing but empty days with now and then an audition for a part he wasn't suited for, and wouldn't be offered anyway, and an irritable agent who forgot his name and said with a shrug there was *nothing out there*. He had no money and, more critically, he had no decent clothes, and as Joan well knew, in the theatre, in the casting room, first impressions mattered. An idea had occurred to her. But first, food.

– This is a cabbage soup, Mr Stone. It might need more salt.

No, it didn't need more salt. That single teardrop had been salt enough for this pot. It was months since anybody had given him a meal. He didn't care how it tasted, for being a guest at a woman's table was feast enough. All this he told her.

– Better a guest than a ghost, said Joan, absently. Have some more.

– You must eat, Mrs Grice.

– I'm not hungry. You've been working. Gricey comes in ravenous, you'd think he'd been down the mines all night.

She was trying to be gay. She touched her pearls. She so rarely wore them now. But they brought out the fineness of the flesh of her throat, and Frank Stone was not insensitive to her sad beauty that night.

– It can feel like that, Mrs Grice.

– You certainly sweat like miners. He comes home stinking. Some nights they're both home late, him in from one theatre, Vera from another—

She fell silent. Those days were over.

– How is Vera?

– Oh, Mr Stone, I do worry about her.

She thought of Vera in her attic room with the sloping ceiling and the dormer window, her frocks hung among the rafters and her mirror propped up against the wall, where she had to stoop and peer just to get her lipstick on straight.

– Mr Stone, I think I might join you. Would you mind reaching me down the gin? I've hardly touched a drop since Gricey died; well, he was the one who liked a drink after the show.

So Frank got the gin down, and Joan had a stiff one while he ate his tinned sausages and potato salad with a nice piece of tongue on the side. It was as he was finishing his semolina that Joan made her suggestion.

– Mr Stone.

– Mrs Grice.

– Mr Stone – Frank – I might have something for you to wear.

She stood by the stove gazing fondly at him.

– His clothes, she said. What am I to do with them?

– I don't think I can, Mrs Grice.

Frank was taken aback. He was troubled, and for this reason. He'd found it disquieting to assume the role of Malvolio because a man died. At times he suspected that he'd come by it in an underhand way, or by false pretences. This was irrational but it was what he felt, and he thought, too, that others in the company were suspicious of him for that reason. Now he was being offered the dead man's clothes.

– But why ever not?

Joan sat down at the table and gazed at him. She gave him her warm smile, then leaned in towards him and extended her hand. She was giving him the full womanly wattage, all she had, and Frank was at once aroused. Her fingers on his arm now, she told him that she had all these suits of Gricey's and if they stayed in the wardrobe she would only get drunk late at night and bury her head in them so as to catch a scent of the man, and weep. Get rid of them! Get them out of the flat! – this was her thought, she told him, these intimacies designed only to help her get her way.

– I don't know.

How helpless he looked for a second or two. Like a schoolboy, she thought. She stood up and came around the table. She reached for his hands and stood gazing down at him. She'd only had the one gin, but it had been a strong one on an empty stomach. She was wearing a pale grey wool cardigan, cashmere, which Gricey had bought her before the war when he was flush. She was also wearing white underthings.

– No, you don't know, and I don't either. I'm sorry I suggested it, Mr Stone. Frank. It was a foolish idea. Let me fill your glass.

– Thank you.

She turned away to get the beer out of the cupboard. Frank was relieved but he felt embarrassed now. It troubled him, how she called him first by one name, then by another. It was late. He should go home. He said so.

– Drink your beer before you go, said Joan. We should at least raise a glass to the show coming down.

She poured him more beer, and a splash more of the gin for herself. They lifted their glasses and drank. At once she began to feel the tears come. He was alarmed.

– What is it, Mrs Grice?

He rose to his feet but she'd already fled the kitchen. When she returned a few minutes later, recovered, he told her he'd changed his mind.

– About what, Mr Stone?

– About the suit.

She hadn't expected this, after what he'd said. It wasn't a pretence, her sudden breakdown, and the tears.

71

– About what, Mr Stone?

– About the suit.

– Are you sure, love?

– Look at me, Mrs Grice. I'm a scarecrow.

– Oh hardly a *scarecrow*, Mr Stone.

She shouldn't have had that splash. She was all at once garrulous.

– But Gricey did have a few nice things and what a shame to throw them out and it's not as though you hadn't already stood in his shoes, if you know what I mean—

– If the shoe fits, Mrs Grice, said Frank, hopelessly.

– If the shoe doesn't fit, Mr Stone, I will have it altered.

She took him into Gricey's room and unlocked the wardrobe.

Oh, that wardrobe. Give us the chills, it did. It was an enormous piece of pale green furniture with fading, flaking paintwork, old browns and rusts under a greeny-blue pallor, and with a broken pediment, and two door panels with carved vines twisting and twining around them as though framing works of art. Opening that wardrobe was never simple now. Her fingers trembled with the key. There was something – untoward – about that wardrobe, for she'd heard noises. There'd been noises she couldn't explain. Mice, she thought, at first, or no, rats. Too big for a mouse, and then she thought no, it was her imagination. But this, now, felt like the most egregious act of betrayal, unless of course – and this hadn't occurred to her before – she was only giving him what was already his. She put the key in the lock, then opened the doors wide. They were stiff and they creaked. Shelving and drawers were up at one end, and a large trunk at the other with suitcases piled on top. And on top of the suitcases, the pot from under her bed, with his ashes in it, which had been giving her dreams. Down the middle ran a rail with clothes hangers on it, suits, coats, jackets, trousers, light to dark, summer to winter—

Joan selected a dark lounge suit she'd always liked seeing him in. He'd had it since before the war, before cloth got rationed and there was nothing to be had unless you got it under the counter. It was navy blue, with a broad lapel, and double-breasted. Board of Trade wouldn't let you have double-breasted, not after the rationing started, nor turn-ups on the trousers. When was it, the last time? They'd been up west for something or other and in the taxi, coming home, he'd slid his hand up her skirt and she'd seen the driver's eyes in the rear-view mirror, and Gricey said, Sid, keep your fucking eyes on the road, and she couldn't help herself, she started laughing, well, she'd had a drop or two, they both had—

– Try this one, Mr Stone, she said. For ordinary day wear. It might do you very nicely.

She laid the suit out on the bed and left the room, closing the door behind her. She went into the kitchen. She sat down with her elbows on the table and her face in her hands. What am I doing? This was what she asked herself, wishing now, oh, *imploring* Gricey, fervently, to speak again. *Tell me what to do! Tell me that this is all right!* Her heart was beating very fast. She was unsure what was happening. More gin? *No. No.* A very, *very* bad idea. She had a splash anyway.

When Frank opened the door of Gricey's room and called out to her she went back in and saw at once that the fit was not bad but not perfect. The trousers were a little too short and they needed taking in at the waist, also some minor alteration on the body of the jacket. A day's work.

– What do you think, Mr Stone?

– It's a good suit, Mrs Grice. This is very generous of you.

Under control now, more or less, she became brisk. She regarded him critically, and in her mind's eye she saw him as he'd look when it fitted him properly; and yes, for just a second she closed her eyes and Gricey was there.

Then she was all business. Out with the tailor's chalk for it was too broad in the shoulder, too deep in the chest. A pin here, a pin there, tighten up the trousers at the back, take it in a touch in the seat, and give him an inch of trouser cuff. She knew what she was doing when a man stood before her in a costume requiring alterations. She handled him with cool impersonality, stepping back every few seconds to see what he looked like. Frank hadn't felt a woman's hands on him since he was fitted for Malvolio and he wanted it never to stop. On her knees before him, working on the turn-ups of the trousers, she glanced up and caught the expression on his face. Yearning, she thought. He was yearning for something. She allowed her hand to linger on his ankle while still holding his downward dreamy gaze, and applied a brief, firm pressure while gripping the ankle as though it were the leg of a table, and how very solid he was, this was the warm hard flesh of a man she had in her hand, and when was the last time she'd felt *that*?

Then she was standing before him, close to him, this tall, slim, elegant, fragrant woman – her fingers on his waistband and pins between her teeth. Each was of course acutely conscious of the other now. They had never been so physically close before. This was a woman who'd often found herself pinning men's clothes but never late at night, and never alone with the man in a bedroom in her home, and fighting down the wild levity aroused by the gin—

She assumed her most professional manner.

– Just stand still, please, she grunted between teeth full of pins, I'll soon be finished.

– Take as long as you need to, Mrs Grice, said Frank, thickly.

It was past midnight. Outside the window the city streets were deathly quiet. Widowed, alone, without attachment or responsibility, she stood close to this lonely man in a bedroom, and did it occur to either of them that should the electricity break down, as it often did in these days of frequent sudden outages, and leave them in a *blackout*—?

But it didn't happen, and the moment passed. Then she was done. She left him to get dressed, and when he emerged he was a scarecrow once more. The suit lay on the bed, pinned and chalked and ready for the tailor, herself.

He left soon after.

*

75

Now when a friendship develops between a man and a woman, much will occur during those periods when the two are apart. Did we say this already? Never mind. It's important. Yes. For the imagination of each is put to work. Scenarios come to life in the mind, the narrative leaps forward, and when they meet again it's with a certain excitement but also a kind of reserve, for there is a suggestion of *trespass* in the thing, particularly for the man; an appropriation of the other one that has yet to be admitted or condoned. Certainly this was true of Frank Stone. He wanted Joan's hands on him again, just as when she'd held his ankle and looked up at him from down on her knees on the floor.

Then when she'd stood close to him, face to face, her scent in his nostrils, her breasts in soft wool just an inch from his beating heart, it was only with some difficulty that he'd restrained himself from removing the pins from between her *teeth*, yes – *with his own teeth* – one by one – as though each were an item of her clothing, of her *underwear* – to be then spat onto the floor, and kicked aside.

She'd told him to come by the following Sunday at six. The suit, she said, would be ready.

8

V ERA WAS IN her mother's flat the night Frank Stone
came for his fitting. She knew him as Dan Francis
who'd played Malvolio after her father died. She'd
observed his discipline. Actors who covered for other
actors were notorious for inventing new business, and it
confused everyone else onstage. This hadn't been the
case with *Twelfth Night*. Dan Francis performed Malvolio
exactly as her father had.

She'd moved in earlier in the day. It was more than a
week after the conversation they'd had in the playground,
she and Joan. The previous night, back in Julius' house,
up in her attic room, she'd realised what was wrong.
She'd been lying on her bed in the attic in her fur coat,
staring at the stars through the dormer window. She'd
screamed. She'd leapt off the bed, scattering the ashtray,
then clattered down the stairs, waking the house, then
fled, hailed a cab, told the driver to take her to Archibald

Street, up by St Clement's, and having rung her mother's doorbell she then banged on the door with both hands. Being admitted she'd come trembling and wailing up the stairs, oh, in floods of tears, and Joan had no clue as to what had happened. Barely had Vera started to talk, gasping and crying in the accounting of it, than Joan stopped her, held her, told her to be quiet, to calm down and talk slowly.

– My poor darling girl, listen to me. Now sit down. Do you want a cup of tea? Do you want a drink?

– Betrayal!

– But you haven't been betrayed—

– Yes!

– You'd better have a drink.

Then they talked. Vera sobbed as Joan reminded her what Julius had done, how he'd saved Auntie Gustl from the Gestapo then brought her to London and given her asylum in his house. This was all common knowledge. When she'd finished she saw her daughter's head come up. She recognised the resilience that at times this girl could command even when total nervous collapse seemed imminent.

– So this is how it feels, she whispered.

She wiped the tears and snot from her face with a handkerchief. She flung back her fine head and ran her fingers through her hair. All at once she was calm, damp but calm.

– What, my darling?

– Betrayal. This is how it feels.

– I'm so sorry—

– Don't be sorry, Mummy.

She was sitting up straight now.

– Don't be sorry? But why ever not? said Joan.

Vera stared at her, astonished that she didn't understand.

– It's not wasted. Don't you see?

Joan Grice was seldom surprised by her daughter but she was surprised now. All passion spent, and calm of mind, Vera sat in her mother's kitchen tapping her fingernails on the table as she gazed out of the window into the night. The sound reminded her mother of a sewing machine with no fabric under the needle, the *tap-tap-tap*, the *thunk-a-thunk-a-thunk*. It was funereal to Joan's ears. Vera was elsewhere, a thousand miles away, and Joan was able to study her in this rare abstracted state. The girl was thinking, but not about her marriage. Joan tried again to explain what Julius had done, and why Vera must not think she had been betrayed, but it was hopeless, because what mattered to Vera now was not whether she had or had not been betrayed but that she *felt* betrayed and she could use it. There were times, and this was one of them, when Joan wished her daughter possessed a more ordinary talent. But what was she doing, defending Julius Glass to her own daughter? And him the man who pushed Gricey down the steps, if she could only prove it. Trying to keep the girl on the rails.

– I had to get out of that house, Vera then said.

It was late in the afternoon. Joan was silent as she moved around the kitchen, unwilling to interfere with this reverie Vera was sunk into. Then all at once the girl seemed to wake up, and retrieved from her handbag her glasses and a well-thumbed Samuel French edition of a play she'd been asked to read. Joan could see her character's speeches underlined in red and black, with pencil notes in the margin. Vera was turning the pages rapidly as some new understanding elucidated that which before had apparently been obscure. She looked up.

– You get what you need, don't you, Mum?

– Do you, my love?

– I needed to know what loss felt like, then I needed to feel betrayed and I got that too.

Was that why Gricey died, so Vera could experience loss? And play the part of a tragic woman? She dared not ask the question. She was afraid what her daughter would say.

The next morning the two women were in a cab turning into Lupus Mews.

– Here they are, said Julius when Vera marched through the front door with her mother behind her.

– I'm leaving you, said Vera, setting off up the stairs. Don't try and stop me.

Julius turned to Joan, as though to say, what's this? Joan lifted her eyes to the ceiling and flattened her mouth in weary resignation, and reached for a cigarette.

– Don't ask me, she murmured. She still here?

– Who?

– Your *refugee*.

– Gustl? She's asleep.

Vera's voice floated down the stairs as she ascended.

– I'm leaving you, Julius!

Joan followed her up the stairs, pausing only to glance down at Julius' sallow, bewildered face. In the attic Vera rapidly took a few frocks on hangers from the cupboard under the eaves and threw them into a suitcase. She seemed careless of what she chose to take and what she left behind. No cabin trunk would be hauled by sweating men down these stairs; or not yet. Vera's mind was clearly on fire and she had no thought for possessions. When they came down again Julius was at the bottom of the stairs. As Vera descended in her black fur, on high heels, stepping slightly sideways on the stairs, Julius asked her what was going on. He appeared not angry, but distinctly annoyed and genuinely astonished.

– I'm leaving you, said Vera for the third time.

– Why, for Christ's sake, darling? What's happened?

A light blazed in Vera's large eyes then, which for a second resembled black lakes on fire.

– Don't pretend you don't know!

Julius didn't know and he turned towards Joan with his mouth open and his shoulders lifting, his hands out-spread. Is she out of her mind? he seemed to say, but Joan wasn't going to get involved in this. Vera meanwhile had reached the bottom of the stairs and with head held high, and a suitcase in her hand, was making for the front door.

– Tell me, Vera!

He seemed about to fling himself against the front door so as to deny her passage out of the house. Vera paused with her hand on the door handle and turned to him. Here it comes, thought Joan.

– There are many injustices I'm prepared to tolerate, Julius, she said, but betrayal is not one of them.

She swept out. Joan thought a round of applause was in order. She followed her daughter in similar manner, glancing at Julius as she left. He had his hand on his head and his lips were pulled back from his teeth in a rictus of aggravated incomprehension. What most concerned Joan now was Frank. He was due for his fitting at six.

Later mother and daughter sat together in the kitchen of the flat in Archibald Street but Vera was again elsewhere and had no wish to talk. She'd come to live in the flat with no thought for Joan's feelings in the matter. She'd assumed her acquiescence. She needed shelter. But darling, thought Joan, could you not at least have asked me?

The bed had been made up in Gricey's room, and although it troubled Joan to have her in there, it had once been Vera's room, and there were still a few of her books on the shelf. The wardrobe was locked, to Vera's surprise, but Joan was firm about this, at least: she'd have to hang her clothes in the hall cupboard. They're all Daddy's things in there, she said, it's still full. One suit was missing but Vera would be told nothing about that just yet, for Frank wasn't expected for several hours. There was at least a decent mirror on the back of the door. But now they were back in the kitchen, where a small moment of grace occurred when Vera looked up from her play.

– Thank you, Mummy, she said, leaning across the table to touch Joan's cheek.

Joan was still troubled. For once in her life she was unsure what was for the best.

– Oh of course, dear.

– I'll need to be quiet here.

– I know you will.

What did she think? That there'd be wild parties, dancing, wine, song? There might be Frank Stone, of course.

It was five o'clock and he was due at six. One scenario had unfolded in Joan's imagination and it troubled her. It involved Vera's reaction to her father's suit being handed over to a stranger.

– Darling, he's a stranger to you but not to me.

– I know who he is, Mum, he's Daddy's cover.

Yes, Daddy's cover. Scorn would be the least of it. The conversation would have to be had before Frank arrived for on no account would she have him embarrassed. Joan was not the woman to defer an unpleasant task in the hope that it might somehow go away, and so she sat down across the table from Vera, who was still reading her play.

– I have something to tell you, dear.

Vera looked up and took her glasses off.

– What is it?

She was alarmed. She was too excited, too alert, altogether too alive. It was the play. Now she sensed danger, or bad news. Joan was familiar with this mood.

– I'm giving one of Daddy's suits to an actor.

– Oh is that all? You had me worried.

– He's coming in an hour for a fitting.

– Do I know him?

– He was Daddy's cover in *Twelfth Night*.

– Oh *him*.

Yes, *oh him,* and for a second Joan was elsewhere, standing on a wet pavement after the pub closed and a damp snow just starting to fall, herself on her bicycle halfway down the street, turning in the saddle to look back and yes, there he was, *oh him*, under a street lamp with his hand lifted in farewell and on his face an expression of, oh what? – yearning. And how long had it been since anyone yearned for her?

– Then you don't mind?

– Mummy, why would I mind?

An hour later Frank arrived. Vera was still in the kitchen with her script. Her hair was piled up with a pencil stuck through it and her glasses were on the end of her nose. She was wearing a black jersey, a black skirt, thick stockings and plimsolls. On the table were scattered her tea things, rolling tobacco, ashtray, pencils, script and a high-heeled shoe. A shoe on the table. Joan might have made a fuss but decided that when Frank arrived they would go straight to the sitting room. She was still in the kitchen with Vera when she heard the doorbell. He was early.

He'd brought a small bottle of gin. She was embarrassed and a little annoyed. She took him into the kitchen. Vera was polite to him. She had no idea why Joan was giving her father's clothes to this man but as it didn't concern her she gave it no further thought. Frank told her he'd seen her *Doll's House* and enjoyed it very much.

Joan watched them with a cold eye as they talked, Vera sitting at the table and he standing in the dim yellow gloom of the one bulb in its shade overhead, in his thin black coat. He told Vera the actor who'd played Dr Rank to her Nora was in a play at the Wyndham and picked up a rat trap backstage and broke his finger.

– Which one? said Vera.

– *Measure for Measure.*

– No, which finger?

He held up his middle finger. It all suggested that he moved in her circles and knew the same people. Joan was irritated – more than irritated, for how much more attractive to him was her daughter, well, how much more attractive to anyone, really, we all agreed, what with her creamy skin and those splendid tits, lucky girl, and of course her teeth, like ivory – not like her mother's poor old tombstones. Oh, but then Joan recognised that it was all irrational, this great flurry of anxiety, just nonsense, for the very premise from which it arose was irrational, the idea that he was in any sense *hers*. But all the same she wanted to get him out of the kitchen. She considered their friendship a private matter.

The radiator sputtered, and watery steam spat up out of the valve.

– Dear, you have to work. I'll take Frank away.

– Who is Frank? Oh I see.

They went down the passage. Joan had earlier hung the suit on a hook on the back of the door. She ushered him in and followed, closing the door and leaning her back against it.

– You shouldn't have brought gin, she said. Listen to me, Frank. I don't want you spending your money on me. So please, no more gifts.

85

How he liked her using his first name and being strict with him. He wanted more of her reprimands.

– I don't like to come empty-handed, he said, when you're doing so much for me.

– I'm doing nothing for you, it's all the other way.

He still hadn't taken his coat off. The little sitting room was wallpapered in green floral patterns with swirls of heavy yellow that caught what little light there was, and an oval mirror hung over the mantelpiece with dark carved acanthus-leaf encrustations on the frame. A small coal fire burned in the hearth. Frank was kneeling in front of it, stirring the coals with a poker. He stood and turned to face Joan who had her back to the window and her hands on the sill.

– No, don't thank me, I don't want Gricey's suits here. I get upset when I look at them. They make me think he's coming back.

He's already back.

Frank had asked himself if he could really be doing her a favour by taking her dead husband's clothes. Now he said this to Joan. She laughed and came towards him, pointing a finger.

– Will you please just take my word for it? Don't be difficult, Mr Stone.

– I'm not sure I can help it, Mrs Grice.

The diffident, twitching grin appeared again.

– You're being difficult. Go and put it on. Use my sewing room.

He left with the suit, and Joan wandered about the room, wringing her hands. Vera was in the kitchen and her presence irritated Joan, for she felt constrained. She and Frank, each time they met, they advanced, she felt, but with Vera nearby Joan was less than fully herself. He must be aware of it. He was such a perceptive man, she thought. Nothing, surely, escaped him. He was a very good actor. He must work more. She must help him. She began to think who she could mention him to and a name occurred to her.

But no, too soon.

Then, silently, suddenly, he materialised in the gloom of the corridor and stood in the doorway. She hadn't heard him. Turning, she suffered a most violent shock. The resemblance was magnified a thousandfold – never had she been so sure of him.

– Come in where I can see you!

She was suddenly full of awe and very frightened.

She moved to the switch on the wall and turned on the overhead light. That was better. But how odd, how very strange it was, to see him standing in the doorway there, and holding himself as *he* once did—

– You look as if you've seen—

He thought better of it.

– Heavens, she said, with a hand on her lifting breast, you did give me a shock. For a second I thought you were him!

– Mrs Grice, it fits me perfectly.

– Oh, Joan, please, for Christ's sake call me Joan. Let me look at you properly. Come here in the light.

Later, when he'd left, and Vera had gone to bed, Joan sat in the kitchen with a glass of the gin he'd brought and saw him again in Gricey's suit. It did fit perfectly, of course it did, she'd done the alterations herself. Of course it was a shock to see it on Frank Stone but still the feeling was there and yes, he was right. It *was* like seeing a ghost.

– Sit down, she'd told him, and cross your legs.

She'd watched the trouser leg rise a little over Frank Stone's raddled wet sock. It fell so nicely, the jacket. How elegant he was now, her scarecrow, how darkly dashing he looked in that navy blue over a white shirt and that old spotted blue tie. And his untidy coal-black hair, of course. Raffish, she'd thought. Dashing.

– Stand up and walk about.

He'd stood up and walked about. Yes, it suited his lanky frame well, the trousers flapping like sailcloth around his long legs. She'd done a nice job, just pulling them in an inch in the seat. Very nice hang.

– Walk like Malvolio.

– Oh, Mrs Grice, he said.

He refused to use her first name.

– What is it?

He was grinning at her again, his long face split into those lovely leathery flaps. The eyes became warm narrow slits with fine lines spreading out like little darts. It didn't happen often. His hair flopped over his forehead and he pushed it back with fingers that were slender and strong like a musician's. She thought him too handsome for words.

– What? she said.

– I'm not Malvolio.

– It doesn't matter. Just do it.

So he pretended to be himself playing Malvolio after the manner of Charlie Grice. It was Gricey stepping onto the stage in the first act, and Joan failed to conceal her flush of warmth.

– Not too tight in the seat?

He'd sat down and again crossed his legs. With one arm thrown over the back of the armchair, he half turned towards her where she stood by the door. He pretended to be suave. He made a face like a matinee idol, a smouldering Valentino now. She regarded him with her hands clasped at her waist and her head a little to one side.

– Perfect in the seat, Mrs Grice, he said.

But at that moment of pleasant intimacy the door had opened and Vera, with a cup of tea and her script, and her tobacco, came in to say goodnight and appraise the fit of the suit.

– Oh it's fine, she said. You look just like Daddy.

She yawned.

– I'm off to bed then. Night, Mum. Night, Dan.

Frank left soon after. Joan had sent him into the night in a double-breasted, navy-blue suit, with the clothes he'd been wearing neatly folded and packed in a brown paper bag. She sat at the kitchen table and felt relieved that it had all gone off as well as it had, meaning Vera had behaved herself.

Frank got off the bus in the Strand and walked past St Martin-in-the-Fields and on up the Charing Cross Road to where he liked to turn into the alley, and past the stage door of the Irving Theatre, where he would remember his brief encounters with Mrs Grice, and their visits to the pub nearby. But tonight – he'd been in her flat, where she'd given him the suit he was wearing now.

He'd felt at home in her flat. The two women, mother and daughter, and the father gone. He entertained a wistful fantasy. He needed not to possess these women but to take the place of the man they'd lost. He paused a second as the idea took shape, briefly, but he didn't pause for long. Far too cold. On he went towards Seven Dials in the belief that if he walked fast enough his quickening heart would heat the blood in his veins and hold off the worst of the cold. He passed down the alley and a couple of tired prostitutes asked him if he'd like to go to a party. He stood before a narrow front door and put his key in the lock. He entered the dank narrow hallway and began to climb the stairs. He heard a scream from out the back of the building. There was no light. There was something unpleasant on the stairs and he almost stepped in it. Up he went to the top floor.

Later that night he remembered he was now a man in possession of a navy-blue suit. He'd been sunk in a chair. Now he sprang to his feet and walked up and down the room, and it felt good, yes, for it had been such a long time, and if he only had a mirror, a long one, floor to ceiling, in which he could properly see himself, for it changed everything. New suit, new man – this was the feeling. He seized up his violin from the top of the piano, and sure now that herself and the boy, his mother, that is, and his sister's child, were asleep, he played a little Mendelssohn, and then, yes, a little of the late, mad Schumann.

Soon he forgot how cold it was up there. He played as he rarely played any more, that is, with real feeling, for he seemed to himself as inspired in that moment as he'd ever been, and there beyond the cracked window, with London's roofs and chimneys black in silhouette against the pale night sky he saw his audience, and it was vast, yes – all of London was out there listening to him! – and in front row centre Joan, dear Joan, dear Mrs Grice, with her daughter Vera beside her.

He grew tired at last. He put away the violin. He hung his suit with care on a wooden hanger, pinching the creases as he'd seen Joan do, and then climbed in under the blankets on the couch. He fell asleep in anticipation of opening his eyes in the light of day to the suit on the hanger on the hook on the back of their peeling, splintered front door.

9

JOAN WAS NOT finding Vera easy to live with. Her hours were unpredictable. Items of clothing and footwear were all over the flat, every cup and glass ending up in Gricey's room, which was now hers again, of course. The ubiquitous flotsam of an actress in rehearsal, this Joan had seen before, but it made it no easier. Then a strange and, oh, a rather ominous development. A few days later she was visited by Gustl Herzfeld. It seems Gustl had caught wind of Vera's suspicions and wanted to clear up any misunderstanding.

Auntie Gustl was a little faded now, a little bit *wilted*, and it was hard to say if she was closer to thirty or forty, and some days she looked older. She was blonde, like Julius, but there all resemblance ended. Her features were fine but puffy at times, bloated even, as though she were a serious drinker. Perhaps she was, thought Joan, although she'd never yet seen evidence of it. Which wasn't to say it wasn't the case. Some women drink only by themselves, and late at night.

It wasn't so late the night Gustl came round to see her but it was cold, although of course every night was cold then. Joan heard the bell and went to the window in Gricey's room from where she could see the street below. Gustl was down there gazing up at her. It was snowing again and she had no umbrella. Joan Grice was not entirely without sympathy for Auntie Gustl, for despite everything she recognised that whatever her mistakes, this woman was not responsible for the collapse of Vera's marriage. Vera could collapse a marriage all by herself.

And here she was, Auntie Gustl, thanking her, tripping a little on the doormat, apologising, somehow getting up the stairs. She was in her good black flannel coat, broad in the shoulder, fringed with black felt, and a gaily patterned headscarf knotted like a turban and damp with snow. She smelled of coal smoke and cigarettes and Joan knew she'd been in a pub. She brought her into the kitchen where it was warm by the stove, and took her coat and hung it steaming on the pulley. There was a tin of biscuits on the table and all the tea things. She thought, I am grieving, bereaved, I am a shadow of the woman I was. Now I have to look after Gustl Herzfeld?

– Good lord, she said, look at the state of you. What's happened, love? Shall we have a cup of tea? Or maybe you'd prefer a drop of something stronger?

Oh Gustl would indeed prefer a drop of something stronger.

– So would I, said Joan, for despite the ambivalence she felt towards this shabby refugee of Julius', she *was* a woman and she *did* arouse Joan's compassion and, too, her admiration, when she thought of what Gustl had survived, what little she knew about it. Gricey had always made it clear he hadn't much time for Auntie Gustl, and uttered dark sneers as to what Julius was doing with a Jewish refugee in his house. Given what Vera was now saying about there being a woman in the garden, and perfume in the bedroom, she didn't know quite what to think. But she was a shrewd woman, Joan, and didn't really believe this blowsy woman was a home wrecker. If it's the only home you've got, why wreck it? Even if it is the home of a swine like Julius Glass? Poor Gustl, what must she put up with in that house. And for a few seconds Joan felt her old lion self rising once more. Her fingers trembled, pouring gin into a couple of tumblers and being not parsimonious about it. I had a good man once, she thought, and Julius Glass destroyed him.

– Drink up, dear, she said, and we'll have another, and you'll tell me all about it.

But Gustl was not the woman to come swiftly to the point. She sat there in her cardigan, shifting about on the chair, frowning. She stopped and started, approached the fence then balked. She sipped her gin. Her English was at times not good, and it seemed to Joan that she was absorbed as much in finding the words as in framing the thought. She tried again. Julius was not a bad man, she said at last – *er ist kein schlechter Mensch* – not like people thought. It was true she was not his *Schwester,* but she was not his *Schickse.* No, no.

– *Schwester?*

– Sister.

– Oh, sister. You're not his sister, and you're not his *Schickse,* so what are you?

Gustl spoke now with the emphatic aplomb of a woman embarked on telling the truth, chin up and hands flat on the table. What emerged was a declaration that Julius had saved her from the fascists in Paris, and now – and this was new – now they were fighting fascists in London.

– But what about the perfume?

– *Was ist mit dem Perfum?*

– In his bedroom. Your perfume, the Jicky, Vera smelled it.

Gustl swelled with indignation.

– *Ich gehe in sein Schlafzimmer, aber ich gehe nicht mit ihm ins Bett!*

– English, dearie! Speak English!

Gustl admitted she went into his room but not his bed.

– Well, I daresay you don't get into his bed but what do you do?

– We talk.

– What do you talk about?

– I cannot tell you this. We are fighting the fascists. *Es ist ein wenig gefährlich, Liebste.* Not safe.

She reached across the table as though to hold Joan's hand but Joan wasn't having it. Fighting the fascists, are you, she thought. They were both smoking now. Joan then thought about her daughter, an untidy girl, eating pork pies with her fingers and drinking beer from the bottle at this very table the night before. She'd had a script in front of her but no other sign of what it was she did for a living, or how very good at it she was. She told Gustl it was Vera she was worried about, not fascists.

– I said to her he's a good man, cried Gustl. *Dass er ein guter Mensch sei!*

– What did she say?

– She said, I am not a fool.

– Why did you pretend to be his sister?

Gustl snorted and said it was her own stupid idea but now she thinks, what was wrong to tell the truth? She was ashamed of herself.

– And at my husband's funeral?

A long silence here. The snow pattered against the kitchen window. A large alarm clock ticked the time, seeming suddenly terribly loud.

– I'm sorry. *Es tut mir leid.*

Joan had not the heart to go on. They sat for some moments in silence. Gustl was staring at the table. Then up came those china-blue eyes, swimming a little in tears and gin, her mascara smudged and running with those she'd already shed.

– Your husband—

It burst out of her. Then she extended a soft white hand, paint-stained, and on the pinkie a thin silvery band with a tiny gem in it, groping for Joan's hand and not finding it.

– Yes?

– I think he was no good.

A silence. Joan stared at Gustl like a basilisk, unblinking.

– Go on, she said quietly, but with steel in her voice.

– You know everything. *Alles.*

– No, I don't. I know nothing.

She stood up and fetched the bottle down again. Oh bloody hell. What on earth was the woman on about?

– I know nothing, and whatever it is you think you know, Auntie, I don't want to hear it.

But Gustl had not the words anyway. Or if she had the words, they were all in German. She was confused, she opened her mouth, she closed it again, she closed her eyes, she brought her hands up to her face. There came a low groan. Joan wasn't angry now, although she'd felt a sharp flare of rage a moment before. Exasperated, rather, but familiar with Gustl's odd ways.

– All right, Auntie, she said. Now drink up, love, and off you go. Better take a cab, it's still snowing hard out there.

Gustl gazed at her. Oh, she *knew* Joan knew.

– Ah no! *Aber ich habe kein Geld. Nichts.*

– *Nichts geld?* No money?

– No money.

Gustl wasn't so bad, thought Joan. She wasn't a slut, as Gricey and Vera both seemed to think. She was disorganised, of course. But she'd spent two years on the run from the Nazis and Julius had saved her life. You had to make allowances. But to let her go out without a penny—!

She was a little shocked. Not a thing Gricey would have done, she thought.

– Finish your drink, dear, she said, then I'll give you what I've got in my purse and you'll have enough to get home at least. The pub on the corner, they'll get you one.

Gustl was weeping again. She didn't think she'd be shown kindness, after telling Joan her husband was no good. But that was what she had come to tell her, in part. She realised she had failed. She found the English incomprehensible.

– Drink up, dear, time I was in bed.

Five minutes later, exit Gustl in her damp flannel coat, two large gins inside her, in some disarray. She makes her unsteady way to the pub on the corner. Her soul is tarnished but there is nothing to be done about that now. Water under the bridge, she thinks. It's a phrase she's recently learned, and she finds it useful. To survive is what matters. All else is water under the bridge. *Wasser unter den Damm.*

She is parked on a stool in the small saloon bar with a gin-and-lemon in front of her. She becomes aware of a man trying to catch her eye from the other end of the counter. And oh yes, here he comes, he's making his move. The master race is on the move. He gets himself comfortable on the stool next to her.

– Buy you a drink, love?

– I don't mind if I do.

This phrase too has been recently acquired.

– And what's your name?

Gustl has assumed a rumbling baritone for this encounter, and with it a heavy Berliner accent.

– Auntie Fensterputzer.

Vera was still out and Joan took the opportunity to go into Gricey's wardrobe. She was disturbed by her conversation with Gustl. She tried to shake it off, dismiss it as the maundering of a sad woman in drink. She wanted to have a look at her husband's overcoats. The black coat in which he'd died was hers now, of course. Oh, Joan. The impulse was a generous one, she told herself, her intention simply to give a poor man something warm to wear in this interminable winter. But what she could not have predicted – although we could, oh yes, we saw it coming – was that the frail structure she had for so long maintained to compensate for the loss she'd suffered, its collapse was imminent. And, all unknowing, Auntie Gustl had brought it to the very point of disintegration.

She kept the key in the bedroom, in a drawer of the small chest under the window. The key to the chest was on a ring in her handbag. She turned off the light in the kitchen and, closing the door behind her so as not to let the heat out and pushing the rug up against it, she went along the passage and into Gricey's room. It was bitterly cold in there and the curtains were closed.

Against the wall stood the immense fastness of the great peeling wardrobe, crowned with its broken pediment. Joan approached with caution. It was silent but its power was undiminished. His garments hung ranked along the rail inside. Eagerly Joan inhaled odours of heather and mothball. How many times now had she pulled clothes off their hangers, then laid herself upon them on the bed like a lover?

Tonight was different. She murmured aloud to him, saying why begrudge a poor actor the use of a coat? She had to ask his permission for he still lived, in a way, in her mind, in this wardrobe, and of course he coexisted with Frank Stone, the two at times discrete entities but often enough a twinned presence, stepping forward and back in ghostly tandem, in a kind of existential minuet. Or so at least it felt to Joan.

But still it was far from easy to stand in front of Gricey's clothes and not be affected. *Courage, dear,* she whispered. There was a particular overcoat she had in mind. She touched first a tailored jacket, a cotton-linen blend he'd worn last summer. Last summer – she stepped away and sank down on the bed, bringing her hands to her face—

She lifted her streaming eyes to the ceiling. To think of all she'd had to look forward to, last summer. Now lost. Just nothing. Meaningless. Just empty days, and little worth waking up for in the morning but memories and old clothes. And thinking this, she told herself, as she had a thousand times before, *now pull yourself together, dear, you stupid bloody woman, you have a task in life.* But at times she couldn't remember what it was.

With what then seemed the most arduous effort of will she stood up from the bed and, wiping her face, stepped forward to find the overcoat that would get that poor bugger through this dreadful winter.

Again she stood before it. Again she pushed the hangers

down the rail. Then she had her hand on the shoulder of the coat Gricey had sometimes worn when he made his wartime rounds in a tin helmet and armband. There was something else, something odd about this coat, and she'd known about it for some time and never confronted it. Until now. And as she lifted it off the rail she felt again a small flat hard thing behind the lapel. What's this? she said aloud, as though she had an audience, and turned it face out.

She stood between the wardrobe doors, holding the lapel in her fingers, the coat itself spilling from her hands onto the floor. She stared at it, disbelieving and believing at the same time. Then she unpinned it, the tin badge she'd found on the underside of the lapel. Again she stared at it as it lay in the palm of her hand. Then she heard a key turning in the front door. She slipped the badge into the pocket of her cardigan. The bedroom door flew open.

– I saw the light from the street and I thought I'd turned it off but maybe I didn't and that's practically *treason*!

– I was just getting something from your father's wardrobe—

– Oh Mum, such a night we had!

– Go into the kitchen, love, while I put these things away.

– A cup of tea, then I want to sleep for a thousand years.

Joan was left alone with the open wardrobe, the overcoat in her hands now and in her pocket that badge. She took it out and regarded it once more. She closed her fingers on it. She turned towards the door and found her reflection in the long mirror, and she was ashen. We knew what it meant all right, that flash of white lightning on blue, didn't we, ladies? Oh yes, and so did Joan.

10

THE NEXT DAY, cycling home in the dusk, she made a detour and stopped into a cinema. She wanted to see the newsreels. She'd thought she could never see them, she hadn't the stomach for it. But she'd changed her mind. She sat in a dark auditorium staring at images of corpses and bulldozers and lime pits. Emaciated people in filthy pyjamas stood behind fences. 'Refugees.' 'Displaced persons.' 'Victims of the Nazis.' They were Jews, of course. Why was this not made clear? She emerged from the cinema feeling ill. That night she sat alone in her kitchen staring at the stove. It didn't occur to her to get the gin down off the shelf tonight. It was after nine when she bestirred herself to make a sandwich, and then she couldn't eat it.

Gricey. The name carried no warmth or softness in Joan's heart that night, and in the days that followed she could think of nothing else. Gricey – the hypocrite.

Gricey the deceiver. The betrayer. The charlatan, the *traitor*. Oh, he was a character all right, he'd come home to her with his stories and she'd sit and listen, sewing or darning, a glass to hand, or a cup of tea, and he never mentioned the badge he wore on the inside of his lapel. Nor how he felt being married to a Jew, either. Or being the father of a Jew, poor Vera's blood tainted by her mother's. Subhuman, were we, thought Joan. Then she thought: Vera must never know, break her heart, it would. No, leave the girl a few illusions about her father. She could only imagine those Saturday afternoons when he didn't have a matinee, and off he'd go to the football, *or so he said*. Then those nights he didn't come home after the show, not until the early hours. Was he out with a bucket of whitewash? Painting swastikas on walls? He should have painted one on our wall, she thought. Or the neighbours' walls: the Bergs, the Silvers. Maybe he had. She'd certainly helped them scrub the fucking things off.

She tried not to think about it but it was all flooding up now. Oh, and was he out marching with the rest of them, in the street, yes, three abreast, proud in their hatred, shouting for the extermination of the men and women she spoke to every day of her life in the shops and caffs and pubs of Mile End, and Dalston, and Hackney and Limehouse and Whitechapel and Bow, was he out there shouting for the burning of the synagogues? At least he couldn't burn her synagogue, she didn't have one. Never observant, saw no point. But so what? He'd still have exterminated her. Why had nobody told her? They must have known. She could hear them in her head, wittering on.

– Ooh, didn't you know, love? Yes, he hated your people. Ooh, proper Blackshirt, your Gricey.

And the work he'd done in the war, a special constable, walking the streets of the West End in his tin hat all through the Blitz. Had he looked up at the night sky, the bombers droning through the clouds, and did he say to himself, go on, friend, drop the fucking lot, right on top of us? All the sorrow he'd caused her, dying as he did then trying to come through again as though he couldn't bear to leave her, and after what he'd done—

She couldn't stop thinking about it. Now she felt she didn't know the first thing about him. He was a stranger to her. And did he fight when the meetings turned ugly, when it got out of hand, chaos and violence in the streets, men screaming in pain and the coppers charging in with their truncheons out, always on the side of the fascists? And some men covered in blood with their teeth smashed in and their fingers broken, there was one man even lost an eye? And her Gricey was in all that, was he, *on the wrong side?* And Cable Street? Autumn of '36, when Mosley tried to bring three thousand fascists into the East End, and encountered barricades, and behind them twenty thousand Londoners, maybe more, Jews, Irish, communists, all sorts, who wanted no part of them *whatsoever*, and fought them to a standstill with sticks and chair legs and rocks, and unloaded on top of them from bedroom windows all the rotten vegetables and kitchen rubbish they could lay their hands on, *and* the contents of their chamber pots? Mosley had to take those fascists back where they'd come from. Wonderful thing, heart-warming it was, to see them turned back, as usual with no help from the coppers, the reverse – they supported *him*. Such pride we felt then, and some of us even thought, well, that's the end of that. Ha. But was *he* there, Gricey, in the fascist ranks?

Well, no. He didn't go in for the actual street fighting. He was more for entertaining the troops, as it were. Stiffening morale.

We saw her in the pub around this time. We thought we should take her out, cheer her up. There were a few of us she knew, old friends, Hattie of course, Delphie Dix, in her wheelchair, poor old thing. Mabel Hatch, two or three others. Oh, but she just sat there gazing into space while the talk ebbed and flowed around her. Have another drink, dear, before you freeze to bloody death, said Delphie – and Joan gazing into space with her mind a thousand miles away. We knew what she was thinking about, it was Gricey, of course, who all that time had had a secret, and herself practically the only one who didn't know it because nobody wanted to be the one to tell her. Well, why would we? She'd have told him.

– Who said that? he'd shout.

And Joan would have to say who it was.

– I'll have that cunt!

11

L ATE ONE SUNDAY morning Frank Stone rang Joan's
doorbell. Vera was out, a small mercy. Joan went
down and opened the front door. An arctic wind swept
into the building and flattened their clothes against their
limbs and went howling up the stairs like an Irish
ghost. He gazed at her for several moments and once
again the curious effect of time apart had occurred, for
she was bathed in light now. He stood on the windswept
pavement apparently unable to move.

– Mr Stone, are you coming in or not?

He stepped across the threshold and pushed the door
closed behind him. The howling continued in the street;
inside all was still. Joan turned and started up the stairs.
He was conscious of her body always, and felt able with
impunity to observe the lift of her heels, the taut calves in
sheer seamed silk – and where did she get silk stockings,
we should like to know, in 1947? – oh, and the sway of

her hips and her bum in the trim skirt, and he loved too
her long slim wrists with the white fingers trailing on the
banister as she ascended. She could feel his eyes upon her
and halfway up she stopped, and turned, and on the narrow staircase, with its thin carpet runner and the dim
light from the hallway above, she regarded him where
he'd halted three steps below.

– You're not wearing your suit.

– I keep it for best.

She turned and resumed the ascent. Then she stopped
again.

– This isn't best?

– Oh, this is very best, he said.

– I'm not royalty, you know, Frank.

He was staring at her intently although she didn't see
him, for she was again climbing the stairs.

– I think you are, Mrs Grice.

– Am what? – with her back to him still.

– Royalty.

She smiled grimly but he didn't see it. She was rarely flip-
pant with him. When it happened his heart sang. He
regarded it as brazen flirtation, any trace of humour he discovered in this composed and haughty and immensely
desirable woman. It was due in some part to what had
happened during the fitting of the blue suit prior to the alterations. He was not used to being the object of the close
physical attention of a woman like this, by which, we suppose, he meant a beautiful woman who so strongly impressed
and aroused him. So yes, she acquired more glamour in his
eyes each time he saw her. He was, to be plain, falling in love.

– Come in here please, she said.

She led him into Gricey's room. It was cold. The morning, although bright, was chill. It had snowed again. Vera's clothing was strewn across the bed and the chair, her stockings, her underwear, her *chemise de nuit,* her slightly tattered *peignoir.* Fragrant odour of Fleur d'Oranger in the cold morning air. Joan gave out a brief exasperated sigh and moved quickly to the bed, and swept the offending lingerie under a tumbled blanket. In her pocket was the key to the wardrobe. Eyes averted, she unlocked it. She had long since tidied and reorganised the contents, and on the rail three suits hung in wintry sunlight, the rest pushed out of sight.

– You are to choose one, Mr Stone.

With what cool formality she addressed him today. Oh, but her heart was breaking. He approached the suits and sorted through them quickly. His choice was soon made.

– I like this one, Mrs Grice.

It was a light Donegal tweed in flecked mustard, single-breasted and with a waistcoat with narrow lapels.

– It was one of his favourites. It's really a winter suit but he used to wear it year round.

How difficult now to speak of him. But it had to be done.

– Did he? Year round?

– Please try it on.

She left the room then stood with her back against the door, her arms at her sides. She took a few deep breaths. Having gone through this once already she was anticipating the shock of seeing her husband again, and this time with dread. She wasn't disappointed. When he appeared she was once again overwhelmed. Tears came. She stepped forward and pressed her forehead to his shoulder, but now it was Frank, him alone. He put his hands on the flatness of her back, beneath the shoulders, and again she was wearing cashmere. She rubbed her cheek against the rough nap of the tweed and let it scratch her skin as once it used to. Oh what was she doing? How could this be happening. She stepped back and they solemnly regarded each other.

– Do you like it?

– Yes, I do, he said. Do you?

The sensation of her body pressed close and warm against his own had almost undone him.

– Come into the sewing room, Mr Stone.

As before, as she pulled and pinned and chalked the fabric, physical intimacy occurred, in the sense that she stood very close to him. His hands had already been on her back for a few seconds, and he felt it would happen again but he wanted her to give him a sign. It came when she'd finished with the shoulders and once more rubbed her cheek on the slightly hairy texture of the tweed. So again he put his arms around her, more confidently this time, with his fingers spread across her lower back, and she shifted her position and lifted her arms up around his neck, Frank Stone's neck, still with her face pressed against his shoulder where she could detect a distant whisper of Gricey's scent. Oddly it didn't disgust her. Then with a groan Frank Stone all at once buried his face in her hair and clutched her very tight to himself.

After a few seconds she lifted her head and pulled back

so as to look into his eyes, and she was frowning now. She was almost as tall as he was. The world stood still.

– It *is* you, she whispered.

– It is.

But the kiss that should have occurred then did not. With her eyes averted she told him to go and change so she could make the alterations. It was clear to both of them that a day would come, and soon, when they would kiss each other, and with that knowledge a certain tension eased, as another came to life in its place.

Later, after he'd gone, she tried to work in her sewing room but it was no good. She had to lie down. With her face in her pillow she wept for several minutes. Then she heard someone enter the bedroom. She sat up at once, pulling down and flattening her skirt.

– Oh Mum.

Joan rarely allowed Vera to see her grief. But for a few minutes that day in February she allowed herself to be comforted by her daughter, for this now was no ordinary grief, this was grief compounded. The two of them lay on the bed staring at the ceiling. Vera reached for her mother's hand. They were silent for a while, no sound from the street outside. Vera spoke.

– That man's covering Harry now.

– What man, love?

She was thinking about the smells in Gricey's wardrobe.

– Dan Francis. The one who took over from Daddy.

Joan sat up on her elbow.

– Why do you mention him now?

– He mentioned you.

Joan was staring at Vera, whose eyes were closed. All at once they opened wide.

– You told him his Malvolio was as good as Daddy's.

– He said that?

Joan lay back down and again stared at the ceiling. It seemed most unlikely. Now it was Vera who was up on an elbow.

– Did you?

– Did I what?

She wouldn't talk to Vera about Frank. She wouldn't do it. Vera rolled over like a big warm seal.

– Tell him that.

– Oh I don't know, dear. It was just after your father died, I could have said anything.

– I think he's soft on you.

Joan said nothing.

– Don't you think that's funny? said Vera.

She was sitting up now and rolling a cigarette.

– Why is it funny? Funny how?

She was getting off the bed. Vera didn't understand why her mother was suddenly irritated. There'd been intimacy and shared tears a moment before.

– It isn't funny, said Vera, of course it isn't, I only meant that Daddy's cover would be like that.

– Like what?

Joan was sitting at her dressing table by this time, staring at her face in the mirror, and at Vera behind her, who was sitting on the bed straightening the seam of her stocking with a roll-up between her lips.

– It doesn't matter, said Vera.

She was sulky now. Joan was rubbing cream into her face.

– Are you going out? said Vera. What is it? Why have you gone all funny, is it because I mentioned that actor?

Silence from Joan.

– Mummy!

– Oh please don't talk about him! Can I just ask you not to do that?

Joan swivelled around on her stool. Her cheeks and forehead gleamed with white face cream. Vera thought it must be Gricey's memory that accounted for it, but it lodged in her memory all the same, and the next day, when she saw Frank Stone – or Dan Francis, as she still thought of him – in the theatre, she remembered her mother's strange mood and the two were now associated in her mind, this man and that mood. And he was wearing another of her father's suits. Not the double-breasted blue one but the light mustard tweed she'd always liked. Vera decided that it made her feel really rather peculiar to see her father's clothes being worn by another man.

Joan heard Frank's news and told him how pleased she was that he was working again, and so soon after *Twelfth Night* had come down. They were in a busy Lyons Corner House off Piccadilly Circus. He'd come from rehearsal and she was on her lunch hour.

– I'm cast as First Madman, he said.

He gazed at her, looking for a flicker of amusement, at least. Her hands were on the table, folded together, white and slender beside her teacup. He noticed she wasn't wearing her wedding ring. An eyebrow lifted, her lips parted slightly. He covered her hand with his own for a second or two. A public gesture of affection like this was by no means usual, for them, in fact it had never occurred before, not in public, but she allowed it, although as she gazed at him a small frown was picked out against the almost translucent skin of her forehead. Then she opened her handbag. She extracted a powder compact and briefly examined her face in the mirror. He'd never seen her do this. They'd only ever met at night, in pubs, and three times in her flat. She closed the compact with a light *snap*.

She smiled at him briefly without showing her teeth.

– I will also play an executioner. I'm going to learn Antonio just in case.

– Mr Stone, I know this. Vera told me. Now when is it you have to be back at the theatre?

He told her.

– Then you should go.

He left soon after. He was disappointed that she did not share his pleasure. She wouldn't allow him to pay for the tea, or for his slightly stale split scone and jam. She watched him thread his way through the people crowding into the teahouse, this tall, shuffling young man in a tweed suit, hatless, frowning, and over his arm his overcoat, which really was a disgrace. He must have one of Gricey's—

She felt weary of the whole thing. He must be kept in check. To touch her hand had thrilled him, she was aware of it, but that was enough. For now. And there was of course this further complication, that he was in the same company as Vera. Only a Madman, but he'd realised it might trouble her.

– Shall I tell them I don't want it? he'd said.

She was touched that he would offer.

– Did you accept it?

– I did accept it. But only two days ago.

– Then of course you must do it.

But after he'd left it was the problem of the overcoat that concerned her. She didn't want to think about the other thing, about Gricey. The winter showed no sign of letting up. There was more snow on the way. And he badly needed shoes too.

Joan found that when she was with Frank Stone she saw herself again reflected in a man's eyes, as for so many years she'd been reflected in Gricey's eyes. As though it were the habit of this remote woman to be loved. And for love Joan would have waited as long as she had to. Her good fortune, or ill, as it may be, she thought, was to find love so very soon after losing it, and losing it so abruptly, with such shocking finality. If there was reserve in her relations with Frank Stone, it had nothing to do with propriety. For was he not Gricey's *vessel*?

No he was not. She was no longer capable of sustaining his memory in one chamber of her heart and entertaining this stranger in another, and regarding them as one and the same. Difficult, perhaps, for some of us to grasp that a grieving woman could discover in one man the living spirit of another, and yet Joan had done so. But now this sense of a mutual identity was fast disappearing. Or put more plainly, a split in the fabric had appeared, a *rent*. She'd thought Gricey was going to come through, Frank Stone being the vessel. But it was *Frank* who was coming through, and *Gricey*, well Gricey was fast receding—

And as for Frank, here was a man bewitched by an older woman, herself, in whose cool demeanour and refined physical allure he had discovered beauty, but who had no way of knowing if she felt as frustrated or as impatient as he did, and if she did, whether loyalty or discretion or something else, he didn't know what, prevented her from telling him so. It would have eased his mind had she been able to. Had she put her hand on his and whispered: *Yes, my dearest heart, I know, and it's as difficult for me as it is for you.* Or words to that effect.

But like so much else it went unspoken. Pacing around late at night, or running his lines, or standing before his mirror, he'd feel the rising hunger, the fierce greedy *need* of her, and have to hold still while the emotion ran through him like a flood of water sluicing down a drain.

116

12

It was Delphie who'd got us all together in the pub that time, and Delphie who Joan went to talk to when she couldn't keep it to herself any longer. Poor Delphie, she'd been much in demand in the London theatre until her looks went. Parts for middle-aged actresses being always scarce, she was out of work for long periods. Joan often used to visit her in her little flat off the Fulham Road. She still dressed in some style, our Delph, for she had an eye for a bargain and a feel for fabric, and she and Joan always had much to say to each other on the subject.

– Now my father, said Delphie, who'd become a florid woman in age, he was a man of the cloth. Everything black except for the collar, and he wore it back to front. You ask me, it was his trousers should have gone on back to front, him a vicar and all.

The two women wheezed over their cigarettes. It was

an old joke but they still liked it. God knows the rest of us had heard it often enough.

– He thought I was a tart. You go on the stage you must be a tart.

Joan sat with her cup of tea.

– Delph, you ever feel your underwear brought you luck?

– Bad luck, oh yes.

Delphie was settled in the little armchair in her parlour. Like every room in London that year it was freezing despite the electric fire and the insulation round the windows and under the door. She seemed to drift off then, possibly thinking of the bad luck her underwear had brought her.

– I always wear white, said Joan, when I need things to go well.

– And what did you wear for Gricey?

Joan made herself busy with the teapot.

– Gricey, she said quietly, he liked me without a stitch.

– You don't surprise me, dear. You're a very good-looking woman. Any man would.

– I'm not so young any more.

– Who is, darling?

His Venus de Mile End, Gricey used to call her. Men would go to war for a woman like you, he said.

Oh dear. All it took was a thought like this and she had to turn her head away. Delphie understood, or she thought she did. She'd buried husbands. Two she'd even loved.

– You've had the worst luck, dear.

The widows drank their tea in companionable silence. No point rushing it, thought Joan. Delphie's cat had died. Septic throat. He'd got thin, weak, very *pinched*, she said. He wouldn't eat. She pressed her tired lips together. Not a tear. Flinty old thing, thought Joan.

– He smelled awful.

– I'm so sorry, love.

Delphie's armchair was by the window. The ashtray was on the arm of the chair beside the Senior Service and a box of matches. She reached for them now. Her trembling fingers were freighted with heavy rings.

– I had the fire in the bedroom going all night, she said.

Joan looked around the little sitting room. The framed photos of Delphie in her salad days, with stars of stage and music hall, many from before Joan's time. The upright piano against the wall. When had she last opened the lid? A year or so ago, it was, when a few old friends gathered in this room to celebrate VE Day. Gricey was present, of course. Songs were sung, with Delphie on the piano and Gricey in good voice.

– He'd had a haemorrhage, that's what the vet said. Bit of trouble with his lungs.

Joan wanted to know if there was trouble with Delphie's own lungs but she didn't say so. She also wanted to know what sort of a fascist Gricey was, but she didn't say that either, not yet. Instead she told Delphie she'd found a badge in one of his coats. She took it out of her handbag. Delphie peered at it, then reached for her glasses. If anyone knew – if anyone would tell her the truth – it was her.

– Was he one of them? said Joan.

Yes, there was a lot of it about in the East End, in the thirties. She found it so very hateful that it was her people who got picked on. Not that she'd ever thought very much about it, but what had we ever done to them? And Vera, she feared for Vera, god forbid she ever fell into the hands of those thugs some dark night. She remembered Friday nights, the old people coming out of synagogue and the fascists waiting round the corner to beat them up. Then there was the Ridley Street market on a Saturday morning, and up the canal, the old towpath under the gasworks, the slums, and Oswald Mosley and his Blackshirts were always making a bloody nuisance of themselves, always where the Jews lived. Why? Joan didn't get it; well, she did of course. It was always the Jews got picked on when times were hard, look at bloody Germany. She'd see them in the pubs, they were the BUF then, civil servants, some of them, schoolteachers, factory workers, all kinds but mostly hard-faced ex-servicemen and young louts from the shops and banks, handing out leaflets, trying to sell their newspapers or get a donation. There were women too, ladies of uncertain age and good family, unattached, and wistfully attracted to the idea of a glorious German past. Half the Mitfords were fascists, *and* their friends. Gricey would never say much about it, which she didn't understand at the time. She did now.

Olympia, that was back then, huge event in Earls Court that Mosley organised with fifteen thousand come to hear him spitting blood and thunder, the rich and important as well as the rest. Oh, and Blackshirts dragging people into corridors and alleys, anyone who dared heckle their precious Leader, and kicking them half to death. First they threw you down the stairs, then they beat you up, twenty or thirty on one, oh yes. The British don't care for that kind of thing. Fucking bullies. Gave Joan a chill just to think of it.

But just a joke, was it, done in the pub one night, some skit they put together and Gricey cast as a Blackshirt, or maybe as Sir Oswald himself? After the first shock wore off Joan tried to think of anything but that badge but she couldn't. She'd never seen him as a political sort of a man, although he talked a bit when he'd had a few. He was a good Labour man, voted for Attlee after the war, or so he'd told her. That's why she thought he wouldn't mind Frank Stone having his coat.

Later, this would be the Sunday afternoon, after Delphie, she stood in the middle of Battersea Bridge, gazing down at the river. What a sluggish, dirty old river it was that day, full of melted snow and all the detritus snow brings, chunks of grey ice, branches and leaves, rubbish. The Thames in winter, she thought, and at its very worst. The sudden unbidden idea of drowning in it almost made her cry out. Thoughts of suicide had occurred to her more than once in the last weeks, and she'd even considered how she'd do it. It was all this death. That cat, and Delphie on her last legs. Delphie had told her what the doctor said, she had to stop smoking.

– Too late, I told him. It's my only pleasure.

There was a spasm of that truly dreadful hacking cough and her eyes streamed a little. It was all very upsetting so Joan did what she'd come down to the river to do, she tossed the badge into the watery mess below, and almost threw her wedding ring after it but at the last moment changed her mind.

– Was he one of them? she'd said to Delphie.

– Yes dear, said Delphie. Oh, he was.

A pause, a silence.

– Not a bad one, said Delphie.

– Not a *bad* one? said Joan, who knew her own mind when it came to fascists. You saying there's good ones?

– I'm saying, not like some. They were proud of him. A famous actor on their side? You can understand it.

Joan was not finding it easy to accept the fact that the man to whom she'd been married almost thirty years had withheld from her a truth about himself that she found frankly an abomination. Now it seemed that Delphie wasn't too bothered about it, and the pair of them friends since Joan looked after her costumes back when Delphie was playing the music halls. She'd come to Vera's wedding. Lord, if she couldn't trust Delphie—

– You know what Englishmen are, love. You remember how it was after the First War.

– How was it, Delphie?

Delphie sighed. She seemed to grow weary of the topic.

She reached for her cigarettes. Joan was close to tears. She was fierce with a rage she could barely contain.

– But why didn't he tell me? she cried.

– I think he was afraid to, dear.

– He was afraid of nothing.

– He was afraid of you.

She thought, afraid of me? *Him?* Of *me?* Why? Because I'm a Jew? Was that it? Ha bloody ha. And she remembered once, out on the street, a Saturday morning, Vera was with them, fourteen years old, and some idiot stuck a BUF flier in her hand. Oh, Joan slapped him, yes, and really very hard. It made her so angry! A child! She wanted to hit him again, have a real go at him, but Gricey stopped her. Of course he did. He was one of them. He liked Mosley, he'd have voted for him, and how was she ever going to explain *that* to Vera? More to the point, how was she going to protect her from it?

She sat in her kitchen with lowered head and wept. What before she'd concealed from herself she could no longer deny. What a fool she was. How could she have been so wilfully blind? But all through the war and the years leading up to the war never once did he say he wanted the Germans to win. But he must have wanted it because he believed what they believed, for why else would he wear the bloody thing pinned behind his lapel where nobody could see it unless he wanted them to? And how many times had she laid her head against it, all unknowing? In a loving moment, say. With her arms round his neck? Leaning into the fucker, loving him and trusting him, and inches, *inches* from her cheek, that horrible little tinny bit of evil? But she'd felt it, and never asked him what it was. Why? Because she didn't want to know. At least he was dead, yes, and dead to her too, she thought so now. Where once she'd wanted him back under any conditions, even in the body of another man, not now, oh no. She was done with him now. Let him rot in hell.

She lifted her head. She dried her tears. She'd surprised herself. Never could she have imagined thinking such a thing. But their beliefs disgusted her.

Later that night Vera was fast asleep in bed and Joan again sitting at the kitchen table. She was drinking. She was trying to sort out her thoughts. To call people vermin, decent people like herself, and what was worse he'd *known* she'd feel like this, which was why he'd told her nothing. But to deceive her so. To live a double life, never opening his mind honestly to her, carrying his secret all that time and those hateful thoughts seething in his skull like corpse beetles in a coffin and pretending every day to be the dependable man, the warm-hearted husband and father, everyone's friend – *old Gricey, good old Gricey* – and never once, not *once* saying what he really thought. She topped up her glass. Thank you, Uncle Alcohol.

So could she trust a single thing he'd said? Their life together now seemed nothing but an elaborate performance of pretence and disguise, yes, his whole life a performance, he'd never stopped performing, the real man was visible only when fascists came together, this she now believed, but she had never seen it and those who were aware of it never spoke of it, not to her. All at once she remembered the men at the funeral she hadn't recognised and didn't know. Fascists! – and actors. Fascists and actors, all gathered here today in the sight of God – was *every* actor a fascist then? – every fascist an actor? – no, stop, that way madness—

Oh Christ. Thank you, Uncle.

13

Like her mother, Vera Grice at this time was far from stable or tranquil or clear in her mind about anything, but she did have her work. She was becoming so thoroughly immersed in the play she was shortly to start rehearsing that the real world receded, and was experienced with immediacy only when it coincided with the play. But to this she did pay attention: the conviction that her mother was not only giving the actor Dan Francis her father's clothes, she was having *assignations* with him. And him in her father's suit, the father for whom she still grieved, and for whom her mother should also still be grieving, unless she lacked all human feeling, and with cold, heartless selfishness had taken up with this obscure actor who doubtless performed her father's role in her mother's bed as once he'd performed it on the stage of the Irving Theatre! There was a Jacobean tendency in this tortured line of thinking, but then it was a Jacobean tragedy that Vera was rehearsing at this time. For she'd agreed to perform the leading role in a play that dripped with treachery and madness and incestuous lust and blood. And a woman who refused to behave as widows should. She was going to play the lead in *The Duchess of Malfi*.

When she returned to the flat that night she found her mother sitting in the kitchen. There was food warming on the stove. Joan had been crying. She rose from the table and moved to the stove, turning her back.

– Sit down, love, she said, while I put the kettle on. Tell me what you did today.

But Vera was in no mood for any of this, and not to be seduced with tears or cups of tea. She sat smoking and glaring, nursing her grievance. It was a mood Joan had known all her daughter's life. She and Gricey used to laugh about it, Vera's *pets*, they called them. She was in one of her *pets*, they said in a theatrical whisper. Little Hamlet, they called her. Vera heard them and hated it. She was about to give voice to her anger when her mother spoke first.

– You're not in one of your pets, are you, dear? she said.

She knew it was a provocation but she was weary of ministering to her daughter's needs when her own needs were becoming so very urgent. Vera sat in a state of stiffened outrage for a few seconds. With this too her mother was familiar.

– I opened a nice tin of pink salmon, she said, with her back still to the table. It was only ninepence and there's some cabbage left from Sunday.

The silence lasted a few seconds more, then Vera abruptly pushed back her chair and left the kitchen, and the door of what once was Gricey's room, but now was hers, slammed. And with all I have to deal with now, thought Joan. Under her breath she said, she'll have to go.

She took her bicycle out the following Sunday afternoon and went to visit Julius in Lupus Mews. Not a meeting she relished, but it had to be done. They had to talk about Vera; also about Gricey. That conversation was long overdue and now of course everything had changed, what with the badge and all. She found him melancholy. There were others at the kitchen table, the man Karsh, also Peter Ryder. He'd been a Spitfire pilot in the war. Joan had met him before. The limping hero, broken in spirit after being shot down over the Channel. Right hand badly burned, hip broken in two places. The war was over now but Peter Ryder still woke screaming in the night. When Joan appeared he rose to his feet with some difficulty. She saw him wince when he put weight on the leg.

– Peter, you don't have to get up for me.

Peter sat down. Joan suspected he'd come round to borrow money for drink. She also believed he had fascist sympathies. She'd seen him in one of the pubs they used, the Two Eagles. Peter Ryder drank in that pub, though to be fair you could say – and it wouldn't be a stretch – what pub did Peter Ryder not drink in?

She had a word with Gustl, who seemed as usual sad, damp, but warm. She turned to the morose Julius. She guessed at once that he missed Vera rather badly and still didn't understand why she'd left him.

– Julius, she said, we must talk.

He lifted his head. She was positively civil, what was going on? She'd been snarling at him for weeks. Her tone was muted; conciliatory, even. Oh but look at him. His eyelids were heavy, his skin more sallow than ever, and the blond head that once had shone in wintry sunlight was lank now, and dull. He was smoking a desultory cigar.

– I have to speak to you in private, she said.

He got to his feet.

– Garden too cold for you?

Still warm from her bicycle ride she told him that no, the garden was fine.

They went down the steps from the back door and sat on a wooden bench. They gazed at the bare hanging branches of the weeping willow at the end of the garden, where Vera had seen the creeping man. Julius had thrown a long grey coat over his shoulders but failed to button it or even put his arms in the sleeves. Let this be brief, Joan thought.

– You want her back, Julius, is that right?

His eyes flickered to hers for a second. He nodded.

– How are you going to convince her?

– Tell me.

– Take flowers. Be humble. Say you can't live without her.

All at once a small black cat was picking its way along the top of the garden wall. Its tail was up like a stick.

– I can't.

– Can't what?

– Live without her.

He turned towards her, this clever, subtle, complicated man, and all she saw was helplessness and pathos. To her mild astonishment she felt sorry for him. What has changed? she thought, but she knew the answer to that.

– It won't be easy. She's in rehearsal. It'll be an upheaval. I don't envy you.

Joan watched a thrush pecking vainly at the hard earth. The cat paused on the wall and stared at the bird. The cold was getting into her bones now. The sky was grey and the earth was like iron. Julius stood up and lit his cigar, which had gone out, then walked back and forth with his head down as though contemplating a military campaign. Joan told him it was too cold, she had to go in.

– One question. Does she still like me?

– Oh you fool, she said. She's mad about you.

Dusk was coming on when she left Lupus Mews. There was a mist rising, and a damp chill. She mounted her bicycle. She hadn't asked Julius about that last conversation they'd had, him and Gricey, nor had he volunteered anything, and now as she cycled east towards Mile End she thought about turning back. But no. It could wait. And Gustl, poor Gustl, who'd almost been murdered by the Gestapo, she knew Gricey was a fascist. So what then did they think of her? That she knew it too, and was *complicit*? This distressed her considerably. When she reached Archibald Street she wheeled her bicycle into the hall then climbed the stairs. Oh Uncle, I shall be requiring the pleasure of your company tonight.

There was a pub on Victoria Street called the Prince of Wales. Frank had suggested it. It was the best he could do. We see them then, during that brief period when they met in the Prince of Wales, we see an island of silent intimacy within a noisy crowd, and odd, no, to think of silence as a conduit of love, and themselves theatre people? Joan had been somewhat reassured. Cycling up Victoria Street that first time, she'd seen him standing outside the pub in the cold, waiting for her. He didn't want her to have to go in unescorted. She knew at once that her fears were unfounded, that no dark spirit resided in him, and it was a kind of awakening, she told us much later, because with Gricey being not in him any more, he was just Frank Stone.

But after an hour, and with this new closeness between them, they knew it was no good. No good this sitting in a pub when it was becoming abundantly clear to both of them that they must be alone in a room, and not just any room, a room with a bed in it and a door that could be locked from the inside. Nothing else would do. Why not Frank Stone's room, his bed? Joan often considered it but she couldn't say this to him, and he didn't suggest it. The absurdity of her position was evident to her when they parted on a cold pavement after last orders.

One day later that week she went round to Lupus Mews again and Gustl let her in. Come in, love, she said, fancy one, do you? I know I do. *Trink doch einen, dann wird*

131

dir warm, Liebste. Go on, love, it'll warm you up. Gustl knew nobody understood her when she spoke German but it made her feel like who she was, a Berliner. Not that there was much of Berlin left any more, it was all rubble, worse even than London. Dear Gustl, Joan was glad to sit down with her, just the two of them, in Julius' warm kitchen. It made it easier. So when they were settled, and had lit their fags, Joan told her about the shock she'd had.

Gustl was wearing her painter's smock. She'd been in the front room when Joan knocked on the door. That was where she'd set up a table and easel so she could paint in peace with the good morning light. Julius had had the carpet taken up and installed an electric fire, and he'd hung blackout curtains on the window to keep the draughts out in the evening. On the one occasion she'd asked Joan to come into her studio, Joan had laid a hand on Gustl's arm and explained that she 'hadn't much of an eye for art'.

– *Ich habe einen Sinn für Kunst, aber das ist auch alles, was ich habe.*

– I didn't understand a word, dear.

– It's all I do have, said Gustl.

– Yes, said Joan, I think you do.

– I would like to paint you, said Gustl, and added, quietly: *Ich würde dich auch gern—*

Joan had thought this a bit off, painting her portrait, but she kept quiet and no more had been said about it. Now they were sitting at the kitchen table and Joan was telling her about the badge, and what Delphie had said, and how she'd thrown the filthy thing into the river off Battersea Bridge.

– Did you know, love? said Joan.

Gustl solemnly nodded her head.

– You did not know, *Liebste*?

– No. I'm so sorry.

– Is not necessary.

– I feel ashamed of myself. And after what you've—

Gustl laid her hand on Joan's and said again that it wasn't necessary.

– He wasn't one of the bad ones, that's what Delphie said, but I don't know if I can believe her.

Gustl shook her head. Gustl didn't believe you could be 'not one of the bad ones' either. Now it was as though there had come into the room an unpleasant smell.

– He had many friends? said Gustl.

– Gricey? He knew everyone. Walk into any pub in London and he always knew somebody. Hello, he'd say, here's Tommy the Crow. Hello, Tommy, still being a cunt, are you? He knew Oswald Mosley. He brought his wife to *Twelfth Night*. They sat in a box.

Joan fell silent. She'd thought at the time Gricey was simply amused that the great fascist liked Shakespeare. Now it was sinister; more than sinister, it was damning. They'd wanted to come round after but it didn't work out for some reason. A problem with Her Ladyship. She was a bloody Mitford.

– Come round to your home?

– Backstage, love.

Gustl then said Julius should hear this.

133

– I don't want him to tell Vera.

– He won't tell Vera. So long a secret, *warum*?

– *Warum*?

– Why? Why to tell her now?

Joan set her elbows on the table and sank her head into her hands.

Julius was in his study. Not a large room and made smaller by the books. Books floor to ceiling, books in heaps on the floor, and only a window over the desk that looked out over the back garden. He had his feet on the desk and was reading a new play and not enjoying it when Gustl appeared. She asked him to come into the kitchen, saying Joan was here. Julius swung his feet down off the desk, stood up and tossed the play into his wastepaper basket. He stretched and coughed. He lit a cigarette off a dog end smouldering in the ashtray and put his jacket on over his jersey. He rubbed his hands together.

– Cold, eh?

They went down the corridor and into the kitchen and there was Joan standing at the window looking out at the garden.

– Hello Julius, she said.

– Hello, dear.

– Tell him, said Gustl.

Julius sat at the table with his head bowed. His hands were laid flat before him. He nodded once or twice. It didn't take long to tell, what Joan knew. Delphie's remarks were included. Delphie knew that Gricey had been to a few meetings but Delphie didn't think so much of it, said

134

Joan. She said I shouldn't worry about it. Just lads being stupid, picking on the Jews again. Giving them a bit of trouble, well, you're not like us so they think it's not so bad.

Julius lifted his head.

– Who said this?

– Delphie Dix, said Joan, not entirely comfortable.

– *You're not like us so it's not so bad.*

Julius repeated the words in grim, flat tones. Joan glanced at Gustl who was gazing at her with some concern. She leaned across the table, and again covered Joan's hand with her own for a few seconds. Joan suddenly and for no apparent reason remembered Frank Stone sitting at her kitchen table, eating tinned salmon and tongue, and doing the same thing, covering her hand with his own. But Gricey was a fascist and it wasn't as Delphie said, it wasn't 'not so odd' or 'not so bad'. They all knew how it had worked in Germany. Knock on the door in the middle of the night, quick march to the cattle truck, and no one knew it better than Gustl.

– You had better to tell her, said Gustl.

So he told her. Yes, Gricey was one of them. Blackshirt. And highly regarded too. Now they'd started up again. The government had to release them after the war and they were back at it. And he, Julius, with Gustl and others, was on the other side, fighting them.

– But maybe she's right, Julius then said, rather suddenly, your friend. Maybe she's right, it's not so bad for these . . . opinions to be expressed, yet again. Perhaps they'll exhaust themselves. And it's not likely these people will command real influence in the country, not now. Pah! Their day has passed.

He spoke now with what sounded like blithe unconcern. His tone was mild, ruminative, scholarly almost in its conjectural speculation. The women gazed at him.

– Draw attention to it, you only make it worse! And, of course, it is a matter of the balanced point of view. Free speech, what we've been fighting for. This appears to be the government position, and perhaps they're right.

He shrugged. He was looking at his own hands now, spread out there on the table. Then up came his eyes, and all at once he was angry. He lifted a hand and brought it down flat on the table, *bang!*

– But it *matters*, he cried. It matters to these men who risked their lives, who *died*, some of them, fighting fascism, and came home from the war, men like Karsh – his eyes were ablaze now – came home to their lives in the East End, to their families, to find men shouting for their destruction *because they are Jews*!

A wintry sun had emerged from among heavy banks of cloud.

– And it was Karsh who started pushing back. Oh yes.

Joan was astonished. A kind of excitement, with which she was unfamiliar, had stirred to life inside her.

– What did he do?

– What did he *do?* cried Julius, leaning forward. Oh, I will tell you what he did. He and three other men broke up a meeting.

– What meeting?

– Fascist street meeting.

136

– It shouldn't be allowed, said Joan.

– You think it, *Liebste*, said Gustl.

Gustl looked at Julius, who was silent now. He was staring at his hands again, the fingers stained a deep tobacco brown at the tips. Faint sunshine drifting in from the garden caught in his pale gold hair. He was shining again. He told Joan how four Jewish ex-servicemen had listened to a fascist on a platform and decided they'd heard enough, so they went in, and they knocked some fascist heads together and overturned their platform. They'd given them a good kicking, yes, really put the boot in. Oh, they were angry. And they broke up that meeting good and proper.

– And you were there, said Joan.

– I drove the car. I knew what we'd done.

– What was that, Julius?

– Changed the situation. Started a fight. Quietly suggested there was no place in this country for fascists.

He paused.

– Then we kicked their arses halfway to Sunday.

– Did Gricey know?

Did Gricey know. Oh, Gricey. Oh, fucking Gricey. The fact of the matter – Julius had spoken of this only to Gustl – the fact of the matter, Gricey was mad at the end. He'd gone mad. Not mad like a rabid dog, but a rabid *exterminationist*. Kill them all, it was frightful. It was as though the mask had got stitched on so tight he couldn't get it off again. Joan must surely have known this, he thought. Didn't she see it, did she have no clue, until she found that badge? He remembered their last furious argument, that bitter cold day in January, himself and Gricey outside the back door at the top of the garden steps. Each was mortally dangerous to the other, for Gricey had seen Julius among the fascists, acting the part. And Julius had heard Gricey talking extermination. More ovens, more gas, sickening stuff. But when the pushing started, it was Gricey who went down.

– Oh yes, Gricey knew. He knew all right.

There was an interesting sort of a silence, full of questions. Then suddenly, a loud knock at the front door! *Bang bang bang bang!* It startled all three of them – a collective lurch of dread, Joan rising from the table, Gustl's eyes wide, a hand over her mouth. Then Julius went off down the corridor, closing the kitchen door behind him. The women heard voices, and a second later in came Peter Ryder, limping, and then Karsh himself. Oh, Karsh. Dear Karsh. He was a short man in a crumpled suit, a flat cap in his hand, no collar or tie, and he was ugly, mottled, unwholesome-looking, with blue eyes and a grey, pock-marked face, and apparently no other name, and Joan stared at him with some fascination. He nodded at her. He leaned across the table to shake her hand, and it was a large dry strong hand he gave her, and she felt oddly reassured by his presence and even a bit excited. She liked him. He made her feel almost tearful, she told us, she couldn't think why. We knew why. Then the three men were talking in low tones at one end of the table, while the two women sat at the other.

Auntie Gustl that day had a shawl around her shoulders, a silky thing, pale blue with tassels. Her blonde hair was pulled back from her face, which brought out the unflattering puffiness of her rouged cheeks. Now she was pouring tea. There was a nice little ruby on her finger. Joan rather distractedly admired it, while still absorbed in the peculiar atmosphere, the weather, or whatever it was, the excitement that Karsh had brought into the room.

– Yes it is nice, isn't it, said Gustl, lifting her hand.

– Where did you get it?

– Oh, a man.

She reached over and absently touched Joan's hand. She was watching Julius at the other end of the table as he quietly talked on, mostly to Karsh, while Peter Ryder glanced at the women and Joan thought: he'd rather be talking to us. Or to Gustl, anyway.

– What kind of a man?

– There's only two kinds—

– Gustl, cried Julius, who's the fellow with the lorry?

Gustl's sad eye lingered on Joan a moment then she turned towards Julius.

– Phil the Soil.

– No, I think it's Bill Bagshaw.

– Julius, Bill Bagshaw is not with lorry.

– I have to go home, said Joan.

– No, stay please a little, said Gustl.

Joan was standing now with her hands on the back of her chair. She sat down again. There was nowhere she had to be other than her empty flat.

– What are the two kinds of men? she said quietly.

– What? Oh I forget now.

139

– Was it in Berlin?

– *Nein! Es war Paris!*

She was suddenly alight. Paris, where Julius had found her, and carried her off to safety. What did Joan know of Paris? Or Berlin, for that matter? Next to nothing.

– Fascists and everybody else.

– What, love?

– The two types.

– I want to help.

– It's not safe, love.

Joan didn't have to say a word. Of course it wasn't bloody safe. One look at Karsh told her that.

– *Wir müssen Informationen haben.*

– In English!

– Information. We need information. What they are thinking, what planning. Who they are—

Joan gripped her arm.

– Tell me what to do!

14

W SEE JOAN and Frank now, sitting in the Prince of Wales on Victoria Street. She'd come from the Beaumont where *Heartbreak House* was in rehearsals. He'd come from *The Duchess of Malfi* rehearsal room in Waterloo. Both were tired. It had been almost four days. She had by now allowed him to cover her hand with his own on several public occasions, sometimes for as long as fifteen seconds. Poor man, his coat, suit, scarf and hat, all had been the property of Charlie Grice. On Frank Stone they created the impression of a dashing gentleman of straitened means, a poor man trying to suggest that he's better off than he actually is.

– Will you let me ask you something, Mr Stone? she said.

It was a Thursday night. The lighting was dim, as ever, the beer was rationed, and who could afford whisky in these times? But the place was thick with smoke and there was an agreeable crush of people around the bar, and the barking laughter of the men amid the lighter voices of the girls suggested a new tone in the air. Was it a rumour of spring? Joan had heard it in the costume shop, a faint lift in the voices of her girls. The gloom of their seemingly interminable winter was lightly punctured now by thin shafts of hope. A better day, or at least a warmer day was coming, this was the feeling abroad. Joan was aware of it but as yet unable to share in it for hers was a different sort of excitement.

Dear Frank, his attention, his affection, his devotion never wavered. He had given her not a single moment of doubt.

– Yes, Mrs Grice.

It was no longer an annoyance, his reluctance to use her first name, and she reciprocated. It was their humour to do so, and her name was invested, on his lips, with warmth, yes, and with longing.

– Why do you never ask me to your home?

He'd been afraid of this. He'd been dreading the question. He'd made up his mind how he would answer it when it came.

– Because I live with my mother.

– But I thought she was dead.

He shook his head.

– But I wonder why you didn't want to tell me, said Joan, the question addressed as much to herself as to him. She seldom smoked but she wanted to smoke now.

– Is she ill?

– She's very ill.

142

– Yes, I see.

She was troubled and wished she were not.

– But I have good news.

– Mrs Grice, said Frank, leaning forward, what is it?

He didn't trouble to apologise for not telling her the truth about his mother. He assumed her trust.

– Vera is moving out.

– Oh!

He sat back, or rather he rocked backwards on his chair. He dared not say what these words at once aroused in him. Joan smiled, and as she was a woman not accustomed to displays of warmth her smile was occluded, although it made fire in Frank's blood. He knew what she was telling him. She turned her head away and exhaled smoke. She lifted her chin. She turned again to his eager face.

– Now stop that this minute, she said. I don't want any trouble from you.

Much about Vera Grice was mysterious to those closest to her. Of predictability there was none. She had told Julius she would return to his house, but that she wished to continue living in the attic, and although Julius disliked the idea he agreed, believing it better that she live under his roof in any circumstances than elsewhere. He'd driven into the East End in the big Wolseley and brought her back in quiet triumph.

We see Joan wandering through the flat later that evening, and discovering that a change has occurred with Vera's brief occupation. Joan has come to think of the kitchen as the single room in which she is safe, and of Gricey's room as the ghost room, for it contains the great wardrobe where the morbid residue of the man endures. Vera's presence has had the effect of diminishing Gricey's. It is as though he's been driven into the very deepest recesses of the wardrobe, or even into the fabric of the building, still there, she thinks, but fainter now, and much less dangerous. She sits on the bed, where Vera in her haste has left behind a scarf, which Joan now fingers absently.

A bit later she's sitting in the kitchen. She covers her face with her hands because it's too much for her. And yes, it *is* too soon to turn to life, and yet she wants to, and knows herself well enough to be confident that despite his wishes she will try.

Frank Stone dislikes deceiving others about his past but finds he can't help it. He wants to stand naked before Joan Grice. He's recognised a quality in her that he wishes to possess, and his attraction is experienced viscerally. He wants *literally* to stand naked before her, and for her to stand naked before him. It is as fierce a thing as he has ever known, he thinks. He doesn't imagine he will reveal these feelings to her when next he sees her, on the Sunday, but in fact he does. For it is on that Sunday, a moonless night in early March, the air sharp as a blade, that she takes him into her bed. Yes. Not the bed in Gricey's room, where Vera has been sleeping, but the big bed that Gricey and Joan had once shared.

Oddly it is Gricey's hat that sets it off. Joan was

144

startled to find it on the hook on the back of the kitchen door. It had been in the wardrobe when she last saw it, and the wardrobe was locked. But now it was on the hook on the back of the kitchen door. It enraged her to see it there because it meant he'd been in the kitchen. That's what started it. She took Frank off down the corridor to the bedroom. And then she again heard Gricey's voice, but by that point she frankly didn't care.

But isn't it enough for you?

But what did he mean? A dead fascist in your wardrobe, isn't that enough for you? And *no* was her answer. No. No. *No.*

When later in the night she rose from the bed she swiftly wrapped herself in her dressing gown and slipped away before Frank Stone could properly see her. He found himself alone. He linked his fingers behind his head and gazed at the ceiling, all in shadow but for the glow through the crack in the curtain from the lamps in the street. He didn't know what this longed-for event meant to her, but he hoped she'd been in heaven, with him. He had no idea there was any question as to whether *he* was a man or a ghost in that bed. Joan meanwhile was in the kitchen. She took Gricey's hat from the back of the door. It was the grey felt trilby. She put it into the stove. There it shrivelled rapidly on the dormant coals and burst briefly into flame before disintegrating with a hissing sound, as of a deflating phantom.

She thought it might have been Vera who'd hung it there. Then she remembered that Julius had come in the car earlier and taken her home. She returned to the bedroom, her heart heaving with resolve. Frank hadn't moved. She sat on the edge of the bed and gazed at him. He wanted to talk but had sense enough to be quiet. Her hair was loose and her eyes were soft. After some seconds of this wordless scrutiny she eased the silky dressing gown from her shoulders, and as it fell to the floor Frank glimpsed her long throat and slim arms as she slipped back under the bedclothes with as little disturbance as a spirit entering seawater from a rock. She took him in her arms and soon they were warm again, for it was bitter cold in the flat in the middle of the night. Her pain began to subside after that.

There was a period of calm. It was Joan's unspoken belief that whatever passion had occurred, and would occur again, she must go forward with utmost prudence. We saw little of her during this time. With the flat all her own now, as she thought, she was able to conduct her life with almost complete discretion. In effect she sank into obscurity. She embraced obscurity. She rode her bicycle to the Beaumont each morning, and in the evenings, sometimes late, returned to Mile End, where it is our belief that she was visited each night by Frank Stone, himself coming from a rehearsal room in Waterloo, perhaps by way of the flat in Seven Dials. They no longer met in public for they had no need to. Nor did they wish to arouse comment in the theatre, which is a place of the most florid gossip, and where a story such as theirs would like wildfire spread from costume shop to dressing room, from the wings up to the flies. Small surprise then that Joan allowed no opportunity for herself and Frank Stone to be seen and commented upon by this peculiar tribe.

Later she would speak of the domestic atmosphere they created, these *shrouded lovers,* in the latter days. Only then did it occur to her how very lonely she had been after Gricey died. But now so much had been recovered – austerity was at an end! For there was again talk in the evening, attention paid to the inconsequential drift of her day which in large part, as it always had, involved the violence encountered in the costume shop. For it was an assault, what was suffered by the costumes in which actors stepped out each night then ripped off between scenes, until Joan and her girls took them in hand, applied sharp needles and, whispering soft words, brought them back good as new before sending them out to be ravaged again the next night.

All this she told Frank Stone, drily, as Gricey had liked it told, with small flares of lip and eyebrow to mark the absurdities of the world in which she worked. He listened to her with pleasure, being one of those who ravaged costumes himself, given half a chance.

– Dear, she said one evening, as they sat in the kitchen, late, him reading a newspaper and herself darning his socks.

He looked up. His face would seem to cloud over with what she liked to believe was love, when he turned to her, and it moved her. It made her soft. This had rarely happened with Gricey in the latter years, for they were at cross purposes often. But Frank did seem to understand that she must make the decisions, and had the good sense to let himself be rendered malleable by the gifts she gave him nightly. She made him want not to oppose her.

– Frank, how is your mother?

A flash of shame. Her glance was sharp.

– I am neglecting her.

– Yes, I thought so.

A few seconds of silence as she continued with quick fingers to darn the toe of a raddled sock.

– And there's nobody else to look after her?

She continued to darn. He was silent. She looked up.

– There's nobody else?

– There is a Hungarian—

– A Hungarian. Frank, what are we to do about her?

She folded her hands on the half-darned sock and gazed at him. She waited for him to pick up his cue. There was a gust of wind against the window, and the big clock tick-tocked on the shelf beside the stove. She was at the table and he was in Gricey's armchair. The bulb was dim and shadows clustered in the corners, plotting. The whispering gods of tragedy.

– I don't know what to do about her.

Then he was on the floor before her, his head against her knees and his arms wrapped around her legs. She gathered his hair in her fists and pulled at it, moaning a little, suddenly strongly moved. He scrambled onto a chair where he could put his arms around her and kiss her throat as she lifted her head to the ceiling, and then with small shushing sounds she pushed him away a little and took his face in her hands. Gazing into his damp

148

eyes from very close she shook her head and then pulled him to her once more.

– We'll go and see her together, my love, she whispered.

– Together?

– Yes.

She was stroking his head, then his face again, and then she kissed him on the lips and he pulled his chair forward, the legs scraping on the floorboards so as to get as close to her as he could and smother the idea.

A little later she sent him home, saying it would be on her conscience if his mother were left on her own another night. From Gricey's room she watched him walk rapidly towards the cemetery with his collar turned up and his breath like billowing smoke. She turned away from the window. How strange and marvellous it all was. None of it disturbed her now. She did not care what she ought to feel, nor about the nightmare of having lost the world when Gricey died. We knew what was in the bed when she first took Frank Stone into it: Death. Then Death was driven out. There was no place for Death any more. Gricey was the ghost now. Of the two of them it was Gricey who clung on, and it was for her now to let *him* go. More than once she had imagined him dangling over a void, hanging on to her fingers and in terror begging her not to let him go – and then, her decision to just open her hands – and *then* the long receding wail as he plummets into darkness, to be heard from no more—

No abject hesitation now! Her own resistance astonished

her. She returned to the kitchen and lit the gas under the kettle. She sat at the table staring at the hissing flame. She reached for the cat, and wanted a cigarette, but she had none. But there was still gin. She stood on a chair and got the bottle down from the top shelf, where she'd hidden it behind the turpentine. *Hello, dear Uncle.*

When next she saw him he said his mother was too unwell to see anyone and Joan said she was sorry. She wasn't in the least sorry because she didn't believe him.

– All the same, love, it's not right, an old woman left on her own.

They were in the kitchen again. He paced up and down, as far as it was possible for a tall man to pace anywhere in that room.

– Come and sit next to me, she said.

She turned her chair around to face the stove, where she'd opened the little door with the tongs so what heat there was poured straight out into the kitchen. It flung a sudden red-gold glow upon her features, and then upon his. They sat close together gazing at the flickering coals, while above them the dim bulb crackled in its stiff linen shade all veined in black, and hanging from a twisted cord, as the clock ticked.

15

WHEN VERA READ the part she remembered it at once for she'd seen it performed as a child. A severed hand presented for a woman's kiss. A family dead in waxen effigy. Incestuous appetite and rampant madness. How they schemed and plotted, grotesquerie abounding, and the minds of the men, all but Antonio, twisted with evil intention.

The author was John Webster. He had read contemporary accounts of the historical duchess, but chose to present her not as others had, as a wanton widow who abandons her duty so as to indulge private desire. No. Instead he gives us a woman who, choosing love, finds affection and friendship in her secret marriage to her steward, Antonio. Reading it now Vera understood how much work lay ahead of her.

For the Duchess was a woman, and Vera until now had played only girls. Nina, Nora, Cordelia. Rosalind. Juliet.

For this reason alone we were all so very curious as to what she'd make of it. She saw a mother, first, a reckless, lusty mother, but an honourable woman, brave, wilful and autocratic, and also cunning. She was wise and deceiving (but not of her husband). Hot blooded, active rather than pensive. Dark like her brothers. Could she do it? we asked one another, had she the imagination for it? Julius thought so. And he would have for his director a woman of broad experience and an iron hand, and consummate theatrical taste. She was thought by many to be old school, a woman of the thirties, they said, but Julius thought otherwise. He hired her. Her name was Elizabeth Morton-Stanley. She agreed with Julius that the times called not for light sentiment but for tragedy, and the darker the better.

> *The worst is not,*
> *So long as we can say, 'This is the worst.'*

This was the spirit, redemption through suffering.

At the first reading Vera had not been impressive; she herself knew this and was not alarmed, and nor was her director. Of the others who'd been cast, she knew her waiting-woman Cariola – Mabel Hatch – and Ed Colefax, playing her twin brother Ferdinand, Duke of Calabria, who goes mad, believes himself to be a wolf, and attacks his own shadow. Him she'd known from a *Lear* in Stratford. And that heart-throb matinee idol, handsome Harry Catermole, he was to be her Antonio, oh a most perfect, gallant and gracious gentleman, later condemned for marrying above his station.

Vera knew Julius would look after her through the long days and nights of the rehearsal period. He expected an anxious, at times panicked and desperate woman, and at other times he knew she would be calm, elated even. Late in the day he would hope, in his exhaustion, for tranquillity, although without any real expectation of getting it.

On the first morning the cast assembled. At about half past nine in an empty hall in Waterloo several affable men and women in hats and overcoats were to be seen standing around in small groups smoking cigarettes and conversing in low tones. The booming laughter of Edmund Colefax erupted at intervals. Elizabeth Morton-Stanley was of course present. She stood by the door engaged in murmured argument with Julius about Harry Catermole's schedule, specifically his contractual release one afternoon a week to do BBC radio work. Elizabeth Morton-Stanley claimed not to have been told about this. Frank Stone stood near the door with May Lyons, a lady-in-waiting who was also covering Vera. Frank overheard this argument.

Vera herself was alone on the other side of the hall. She and Julius had stayed up late talking in the kitchen. He knew what she was going through. It was the traveller's unease before the start of a journey into the unknown. It is not true that the terror lessens with every step. Often the reverse is true. Julius had been patient and understanding, and wise enough to make the same point over and over.

– Vera, listen to me, dear. You've done this before.

– It's never been like this.

– Oh yes it has.

– It hasn't! Christ, Julius, you've never done it!

They're both smoking cigarettes. Outside the kitchen window the snow on the back lawn has only partially melted. The wall is seamed with ice, and icicles still hang dripping from the branches of the weeping willow at the bottom of the garden. There's no moon. The only sounds are the shunting trains, and the banshee screeching of iron wheels on rails. Julius knew it would be a long night.

– I've never done it but I've seen you do it, and nobody does it better than you, you know that, darling, but it's always like this and then you start to see a way. Don't you remember? Sweetheart?

Vera was standing by the back door, her arms folded, half turned away from him. She was flinging glances at him over her shoulder, fiery darts of resentment, resistance—

He was waiting for petulance. He realised that before they were married this had been Gricey's task, to reassure her in her panic. He wondered how he'd done it, what he'd said to her. He regarded his wife carefully. When he saw petulance he'd know she was starting to surrender. She was in a tight black skirt and high heels and a pale blue cardigan, and she had a scarf wrapped around her neck to protect her voice. Her hair was in a great tumble and her eyes were glorious in their damp black-lashed fury as she flung at him those fearsome glances, and

154

insisted with no small contempt that he knew nothing, nothing, of what it was she was about to endure. Then she appeared to come to a decision.

– I'm not doing it, Julius. You can forget about your fucking *Duchess of Malfi* right now.

– What about Elizabeth?

He referred to Elizabeth Morton-Stanley.

– I don't care about Elizabeth!

– You don't care about *Elizabeth*?

A weak spot in her argument, this. Vera was afraid of Elizabeth Morton-Stanley, everybody was, except perhaps Julius. She laid her forehead against the wall, and now her back was fully turned to him. Her arms were folded tight across her heaving chest, while Julius stood beside the stove, the length of the kitchen table between them. He watched her coolly. He lifted his glass to his lips. He waited.

Later she sat at the table and wept. After the mention of Elizabeth Morton-Stanley the first chink of petulance had opened, and a fretful child appeared. She'd sat down at the table, elbows planted close together, her head clasped tight in her long, pale hands.

– Oh give me a drink for Christ's sake before I kill myself.

Julius poured her a weak gin and put it in front of her. She took a few rapid sips then buried her face in her hands again. There was a long silence in the kitchen. Distant railway noises could still be heard. Then she started to talk.

– You're right, of course, you're always right, damn

you, darling, this happens every time but it doesn't make it any easier because you think, oh, this time it's too much for you and it *is* too much for me, it's an unnatural act, you see that. It's just – oh, it's *impossible*. What am I supposed to *do*? I mean, why does she let Ferdinand destroy her, why does she provoke him? She doesn't have to marry Antonio! Nobody has to *marry* someone—

Julius let out a small grunt of pleasure. He'd wanted to marry Vera about ten minutes after he met her. If that. It broke her ill temper. She briefly hammered the table with both fists then started to laugh and cry at the same time.

– What a fool I am, she murmured as the outburst subsided, her head came up, she pushed a hand through her hair and reached for a handkerchief.

By then he was sitting opposite her, leaning forward.

– You've done this before, he said again.

– Yes yes yes, I know. I'm going to bed, Julius.

– Where are you going to sleep?

– In the attic.

A pause here.

– Oh, in our room, she said, and then, with a rising inflection: *can* I sleep with you?

– Yes, dear.

Thus the night for Julius and Vera, on the eve of rehearsals. Some hours later, in that cold hall in Waterloo with the view of St Paul's, Elizabeth Morton-Stanley called her actors together. She was a woman of some heft, both of personality and physiognomy. A small female giant, then, with broad forehead and narrow, probing eyes, nose of an eagle, stout chins and a vast heap of reddish hair piled on top, she bestrode the London stage like a colossa. In a hoarse whisky baritone she told them what she wanted. It wasn't so much. Be punctual, she said. Be sober. Know your lines. Vera was composed now for it had started. She was setting off. In front of her she saw a sort of tunnel. It was long and dark and it would take her some time to reach the end of it. But what she'd find at the end of this tunnel was a truth. Yes. That's what she was after. The truth about the Duchess. Why it is that she does what she does and says what she says at every bloody moment of the drama. That was all.

Frank Stone was watching her, at least when he wasn't watching Harry Catermole. He had already decided that he would learn his own part, and that he would learn Antonio as well. This would not be easy but for Frank it felt like no obstacle at all. His appetite for the thing was huge. He would learn the part of Antonio exactly as Harry did it, which is what he'd done with Malvolio. He'd studied Gricey day in and day out and missed nothing. Saw it, and practised it. Made it perfect in his own image, so perfect in fact that when the man died and dear Joan first came to the theatre she couldn't tell the difference.

Then, to his astonishment, he felt rather nauseous. He felt very odd indeed – and had anyone been watching him, they'd have seen him turn grey, and then white, and even his lips grew white, for he had suddenly glimpsed that who he was – his *very self* – was as nothing. A tiny shadow self. Cowering behind the persona projected. Nothing. Certainly his identification with Gricey had been sustained far beyond the stage door, and often during *Twelfth Night* he'd walked out of the theatre a star, at least in his own mind, a being on a higher plane than the scruffy shivering fellow who sloped home through the dark streets of London. Yes, and in Gricey's bed, with Joan, even there he was something other—

And this is sometimes the case, we have observed, in the *genuine* actor, the real thing, that is, that the sense of self is weak to the point of incoherence. Yes. It is the way of the mask. Vera was watching him now, seeing him turn a most peculiar colour, and catching her eye he realised that *she* didn't think he was Gricey. No, it was only Joan, only Joan—

Oh, but that strange woman, Frank then thought, with all her impossible mystery—! She absorbed his every waking moment when he wasn't thinking about the play. So opaque, he thought, so very unreadable. And as the actors sat around the table that day, and read the play aloud, and Frank recovered from his momentary – *vastation* – he recognised in Antonio's dealings with this duchess, whose love he's aroused, a reflection of his own story. For he too possessed a duchess. He too, all undeserving, had won the love of a duchess. He glimpsed the revelation of a symmetry, and how often does that happen? We thought him a most unfortunate man. Yes, a very nice symmetry, life and the drama, that's what he saw; but we know what happens when symmetries appear, don't we, ladies? Bad tidings all round.

*

They read the play through. Elizabeth Morton-Stanley sat at the head of the table, and the frown barely lifted from her great blasted heath of a forehead. There was a pipe in the top pocket of her shapeless black blazer and she pulled it out at times to hit it on the table while she talked to an actor.

– Dear boy, would you please just read the bloody line as the man wrote it and stop trying to pull the wool over my eyes, I don't care what you think the character's really thinking, just say the bloody line.

Actors glanced at one another and made small illegible movements with fingers and lips, for they knew you can't just say the bloody line, you might as well get a machine in. Christ knows what the old girl wants, this was the feeling. At least they'd be on their feet in a day or two.

Then when they were on their feet it wasn't much better. Ed Colefax got it in the nose before he'd moved three steps downstage.

– Don't *mince*, man!

This was shouted from the chairs out front, where Elizabeth Morton-Stanley sat with her assistant, a weary homosexual called Sidney Temple who'd been at her side for years. The idea of Ed Colefax *mincing* provided amusement to the company and the tension briefly lifted. Ed swore audibly, although he wasn't heard out front, and then tried to move downstage again.

– Who are you? cried the director.

Again everything came to a halt. Ed knew enough to say nothing. The question expired in the cold air of the rehearsal hall. Elizabeth Morton-Stanley didn't shout at

159

Vera at all. It seemed she understood that she was working with delicate porcelain here. She would tread softly and keep her stick for the big beasts like Duke Ferdinand and his brother the Cardinal, played by the languid David Jekyll, a very well respected actor, and of course Bosola the melancholy spy. From the lovers she would coax with gentle tact the performances she required.

Vera came home exhausted but not desperate. She'd started to glimpse the invisible currents, the attitudes, the prospects of the other actors, around which she'd have to navigate in her own work. She'd been wearing her fur coat all day, it was still that cold, in *April*. Elizabeth Morton-Stanley liked the coat. She let others of the cast wear overcoats but not Harry Catermole. She said Antonio must be always vulnerable. Others thought she was punishing him for being absent once a week to do his BBC radio parts as contracted. It forced the director to use another actor for Antonio, which irritated her. Fortunately another member of the cast knew the part.

Later, in the kitchen, Julius asked Vera if she'd like to go out but he knew what she'd say. What she needed now was peace and quiet and early nights so she could think about the work. So she could be clear-headed for rehearsal, and protect her voice, her skin and her mood. And her bowels. Once the play was on, it would be different. By then she'd have been down that tunnel and got at John Webster's truth and come back out again a different woman. She was then supposed to put her on and take her off like a garment. But that's what she found so difficult. She always had trouble taking off the garment, perhaps because like Frank she hadn't got that much on underneath.

Julius was waiting for her when she came home in the evening, just as Joan would greet her Frank. Well, she'd had Gricey all these years, of course, but it had been different with him. Gricey never took it seriously. He was not a man for whom the drama mattered beyond its being his livelihood. The engagement of his true self, whatever that elusive and probably specious entity might be, or the idea of going down a tunnel and finding truth at the end of it, this was the stuff of humour for Gricey. The man without illusions, that's how he saw himself. Capable of playing the role he was asked to, and taking his pleasure where he found it, that for him was the meaning of life in its entirety, or so he'd led her to believe.

She remembered him coming home after the show, and how they'd sit and talk, just as she now sat with Frank Stone. But this was the difference – here was an actor who did take it seriously, so much so that Joan at times became alarmed and didn't know what to say to him. She was silent when he talked about his ambitions, and her silence seemed only to encourage him, and then he'd be walking back and forth in that little kitchen, telling her how Harry Catermole would be missing from rehearsals and he'd be on instead, for he'd let it be known that he'd learned the part. Joan thought about him working with Vera, and of this she was sure, that she couldn't return to the loneliness of those first weeks without Gricey; she'd rather die. Frank Stone made the world tolerable again. She strongly suspected that without him she would sink.

He'd fallen silent. As usual she had a needle in one hand, fabric in the other.

– How is your mother? she said.

He stood gazing down at her as she sat at the table. She had no idea what he'd been talking about.

– I'm sorry, love. What did you say?

– I asked you if you knew her.

– Who's that, dear?

– Elizabeth Morton-Stanley.

She'd worked on productions of hers. An impatient, unpleasant woman, she thought. The girls hated her. A bully. She would come to the stockroom and go through the racks. There were disagreements always. Joan would tell her what was possible, and often she trusted Joan more than she did her costume designer. It made it no easier dealing with her.

– I've worked with her.

– Could you speak to her about me?

Joan put her mending on the table and stood up. She was frowning. There was an unpleasantness in the air. She took the lapels of his jacket in her fingers. He'd asked her a few days before if he might have a new jacket, and she'd gone into Gricey's wardrobe and found one. Now she was angry. For a few seconds she examined the material. Then she looked him right in the eye. He was a grown man, talking like a boy.

– No, Mr Stone, I could not. Don't be so impatient. You'll get what you want.

– You think I will?

She sat down.

– Yes Mr Stone. Frank. I do.

– Why?

– It's always why. I won't tell you.

He was beside her now, he was sitting close to her, begging her to tell him why he'd get what he wanted. He was grinning. It was undignified.

– Because you want it too much. It's a bloody curse.

– What do you mean?

– That's enough. No more of this.

He laid his face on her breast and she ran her fingers through his thick hair and gazed out the window, thinking, he'll fall in love with someone else, that's what'll happen next. Someone who can do more for him than I can. Then he'll see me as a gargoyle. I must be prepared for this. He's got his confidence now. It's the new clothes. So it's all my doing. Oh, I am an *idiot*!

So something between them died a little that night.

Later as he slept she lay awake beside him and watched him, thinking that once she'd believed he was a vessel for her husband, whose spirit was in him. What she saw now was just a man, with his head on her pillow and his mouth open, and his arm flung across her body. Not a vessel, not a spirit, just a man, another vain, ambitious man. She eased him off her so she could turn and face the wall. It was warm at least in the bed with another living body. She didn't know what she wanted now, perhaps only to grieve for a good man, and Gricey had denied her that. The anger again rose up in her and she had to clench her fists and squeeze her eyes shut so as not to disturb the other one, whose breath was warm on her back. She pushed against him just a little and he stirred in his sleep.

For some minutes she was comforted by his closeness. She was growing drowsy. What was she to say to Vera about her father? Nothing. Vera was not to be disturbed by any of this, not yet. After they'd finished rehearsals, after they'd been on for a week or so, then she'd tell her. She'd have to, before someone else did. Or maybe let her finish the run. Who was looking after Frank Stone's mother? He wasn't supposed to be spending the night. What if the old woman took ill? What if she died, and him not there? What would they say? It would all come out. Vera would be hysterical. She turned in the bed to shake him awake and tell him he had to go home. But even as her hand hung in the dark there, close to his shoulder, she thought, it's all right. Let him sleep. The old woman was asleep. She would soon be asleep herself, she thought; and then she was. But not before she'd again pondered what Julius was asking her to do. *Es ist ein wenig gefährlich, Liebste,* Gustl had said. Yes, said Joan, when she'd got her to say it in English, she knew it was a bit dangerous. Her last thought was, I still don't know what to say to them.

16

JOAN BEGAN SITTING for her portrait. Gustl had told her several times she wanted to 'do' her and Joan hadn't seen the point. Me? Why me? Then finally: if you must. It was still cold but the light was clear when the blackout curtains were open. Since *Heartbreak House* had finished she was sometimes free in the afternoon. She still had much to do in the empty theatre. There were sewing machines to be cleaned and oiled, a thousand small necessary tasks to be delegated and overseen, but she could get away in the afternoon and Gustl was grateful, for she preferred to paint by natural light and Joan was a good subject. Such strong features, with her unblemished skin, her coal-black hair, her fine hands.

– Don't move so, said Gustl, and Joan smiled a little, seated there on a high-backed wooden chair with her back straight, her chin lifted, and her hands folded in her lap. She was wearing the black dress she'd made for

Gricey's funeral. She'd wanted to wear the veil too, but that request was met with laughter. Behind her Gustl had placed a small round table on high legs with a white china vase on it, and in the vase an off-white, almost yellowish rose. It was the smile Gustl wanted. Joan's lips never truly parted, for reasons already established concerning her teeth, and the lips themselves curved only slightly, and downward. But in the marble pallor of her cheek, there the smile was briefly evident as an almost imperceptible lift in the flesh, and because it was so fleeting, so *arcane*, it had aroused the imagination of the painter.

– So restless, she said.

She liked to paint portraits. There was a yellow one of Julius where his fingers were the focus. There was a small, half-finished study in oils for which Vera had briefly sat, then grown impatient and walked out of the room; never to return. And there were others stored at the top of the house, in the attic, including a number of self-portraits. She mentioned once to Joan that she'd lost ten years' work when she fled Germany.

Then there was one large work, painted here in London and hanging in the corridor above the kitchen door so you saw it as soon as you came in through the front door. The sky was dark and a woman was fleeing an unseen terror with a baby in her arms. She was looking over her shoulder. It was stark and fearful and Joan was very much impressed with it, for while she understood little about Gustl's flight to England she saw there in the painting how her friend must have experienced it. She didn't ask her about the baby. She associated this painting with the turmoil she was herself enduring with Gricey. It touched her dread and, too, it touched her sense of violation and shame. Although she didn't like it she seized on it as a sort of confirmation of what she felt. It affected her friendship with Gustl. It aroused trust.

Her mind drifted. In Gustl's studio a large canvas was propped against the wall that showed a group of refugees in a rowing boat on a stormy sea at dusk. The woman in flight from the unseen terror, the one in the painting in the hallway over the kitchen door, she was also in the rowing boat. It occurred to Joan to ask Gustl who she was but she would wait until she knew her better. Her thoughts wandered, but she always returned to Frank Stone and his pitiful desperation to succeed, and then to the sick mother in the cold flat he'd described to her in the alley off Seven Dials.

One day Joan went to visit her. She knew Seven Dials and she found the building. It was what her own mother would have done, tried to help a neighbour in need. She took a tin of tea. It was the middle of the day and the West End streets were crowded. The sun was out but it was very cold still, dirty snow in frozen heaps beside the pavement. She rode her bicycle up Shaftesbury Avenue to Cambridge Circus and in heavy traffic made a left turn with arm extended, the large bicycle swinging around the corner in a wide soaring arc, the tin of tea rattling about in the basket on the front mudguard. Her breath came like gusts of fog as she pushed on into the

Charing Cross Road and up the hill, her backside lifted off the saddle and her eyes ablaze with exertion; her mouth in a fierce rictus with her wide-spaced, blackened teeth exposed.

She saw old imposing buildings reduced to mere facades, skeletal, unsafe to enter, with wintry light spilling out of empty windows because the roof was gone. The crowds she saw on the pavements were poorly dressed and all worn out by this hard winter that still seemed to have no end in sight: everything grim and austere; everything cold. No work, the government useless, decline and fall wherever you looked. Just like '31, when Mosley started up. She slowed and turned into the alley off Seven Dials, and dismounting, leaned her bicycle against a lamp post. As usual there were a few prostitutes about, hugging thin coats to their scrawny frames, shivering. The front door of the narrow tenement opened at her touch.

She ascended a steep staircase. She was aware of cooking smells some of which she recognised, others not, as she passed through narrow landings. On the top floor she tapped at a door, believing it to be Frank's flat.

The woman was small, weary, unkempt, and spoke imperfect English with a strong German accent. She was no more, surely, than fifty years old, although the first impression suggested otherwise.

– Rosa Stone?

– I am Rosza Stein.

Joan stood there with her tin of tea. She stared at this little German woman and felt that she had met her before. After a silence Rosza Stein said: I am the mother of Franz.

– I am his friend, Joan said.

– Please come in, said the woman.

– I am Joan Grice.

– Yes.

She led Joan into a small, poorly furnished room, with a few objects and pictures that at once confirmed to Joan that this was a Jewish home she'd entered. The Sabbath candlesticks, a menorah. Rosza brought her to the couch and had her sit next to the unlit gas fire. She then sank to her knees, brushing her hair from her face, and with unsteady fingers struck a match and lit the gas. Behind the armchair stood an old piano and a kitchen chair, and on the chair a violin.

– Sit, please, Mrs Grice, soon it will be warm. Franz has told me about you.

Joan sat down slowly on the couch. Rosza disappeared. Joan did not take her coat off. She was still holding the tin of tea. There was a threadbare rug on bare boards and a few mean sticks of furniture: a table, some chairs, a worn-out couch, and she was startled to see a child on it, asleep beneath a blanket. There was only a thatch of black hair visible, a bare ankle, and a foot in a little sandal. The window frame was warped and the cracks were stuffed with rags. A stained ceiling, a single bulb, and a door into what must be a bedroom. This was Frank's home. Joan experienced a sudden fierce sadness. Much had become clear to her in the last seconds, and she didn't regret the impulse to descend upon the woman

169

unannounced. If you sat close enough to it, the fire took the chill off the room a little. There was a history here that Joan knew only from Frank's telling of it, which was certainly incomplete.

Rosza Stein reappeared with a plate of what Joan at once recognised as latkes. She accepted one, and oh, the taste took her straight back to her childhood. On the mantelpiece, a framed photograph of a large family, with a bearded father seated in the middle. Beside him stood a child who might have been Frank. On the wall a Jewish calendar. She gave Rosza the tin of tea, and was thanked. The woman gazed at her.

– Why did you leave Germany? said Joan, and knew it for a stupid question as soon as it was out of her mouth.

But she was nothing if not direct, and Rosza Stein the same.

– Because we're Jews. As you are, Mrs Grice.

– How did you get out?

– You wish to know?

Joan said that yes, she did wish to know, and the woman began to talk, and it seemed to Joan that she had not told this story often. It seemed not to have been organised by means of repetition. It required of her a kind of trance, and Joan understood that she must not be interrupted or it would be lost. A friend had come to Rosza's husband and said they had to go, just take whatever money they had, and go. This was a year before the war. They lived in Berlin. No, no, you must not wait, you must go now. The woman remembered the urgency, it had terrified her. So they went to the station but there was a problem because they had no transit visa, and her husband – this was poor Edvard, she said – she paused – he went to the consulate for the visas. But they did have a passport, they were all three on the passport, Edvard and Franz and herself—

So they had to go back and wait for the consul, who told Edvard that he would bring the visas. Others were leaving because they had their visas, but weeks passed and they were still waiting for the consul. Edvard said the consul would come tomorrow; every day, tomorrow. They lived in fear. They had to get out. Their bags were packed. And it seemed he did come, the consul with the visas but it was too late for Edvard. He had gone into his study the day before and shot himself.

Rosza stared at the little gas fire and became very still, as did Joan. It was as though this death, out of all the millions, was held in a tiny egg with a very thin shell and must not be dropped.

They went to the station, she and Franz, and now they had the child too, he was her daughter's baby son. And her daughter? said Joan.

Rosza stared at her, her eyes dry and her tone flat.

– *In den Osten gegangen. Adresse unbekannt.*

– English, dear?

– Gone East. Address unknown.

Joan felt sick. Rosza continued. Their friends told them go, go, they would look after Edvard, they would make the arrangements. They had packed of course, they'd been packed for weeks, and they had tickets but by now all the frontiers were closing. But they went to the station

171

all the same and it was the blackout. They were practising the blackout and it was all dark, thousands of people in the dark. More people were arriving, and such rumours they heard, terrible rumours, but Franz was very good, he said they would be OK, their papers were in order now but of course they had no papers for the baby. Then Franz got them on the train, she didn't know how he did it, but they went to Köln, and SS men came through and asked her how much money she had. They took it, also her jewellery, hidden in her clothing. They let them keep thirty schillings, which was nothing, then another one came and told Franz to get their luggage because they had to go with him. The child was inside Franz's coat and began to cry, and she said to herself, now we are all lost. But then as they were about to step off the train the SS man said, that is your child? And Franz said yes, and he said, go up again, and then the train started to move and they were saved. Why? She didn't know.

All her jewellery they'd taken but they let her keep her wedding ring. And then they were in the train and a man died and nobody knew what to do. But nobody wanted to leave the train. So they sat with him for hours, all through the night, and then when they crossed the border into Belgium they told a guard and the dead man was taken away.

She fell silent. With her hands clasped together and her head lowered, she sat profoundly still. The fire hissed. The child slept on, stirring only once but not awakening.

– Then what happened?

They left the train at Calais and were allowed into

172

England because they had their papers and there was Edvard's cousin in Hampstead who Franz told them was going to help them, and Franz's English was so good they believed him when he said his cousin's letter with the offer of help had been taken from him. He had studied English for many years, since he was small. He had been one year in the *Universität*, and of course he was *Musiker*—

Joan listened until Rosza seemed to have nothing left to say, and had begun to weep, although not for her husband, she said, but for her jewellery, which had come to her mother from *her* mother, and now she had lost it all.

17

H AD YOU BEEN passing down that dead-end mews street in Pimlico, not far from the Builders Arms and the small square with the defaced synagogue and the ruin of a house supposedly haunted by a German soldier, you might at around ten in the morning one cold day that spring have seen two persons emerge from the last house on the left. He was in a camel-hair coat, double breasted, with a silk scarf and a black beret. She wore a dark cloth coat, broad in the shoulder, tight in the breast and waist, stockings of a heavy grey wool, and men's walking shoes. And on her head, at a rakish angle, a slope-brimmed grey felt hat with a jaunty feather and pinned with a silver hat-pin that had a small precious stone set in its head. Around her neck hung a tippet of red fox fur. She carried a bulky handbag, and he a tight-furled umbrella. There was a brief conversation, irritable on both sides, as to whether she had locked the front door behind her. Then they were on the pavement arm-in-arm, turning up the road towards the bus stop. There was that about them which suggested that they were not husband and wife, or, if they were, remarkably ill-suited to one another. There were stoppages, shiftings and annoyances. To walk together in that manner was apparently irksome to both.

– Julius, don't go so fast.

– Please, Gustl, just pick up your feet. It's like walking with a distracted child. We must always convince. There must be no question.

– Yes yes. *Sag mir nochmals ihren Namen.*

– Hilda Bacon.

– My god. *Frau Speck. Gib mir eine Zigarette.*

On they tottered, blowing smoke in the chill morning air, to join a bus queue by a bomb site near St George's. There were three housewives with rollers under hairnets under headscarves knotted at the back, with empty shopping bags. There was a gent in a bowler hat with a briefcase and a face like a collapsing pastry. And two youths stamping their feet to stay warm. At last a bus. The uncoordinated couple sat upstairs at the front, their destination a small street off the Fulham Road.

We see them next at the front door of a terraced, three-storey white building with a small bookshop on the ground floor. In the window are displayed academic volumes of modern European history, German mostly. There is a black door to the side with a polished plaque that identifies it as the home of the Brompton Club. After a minute this door is opened by a tall woman of heavy build with blonde hair piled atop her head in braided

175

heaps. She wears a dark green tweed suit. Her eyes are heavy-lidded. There is a spark in her, on seeing them, for Julius is known to her, as is Gustl. It's the man who owned the theatre that got bombed, and his sister, the eccentric German lady.

– Come in, please, she says, and glances up and down the street as they enter.

She leads them upstairs and into a large pale living room with a pleasant outlook over a walled garden. Above the mantelpiece hangs a framed photograph of a thin-faced man in a black uniform. One of his eyes is out of alignment.

Hilda Bacon has no need to tell them, as her guests' eyes wander to the portrait, that this is the Leader. Mosley. High-born parliamentarian who threw it all away to found the British Union of Fascists. He'd spent most of the war in Holloway Prison. Released in 1943 on humanitarian grounds. Phlebitis.

They sit in low armchairs around the fireplace. There are mounted sepia-tinted photographs on a low table of a man in flowing Arab dress with camels. Hilda Bacon explains that her husband has been delayed. Julius reclines in the armchair, gazing at Hilda and smoking a cigarette. Hilda Bacon sits in placid majesty and only once betrays unease when picking at a wisp of lint on her skirt.

Beside Gustl on a table lie stapled newsletters, the top one titled, in Gothic script, *Imperial British Patriot*, and elsewhere on the page the initials, *IBP*. The subtitle is *Wir Kommen Wieder*. Gustl glances at Julius. We Come Again.

Ten uncomfortable minutes later they hear voices on the stairs and five men loudly enter the room, including Hilda's husband, Frederic Bacon. He is a balding, frowning man of fifty with a clipped moustache, in a black three-piece suit and a dark blue tie over a grey shirt with a silver tiepin in the form of an arrow. When he shoots his cuffs it's apparent he's wearing swastika cufflinks. Julius knows this about him. He is thought to be one of Mosley's most trusted officers. Earlier he had served with T. E. Lawrence in the Middle East, where he'd become an expert on the diseases of the camel. He is a devout Catholic with a religious conception of the State, and known to his subordinates as an inflexible martinet. His four companions are men in their late twenties in raincoats and duffel coats, all ex-Blackshirts.

Hilda takes her husband's coat and he comes to the fire, rubbing his hands. Nods are exchanged, for Julius and Gustl are known to these men. There are mumbled *Heils* and a bit of heel clicking. Several of these men spent the war in prison. They sustain a belief in themselves as diehard idealists fighting for a lost cause that may still come good. Their faith in their leaders is intense. All are virulently anti-Semitic. Gustl is as impassive as marble, and Julius is impressed, as always, by her composure. Frederic Bacon stands with his back to the fire then claps his hands.

– To business, he barks. There is a problem, gentlemen. We have a problem.

They all know what it is. It concerns security. Gustl watches the men scattered about the room. They are very dreadful to her. They frighten her. Julius has steepled his fingers under his chin and gazes at the ceiling. He shifts his position in his chair and shakes his head. Muttering is heard from the back of the room but Frederic silences it.

– What is it you have to say, Edgar?

A young man with a shock of black hair is sitting forward with his elbows on his knees. All at once he sits up. He seems angry.

– It's not us talking in the pub, he says. It's worse than that.

– What do you mean, Edgar?

– They know everything. They even get there before us. They know our numbers, they fucking know who the speakers are—

Gustl glances at Hilda with lifted eyebrows and pursed lips, as though to say, rough talk for the drawing room.

– Shut up, Edgar, says Hilda Bacon, you're not in a public house now.

Edgar turns his head away. He flushes at the rebuke.

– Nevertheless, he has a point, says Frederic Bacon.

– What is his point? says Julius.

Gustl marvels that he seizes the nettle so boldly. Someone's giving their plans to the enemy, and otherwise disrupting their activities. There have been cancellations when landlords and local councils have been warned who it is they're renting a hall to, and that there will be trouble. With outdoor meetings, when Bacon's men arrive to set up the platform, they find the enemy already in possession of the site, whatever East End street corner or piece of waste ground or bomb site they've chosen. Who is the enemy? A group of Jewish ex-servicemen, returned from the war to discover that what they'd been fighting against is flourishing in their own neighbourhoods. It's now clear they've infiltrated the resurgent fascist movement. Peter Ryder's name is mentioned.

– The point? cries Frederic Bacon. The point, my dear Julius, is the quality of their information. Edgar is right. It doesn't come only from the rank and file. And Peter Ryder is not the only one.

The persona Julius assumes for this meeting, and has sustained since he was first introduced to Frederic Bacon and the IBP, is one of careless lethargy at times interrupted by a vicious expression of xenophobic profanity, most often directed at the plight of the honest businessman, like himself, in this Jew-ridden country. As a blond Englishman with a Germanic surname and a glamorous actress wife, his credentials have gone unquestioned. Gustl, as his sister, is a more scattered species of anti-Semite. Nobody listens to her, but they like big women with fur round their neck who believe in the destiny of a greater Germany.

– Then where precisely is it coming from, says Julius. One of you boys?

He sits up in his chair and with his hands planted on the arms, elbows out, peers around the drawing room. He subjects even Hilda Bacon to scrutiny.

– Julius, please, says Frederic Bacon.

– In this room? says Gustl. *Mein Gott!*

There is animosity, sneering. The young man in the

179

corner, Edgar Cartridge, seething, resentful, leans against a table and watches with hooded eyes.

– Enough of this, says Frederic Bacon. I will deal with Peter Ryder in good time.

The meeting rambles on. There is discussion about a quantity of fascist literature to be moved from a printer in Hammersmith to the bookshop on the ground floor of the building. Other matters come up. Eventually Julius rises to his feet. On his face, the suggestion of boredom.

– You won't stay for a little sherry, Mr Glass? says Hilda Bacon.

– I'm afraid not, my dear. My sister and I have a luncheon appointment in town.

– Wait! says Frederic Bacon, bending to crush out his cigarette in an ashtray. Julius and Gustl stand startled for a few seconds.

– What news of the Grice woman?

– She is with us. She wants to help.

Frederic Bacon glances at the others.

– The widow of Charlie Grice is with us. What do you think of that, gentlemen?

There is some satisfied murmuring. Gricey had told none of them what sort of a woman he was married to. Oh, he wouldn't have been so very popular if that were known! No, they'd have kicked him out, and pretty sharpish too. He'd kept quiet about Joan all right.

– We may expect her then on the fifth?

– Yes, said Julius. We will bring her here. She is eager to meet you. But now, I'm afraid—

He looks at his watch.

– Then I will show you out, says Hilda.

As the door closes behind them, Edgar Cartridge looks at Frederic Bacon, who shrugs.

Julius and Gustl are sitting on the top floor of a double-decker bus bound for Pimlico.

– You were brilliant, *Liebste*, says Gustl.

– Such a tricky bastard he is. The printed matter isn't in Hammersmith. They'll point the finger at us when it's lost.

They sit gazing straight ahead as the bus wheezes down Ebury Street. They understand the danger they're in. But it had gone well this morning, considering.

– They're on to us, of course.

– But they like Joan.

– It's Gricey they like. But if Joan comes in we have more time. Our secret weapon.

Gustl laughs quietly, and under the red fur tippet her shoulders heave.

18

THEY WERE A week into rehearsals and it wasn't going so well. Vera was having difficulty with her lines. Webster's dark poetry was not easy. When she wasn't in the rehearsal hall she was pacing the attic of the house in Pimlico. She was determined to be off-book by the end of next week. Julius and Gustl could hear her up there as she flung about, stamping back and forth on the bare boards, shouting her lines, and swearing wildly when the words didn't at once come to her, or came wrong. They sat trying to read or, in Gustl's case, paint, but their eyes went constantly, nervously to the ceiling.

Eventually she came clattering downstairs and sat at the long kitchen table, snorting, and pushing her hands through her hair. Gustl entered the kitchen in spattered smock and turban.

– Going not well, love?

– Fucking nightmare.

– It comes, I hear it. Cup of tea?

– You think so?

– I think so. Here's Julius.

Julius had left his work in the small back office to see what was amiss.

– Not going well, love?

– It's coming but it's so fucking *slow*. I'll never be ready.

– Oh you will. Won't she? Tell her she'll be ready.

– She will, *nicht wahr*. Here's your tea, love.

And so it went at home. And back in the rehearsal space, the chilly church hall in Waterloo, some knots were untied, others they just pushed further down the piece of string for later. Was there progress? It wasn't the question. The question was: was there time?

– Brighton would be nice, said Edmund Colefax as he and Vera and the actor playing Bosola, Freddie Campion, sat on wooden boxes smoking cigarettes during the break. He'd have liked them to open out of town.

– Just to break the ice.

– I hate Brighton, said Freddie Campion.

– I was born in Brighton, said Vera. Daddy was playing the Royal.

– Nice to have memories then.

While they were enjoying this bit of wit Frank Stone wandered by but they didn't ask him to join them. He was playing First Madman in Act IV. He'd also learned Antonio. Then came the day Harry Catermole was off, released to fulfil his contractual obligations with the BBC. Vera was asking for more work on the last pages of

183

the first act. This was the wooing scene, which involved her romantic assault on Antonio.

– Yes, damn it, we'll have to use the First Madman. Does he know it?

Sidney Temple supervised the secondary parts.

– He knows it.

– Let's get it over then.

Frank was of course aware that Harry would not be present and that those pages were in the schedule because Vera wanted them in. Also that Vera was unhappy with how they'd been played in the first run-through. So there was more than a chance he would get to work with the Duchess, and oh yes, he was ready. It was just a hundred lines earlier that Duke Ferdinand says to Bosola: *She's a young widow, I would not have her marry again.* And a bit later he makes it clear to the Duchess herself: *Marry and you die.*

But she will defy him. And it is in this scene that she does so. Much will be revealed about the Duchess. That she is brave. That she knows her heart, that she is a passionate woman, and that she has chosen well. And is nothing if not decisive. She drives the matter forward and Antonio is pleased to be driven. She tells him she wishes to make a will. He suggests she first find a husband as beneficiary. *Go, go brag* – she says – *you have left me heartless, mine is in your bosom.* And later still she commands him, *Kneel* – and with her servant Cariola – Mabel Hatch, that is – stepping out from behind an arras, as witness, they declare themselves married. That's all it took in those days. The newly-weds then depart and Cariola says: *Whether the spirit of greatness or of woman, reign*

184

most in her, I know not, but it shows a fearful madness. I owe her much of pity.

Ominous words. End of Act I.

Frank Stone was fine. We were all impressed. Elizabeth Morton-Stanley stopped him only twice. First, to demand a stronger response when the Duchess closes his lips with a kiss. So they do it again, and this time she wraps an arm around his neck, and slips her other hand into the side pocket of his jacket. When he breaks free of her, hearing a sound behind the arras, it is done with such passionate urgency that the seam of the pocket rips and hangs off like a flap. The second time is when the Duchess commands him to kneel, and in the same moment Cariola emerges from behind the arras. Antonio's line is: *Ha?* The director wants this stronger too. But that was all.

When they were finished Vera laid a brief distracted hand on Frank's arm then went off to talk to the director. Frank wandered away. He was exhilarated. It was clear to him that he could play the scene much better than Harry Catermole. And he could still taste Vera's kiss. It was awkward, later, to tell Joan how well he'd done. She listened to him as she cooked their dinner. Shredded cabbage and corned beef, with cold semolina for pudding as a treat. Frank mentioned only that the director had had very little to say to him.

– What *did* she say to you?

Joan knew the cruelty towards actors of which Elizabeth Morton-Stanley was capable.

– Oh in one place, do more.

– What place was that, love?

She was not paying close attention. This was two days after her conversation with Frank's mother. She'd decided to say nothing about it yet, and so apparently had Rosza.

– When I have to kiss her.

– The Duchess?

– Yes.

– Vera?

– Yes.

Joan set her glass on the table and crushed out her cigarette in the ashtray. She stared at him with a stricken solemnity. He understood her concern, or thought he did.

– Should I not have said?

– No, you should have said. I am very tired, dear. I think I must go to bed. And you are to go home. I don't like your mother left on her own.

– You're displeased with me.

His distress was palpable, for a few seconds; then settled to resignation. But her heart was sick, she could not pretend otherwise. She reached across the table and laid her palm against his cheek. He was white as a sheet, and his eyes were alive with anxiety. Yes, and guilt, she knew, she could see it now. He may have been a good actor but he was a poor liar. How was that possible?

– No, my sweetheart, I am not displeased. I'm just tired.

He had to be reassured, then he had to be sent away. She wept a little in bed. She lay awake for an hour and then she fell asleep. She seldom had difficulty falling asleep. She was sad in the morning, as she sat at her mirror. Vera was hysterical but not recklessly so. Anyway she was far more preoccupied with her work than she ever was with sex, or so Joan told herself: nothing would come of it. She slipped her coat on, locked the door and went downstairs and out into the cold. Then she was on her bicycle and gliding past the bombed-out buildings near the docks, with their high, empty windows and air of unutterable desolation. The days were past when they still smouldered and stank but Joan was swept with sadness all the same. Wherever she looked, all she saw was ruin and waste.

Later, in Julius' house, sitting in the high-backed chair against the peeling, off-white plaster wall, with behind her the vase with the dead rose in it, and dead petals strewn across the table now, Joan gave Gustl her decision.

– I will come with you.

Gustl was behind the easel wiping a brush on a rag.

– *Gott sei Dank*, she whispered. I will tell Julius.

She could say nothing of any of this to Frank Stone. He came to supper on the Thursday, a cold, wet night. It was fortunate there was the matter of his jacket pocket, for it allowed them to avoid the topics about which for the first time they found they could not speak. It was when he took off his overcoat that she saw that it was ripped and hanging askew, and she at once told him to remove the jacket so she could inspect the damage.

187

– What happened, love?

– I had a book in the pocket and I tried to stuff my script in beside it. I wasn't thinking.

No, thought Joan, you were thinking about my Vera. He sat by the stove in his shirtsleeves and Joan put on her spectacles.

– Come into the sewing room, she said. Put your coat back on, dear, it's cold.

He followed her, she carrying the torn jacket. He'd seen her at her machine before. It gave him a curious pleasure. It was one of Gricey's jackets he'd torn, of course. She dropped it on her chair and from the shelf she pulled down a box of spools of thread. She selected what she wanted and sat at the machine. She put the spool on the pin and passed the thread onto the bobbin. How quick her fingers were, he thought, as she frowned over her spectacles, then selected a needle – and what was she doing now? She was humming as she pulled the thread through the machine then into the eye and with a turn of the wheel she was ready to feed the material onto the plate. She pressed the treadle and the sewing commenced. *Whirr-pause. Whirr-pause.*

It was soon done. When the material started to rise with the needle she paused to lighten the pressure on the thumb screw, and murmured to herself as she did so, for she'd forgotten how heavy it was and Frank, watching her, agreed.

– It *is* heavy, he said.

Again she paused, and turned to him where he stood behind her.

– Yes dear, she said, isn't it?

It amused her, and she resumed humming.

– I'm using a short stitch in case you want to stuff more books in your pocket.

– Oh I don't think I'll try that again, said Frank Stone.

– You never know. Heat of the moment.

She glanced up at him. In her spectacles she looked like a schoolmistress. He said nothing. He laid his hand on her shoulder and turned his head away.

– There!

She took her foot off the treadle, withdrew the garment and, lifting it, bit off the trailing thread. She inspected the mended pocket then turned to him and told him to put the jacket on.

– Put your hand in the pocket.

Gingerly he did so.

– Make a fist. Move it around.

– I don't want to tear it again.

– You won't.

He could feel the strength of the stitching.

– Good, she said. Let's have supper.

They went back to the kitchen, into the warmth, and the earlier awkwardness, when their secrets hung thick in the air, was dissipated now. Joan was even able to ask him how it had gone that day, and poor Frank Stone, he had not the guile to conceal his satisfaction at having played Antonio to Vera's Duchess once more. He was careless enough to suggest that if Harry never returned, and he, Frank, took on the role instead—

He stopped, appalled. It was as though he wanted

189

Harry dead, as he might once have wanted Gricey dead – and if he hadn't, then Joan would think he had—

She saw all this going through his mind and told him that every actor had such thoughts. It was only natural. Only human.

– Only human, said Frank, faintly.

The meeting was on Sunday. Julius was to drive them in to the East End, where they would leave the car in a side street close to the event. The day was overcast. Everything seemed turned to metal, everything the colour of lead, or iron or steel. Strong gusts of wind lifted sheets of newspaper from the pavement and sent tin cans and bottles clattering along the gutters. Men in overcoats and flat caps in twos and threes pushed through the wind; women and children, too. The meeting was at noon and Frederic Bacon was to speak. Joan walked between Julius and Gustl, the three arm-in-arm. Her face was like stone. She was anxious. She feared she would let down her companions through some display of weakness. But she was committed to it now.

About sixty people were gathered on a patch of ground where a house had come down and the ruins were only partly cleared from the site. Nearby stood other buildings with empty windows and no roofs. It was rough ground with a few heaps of rubble still, and the sky was blustery and grey, the clouds thick and low overhead. There were a dozen policemen. The platform was a crude wooden stage four feet high, rough-carpentered with old planks, a short leg at each corner. Four men in raincoats and hats stood on it. They were talking in low tones and casting glances at the crowd.

Frederic Bacon wore a pale shearling coat and carried a polished black stick. He made a short bow to Joan, whom he had not yet met. He then descended from the platform, helped down by a young man in a belted raincoat who was eyeing the crowd from the side of the platform. Julius recognised him as Edgar Cartridge. Later he pointed him out to the two women, saying under his breath that he was a *particularly* nasty specimen. Several more men gathered around the platform but the crowd remained sparse.

Frederic Bacon stood in front of Joan. She heard his heels click. This time he bowed deeply from the waist, then held his hand out. She gave him hers. He bent low over it, and applied his lips; fortunately she was wearing gloves. There was a little ragged singing in the crowd and then a black van, backfiring, appeared from the direction of Ridley Road. It mounted the pavement and came bumping and rattling across the waste ground to the side of the stage. Two men got out, and from the back of the van they lifted down a table. They manhandled it onto the stage.

– Here comes the flag, said Julius. Raise your voices.

Joan was cold. She hated this. She now bitterly regretted agreeing to become involved with these people. She watched a black flag with a swastika being draped over the table. As a gust of wind picked it off the table it fluttered wildly, and had not the two men held it down it would have gone flapping off across the waste ground, oh, with a gang of fascists chasing after it, and kicking it to death for insubordination. It seemed then the decision was made to get started. Chairs had been handed up onto the stage. The men sat down as Frederic Bacon stepped forward with a megaphone.

There was shouting, a disturbance, some kind of scuffle in the crowd but Joan had no clear view of what was happening. She felt violence was imminent and wanted only to leave. Gustl again slipped an arm through hers and murmured that she wasn't to worry for she would come to no harm.

– I'm not so sure, said Joan. Look at them all.

A limping man in a long RAF overcoat was meanwhile moving through the crowd. He was handing out pamphlets and collecting coins in a box. It was Peter Ryder.

– You've met Joan Grice, have you, Peter? said Julius.

– I have, he said, and lifted his hat.

Joan took the pamphlet he offered her. The words *Britain for the British* were printed across the top. Julius put some coins in the box. Peter Ryder moved off, but not before exchanging a whispered word or two with Julius.

– Karsh is coming, Julius then murmured to Gustl and Joan.

– Can you hear me? shouted Frederic Bacon. His megaphone wasn't working

There was shouting from the crowd, much of it unfriendly.

– Never has Britain faced a crisis like the one we face today!

192

– That's your bloody fault!

There was laughter. The young men standing around the platform moved towards the source of the barracking. Bacon was calling for order.

– Let me speak! he cried. Hear me out!

Some kind of fracas had occurred but it ceased abruptly when the police started to move in. The first rain was felt in the gusting wind.

– England cannot afford to drop her guard! We are under attack as never before. But it comes not from the skies, no, but from within! From within! *We must be rid of the alien parasite! The Jew power must be stopped!*

There was more of this.

– Hear hear! shouted Julius, and Gustl echoed him. They attracted sharp looks from people around them. There was muttering.

– Shout, love, she murmured to Joan. Make them know you are on what side.

Was it what Gricey did? That fine baritone, with which he'd filled theatres, speaking, oh, speaking the finest English verse, in the service of this contemptible tosh? Frederic Bacon was shouting himself hoarse. He was flinging his arms up as though directing traffic, although clearly it was a very low form of traffic. *Alien filth!* he shouted. *Inhuman scum! Bacteria! You pass him on the street, you push him in the gutter! You see him on the bus, you throw him off the bus!*

There were scattered shouts and jeers. Joan realised it was performance, merely, and her disgust deepened. They were pathetic, despicable. How could Julius think them so dangerous? All at once she was aware of movement, of something happening, and turning, she saw Karsh running through the crowd like a small bull, coming fast, a bomb of a man with his coat flapping out behind him, and men running with him, towards the platform, a group of three or four – no, two groups, another over on the far side, fascists now rushing from the platform at these running men and screaming with rage, and the crowd falling back and hustling themselves clear even as the groups clashed and were at once swinging and kicking at each other—

Then Karsh and another man had seized hold of the edge of the platform and from his now unstable footing Frederic Bacon lashed at them with his stick but he was losing his balance – the stick flew up – then he was tumbling backwards – the platform rose higher, steeply canted, and table, chairs, the other men on top, all were sliding backwards, Frederic Bacon screaming, 'The flag! Get the bloody flag!' – and the fascists below were being set upon by more and more men emerging from the back of the crowd, much shouting and screaming now as people in genuine panic tried to get away, and then in came the police striking out wildly with their truncheons until suddenly, with a great roar, the platform was overturned, it toppled over backwards, and there was more cheering—

Then the rain started coming down in earnest.

They were all dispersing rapidly now as though by some prearranged signal. Joan and Gustl were hurried away by Julius and they crossed the street among the throngs and then they were in the car again and moving through the now busy streets, honking at people in the road, edging slowly forward, being jeered, and Joan sat upright in the back seat trembling, for the violence had terrified her. Julius soon had them clear away from the crowd.

– Sorry about that, love, he said, Karsh thought it was a good day for a rumble.

Later the three of them were sitting in a warm pub.

– Why do you take them seriously? said Joan.

– It doesn't die on its own, said Julius.

But it was Gricey she was thinking about. Where had it come from, all that hatred? She wasn't rid of him yet, she realised, and thinking this, she heard Gustl saying that they couldn't let it happen again, never again, and herself now saying silently that yes, it can happen again, it *is*. It *is* happening again, Gricey is still out there, she'd heard him.

19

FRANK WAS PLAYING First Madman, who appears in Act IV, and speaks the immortal line: *Doomsday not come yet?* Vera had liked his Antonio, what little she'd had of him in the two days of rehearsals when Harry Catermole was absent. There was something in Frank's Antonio she missed in Harry's, and among those who watched them many recognised a quality of affection and of tenderness and, too, urgency – of passion restrained – in Frank that Harry had never offered the Duchess. The director was worried about it.

– That's what's missing when she acts with Harry, you see it, Sidney, when she's with the other one.

Sidney saw it all right.

– Damn. Damn.

Elizabeth Morton-Stanley hated this kind of thing. She created complication constantly but she hated it. A short break was called in the middle of the morning and

Vera went looking for Frank. He was in the back of the hall, sitting on a crate.

– Hello, she said.

– Oh hello!

He hadn't seen her coming. He was on his feet at once.

– Sit down, she said. Move over. What are you reading?

– Act IV.

– Oh Act IV. Let's have a drink later. You want to?

Vera never went out for a drink after rehearsal. And Frank Stone was planning to go to Archibald Street where Joan was giving him supper. But at once he said yes.

When he arrived at Joan's, much later that evening, he found her in some distress. She'd cooked him a meal but it was ruined in the oven. She was haunted still by what she'd heard at the street meeting on Sunday. She was confused and miserable and she needed Frank but he hadn't come.

She'd been unable to tell Julius and Gustl that she'd heard Gricey's voice. But who knew that voice better than she did? It had rung out with volume and clarity within the coarse incoherence of the rest, she could hear it still. And now she'd convinced herself that she'd *seen him too.*

Several times earlier that evening, when there was a footstep on the pavement, she'd gone into Gricey's room and looked down into the street. She would then unlock the wardrobe, and such a disquieting stillness there was, there among the clothes left hanging. Briefly she'd fondled the pale silk lining of a good wool overcoat, then heard a whistling in the street. From the window she saw Frank Stone on the pavement, gazing up.

She flew down the stairs without troubling to lock the wardrobe and flung open the door into the street. She clutched him, whispering, oh thank god, thank god. Frank had an explanation prepared but it wasn't required; to have come at all was enough. Up the stairs they went together, and into the flat, to the kitchen where it was warm. For the first time he saw her in tears. She set her elbows on the table, covering her face with her hands, and Frank sat helpless before her heaving shoulders and muffled sobs until, one hand still clasped to her face, she reached with groping fingers for his hand.

How could he tell her what had happened to him?

That night he stayed with her for she wouldn't allow him to leave. She had no thought for his mother. Never had she clung to him as she did that night, and never before had he felt ambivalence towards her. He wanted to leave the flat, not to be in his own home, no, but so as to be by himself. What was he doing, playing Vera's lover then coming to the bed of her mother? It wasn't funny any more. Was he mad? Well, we asked ourselves the same question! Only when the first grey light was apparent in the crack in the curtain did he slip silently out of her bed and, gathering his clothes up, make his way down the passage to the kitchen. Joan didn't awaken. He quickly dressed then let himself out, and walked past the cemetery to the bus stop in the dawn.

*

Well, Vera had kissed him, but so what? Boy meets girl, so what? She'd liked doing the wooing scene with him in the first act. She liked the delicacy of his flirting, and his seriousness late in the scene when he tells her that he'll be the 'constant sanctuary' of her good name. What had he meant by it? That he promised discretion. And then there'd been the headlong rush into the marriage vows, which the pair of them took at the gallop, pouring the words out in front of Cariola and the deed was done. They were man and wife. It had aroused her, the haste and heat of it, with its palpable undertow of lust, so she took him for a drink and when they left the pub she led him into an alley and pushed him up against the wall and kissed him hard on the mouth. She was a very forward girl, Vera, very pushy when she chose to be. She opened her mouth and used her tongue on his lips and on his own tongue, flicking and licking. Startled at first, he became at once excited, and kissed her back, and was given some freedom with his hands, there in the chattering cold with their panting breath turning to smoke in the darkness. He tried to get his fingers up under her skirt but only managed the top of her stockings, a touch of womanly thigh, no further. Well, why not? He was in a state of some violent confusion, with this flurry of passion—

Then she pulled away from him.

– Remember, she said, panting a little, and put her finger on his lips.

– What?

He stared at her with wild eyes, hard as coal in his trousers and desperate to finish.

– Constant sanctuary.

He nodded, breathless. Oh, *he* had no wish to betray their secret, and for Christ's sake, Vera, lift your skirt, won't you, so we can bloody *have* a secret!

– Cheer up, sweetheart, she whispered, then again laid her fingers briefly on his lips and left him, her coat wrapped tight around her and her heels tapping on the cobbles down the alley.

– Bloody hell, said Frank.

Joan awoke to find him gone from her bed but this had happened before. She still felt she could trust him, although she would never tell him what she was doing with Julius and Gustl, no. In a way she was doing it for him, or maybe for his mother. She wanted to believe that.

Meanwhile rehearsals went forward and Elizabeth Morton-Stanley made it clear to Harry that she wanted more from his Antonio, and particularly in the first act, when the foundation is laid for the horror to come. Harry listened in silence and understood that Frank Stone must have produced some kind of an effect that he as yet had not. He thought: if passion and tenderness is what they require then that is what they shall have. Frank Stone looked on as his rival became more amorous and tactile, his glances more burning, his words now soft, now husky with emotion. Any actor can do love, love is easy, as well we know, don't we, ladies? We do. Love onstage is like hate, like rage, like anything with passion in it, and all you do is produce the passion and it reads like love if that's what the words say. Harry was probably a bit angry. And

200

Frank, watching him, was at once resentful because he still thought he could play it better.

Then came the day the cast left the rehearsal room and entered the theatre, the New Apollo. It was a big, old, square building, dark too long. They got onto the stage and had their first real look at the set, which had gone up the previous night. They stood around in their overcoats and scarves, smoking and making jokes, and gazing up into the flies and out into the empty auditorium. Never a simple occasion for an actor. For he now finds actual walls where before he'd walked through them as though they were invisible. There were real doors too, by which we mean flimsy hinged openings in vertical flats, where before there were chalk marks on a floor. There was *furniture*.

– This is *here*? cried the Duke Ferdinand of Calabria, twin brother of the Duchess of Malfi – Ed Colefax, that is – coming upon a table where he'd intended to make a vigorous upstage exit. Stagehands watched with amusement as he stared at the table, became bewildered, gazed out into the auditorium with a hand on his forehead as though an answer would come from a voice in the back stalls regarding the peculiar fact of the presence of a *table*. They'd all seen this before. Actors were constantly astonished to encounter actual furniture on a stage. Elizabeth Morton-Stanley allowed the silence to go on for a while. Then she lit a cigarette and lay back, closing her eyes.

– It was always on the floor plan, Edmund.

Later each of the actors flung a few words into the

empty auditorium to hear what bounced back. Then they went off to find their dressing rooms and discover just how far from the stage they'd be.

Frank Stone was sharing a dressing room with four others, two of them Madmen, one a Pilgrim, all Executioners, and other minor roles such as Officers, Servants, Churchmen. They were deep in the bowels of the building, and it was impossible to reach the stage in under three minutes. The others were already there, each laying out his make-up and his rabbit's feet and what-have-you, including a man called Willy Ogilvie. Frank had the chair furthest from the door. The chatter was genial, these actors relieved to have at last come into the theatre.

Well, we all know the feeling. It's jaded you'd have to be if you're not quickened to the marrow by getting into the theatre with real work to do on a stage, even if only to play a lady-in-waiting or a servant or a whore, or maybe all three, in the course of one evening. The dressing room was stifling hot where Frank had his chair, at the end next to the wall, there being no window but several very hot steam pipes with ancient ring brackets attached to the bricks and painted a muddy yellow colour. The door was wide open so as to cool the room but it made little difference to Frank. He didn't complain. It would do no good. And he knew now for sure that he would again show them how Antonio was to be played. It was with a kind of pent impatience that he anticipated his opportunity, for he didn't for a moment doubt it would come.

All this going through his head as he sat before his mirror on an old rickety bentwood chair with hooped curved legs and a round wooden seat with little holes in it. He stared at his face in the bright glare of the three good bulbs he'd been left. He turned his head this way, that way. He lifted his handsome chin, and after a few seconds he darkly frowned. He tossed his shaggy head. He pulled his lips back in a feral sneer to expose his strong white teeth. Then hearing his name called he turned to see none other than Vera Grice leaning in the doorway of the dressing room. She was in a baggy maroon sweater, and a tight black skirt. She was eating an apple and grinning at the line of actors each in front of his own mirror, all now turned in her direction.

– Hello, boys, she said.

– Hello, Miss Grice! Come to join us, have you?

Frank could hear the distant shouts of stagehands as the company got settled, and he rose to his feet. He edged along the narrow space between the back wall and the costume rack and the long dressing table. He was grinning now. The other actors' chairs were pulled in close to their mirrors, each with its light bulbs all burning at once. There was more banter. He was sweating and still grinning when he got out into the corridor. He was wearing one of Gricey's heavy winter tweeds. He wanted to seize her by the hips, by the shoulders, crush her lovely splendid bosomy voluptuous body to his own, for he was aware of vigorous fresh business within his trousers. He asked her how it was in her dressing room.

– Cold, she said. I might move in with you boys.

– We'd like that.

– I bet you would. This Daddy's?

She fingered his jacket.

– The suit? Yes.

He watched her reaction closely. All at once he was uneasy. Her smile was strange, cryptic. Oh, he was bewildered by this new friendship he seemed to have stumbled into and was powerless to control. If Vera Grice chose to toy with him, why then he would be toyed with. This at least was what he felt at that moment, being taken by surprise by her visit to what he thought of as the very *intestines* of the theatre. It was hard for him to forget how she'd pushed him against the wall in that alley behind the pub, the memory of which in equal measure excited him to madness and maddened him with guilt. How could he love the mother, and at the same time lust after the daughter?

– Will I see you later, my fearless one? she said.

She touched his sleeve, rolled the fabric between her fingers, and mouthed the word, *Daddy*.

Such a look she gave him, and such a helpless, lost gaze he gave her in return, and we were all moved, just a little, but amused, of course, how could we not be? – she blinks her big dark peepers at him, calls him Daddy and reduces him at once to a wreck of carnal confusion and servitude – and there it all is, in his long, worried, happy, frowning face, as he looms over her, leaning in, and pushes his fingers through her hair – oh what a silly fellow—

– Constant sanctuary, she whispers, and steps off down the corridor in the direction of the stage. Constant sanctuary? *Discretion?* Everyone knows now! The other actors gaze at him with smiles of sweet disingenuous curiosity as he comes back into the dressing room. Bastards, he thinks.

He tells himself they'll have a drink but he won't go with her into an alley again, whatever she says. It was foolish, what happened. But what exactly did she know about his relationship with her mother – just that Joan had given him some of Gricey's clothes? She surely couldn't know that he was spending the night, not every night, but some nights, lots of nights, in her mother's bed, the bed in which Joan had slept with Gricey – could she know that? But then how was he to tell her he couldn't kiss her in an alley any more? From her point of view there was no reason for him not to want to kiss her in an alley, for he had no attachments, seemingly, and what's more he needed her, because he wanted to play Antonio to her Duchess.

If he kissed her in an alley again, would she tell her mother?

Would her mother find out anyway?

Was he doomed whatever he did? Doomsday not come yet, but just around the bloody corner, oh yes. Oh hell, thinks Frank Stone, and decides to wait and see what happens to him later.

When he found Vera in the pub down the street from the theatre she wasn't alone. He'd intended to explain to her that, for the sake of her own reputation, they must stop going into alleys. But actually – who'd be the wiser? He knew that the romances, quarrels, deceptions, heartbreaks – the rumours and scandals and betrayals – the revenge tragedies and high comedies that went on among us, among any company of actors, were not the exception but the norm. And that what we performed onstage paled in comparison to what we got up to backstage. So a couple of snogs with the leading lady in fact amounted to precisely nothing.

And here was Vera with that idiot Harry Catermole, and their gossipy, odious stage manager, Jasper Speke, and there were one or two others, and what sort of a dalliance had this turned into now? What was he to do with himself now, his loins already eager, *strident* for an alley?

– Hello, Frank darling, said Vera. Have a drink.

Harry made room for him at the bar, and Jasper Speke insinuated his hand onto Frank's shoulder.

– Now you two behave, said Vera, Frank Stone is my friend.

– Frank Stone is everyone's friend, said Jasper Speke. How's the dressing room, Frankie?

– Too bloody hot.

They laughed. What a wag. He was still finding his way with this company. They'd seen his work when Harry was away, and they knew he'd found favour with Vera, who was known to be difficult. After about ten minutes this dawned on Frank and he began to take their friendliness at face value. He started to enjoy himself.

– Frankie Stone, said Jasper Speke, when they were on their second round, is it true you weren't born in England? Nobody seems to know very much about you.

And when was it, thought Frank, that they stopped

calling me Dan Francis? When they heard Vera call me Frank.

– A man of elusive mystery, a shadowy figure of dark intrigue, that's right, isn't it, Vera, said Harry, who was a tall, heavy man in a sweeping overcoat, unbuttoned and with the collar turned up, who stood with one hand on the bar and his large leonine head, with its splendid shining temples and lustrous golden mane, thrown back. He'd become a leading man, something of a matinee idol, in fact, on the strength of his fine legs and good hair, but as Vera well knew he rarely had both oars in the water.

– I was born in Germany, said Frank Stone, and I came to England with my mother before the war.

– Had to get out?

– Yes.

There. Now they knew.

– Lucky to get out in time. That was the Committee, eh?

– No, we got here without them.

He was astonished that his story should be in the least familiar to them. Vera grinned at him. Did she know? Did she know she'd been snogging another Jew? Yes, he thought, she did. So did it matter? Apparently not. What luck.

– Saved your bacon, did she?

– Who?

– Your mother.

Some genial laughter here but Frank detected little malice. This Jasper Speke probably knew all about him.

All at once the beer he'd drunk seemed to go to Frank's head. He felt light-hearted; euphoric, even. They knew about him and it didn't matter. It could still surprise him, to realise he'd become a member in good standing of the society of the London stage.

Curious to think that at one time he'd felt he didn't belong and would never belong. It was often said how tribal the English were, how closed off as a people, but it was only Gricey, now he came to think about it, who'd found ways of making him feel unwanted. Oh, he'd been curt, dismissive, never gave him the time of day or looked him in the eye. It had sharpened his resolve. But that evening in the pub with Vera and the others, Frank Stone had it confirmed that the theatre didn't care who you were, or where you were from, all that mattered was that you worked hard. And didn't behave like a shit.

It was a good night, a happy night, but it made for difficulties in Archibald Street, of course it did. For he didn't visit Joan after the pub, even though there'd been no snogging, and that was because Vera needed her beauty sleep, or so she said. He made his way home on foot. His step was less than steady for he was in the throes of various forms of intoxication. Rosza was asleep, the boy was in the bed with her, and Frank was soon on the couch and dead to the world. But when he awoke he felt as though he was awakening to a new dawn, like the man in the silent film, the early sunlight shining full upon a face once dismal but now radiant with hope.

He sat on the edge of the old couch in the clothes he'd worn the day before, then slept in, and with his elbows on his knees, and his long hands hanging loose, he stared at his shoes and reflected on his good fortune. But oh, callow man, had he yet given a thought to the poor widow in Mile End? Did Joan Grice not pull at his swelling heart, did her voice not murmur to him in this happy dawn, *but what about me*? No, not yet it didn't.

Joan meanwhile sat in her kitchen waiting for the kettle to come to the boil. Again she had cooked a meal for him and he hadn't appeared. Perhaps his mother was ill. Joan Grice was a proud woman. It was not easy for her to accept that she had become dependent on a man upon whom another woman had a prior claim. Of course Frank must care for his mother, but could he not stop in, oh, for ten minutes, at least? Didn't he know that would be enough to reassure her in what was for her a most anxious time? No, he couldn't know: nor had she explained anything of her predicament to him, of the risks she was being asked to take by her friend Gustl Herzfeld.

Joan was not so foolish as to think she would hold Frank Stone for ever. But in some fond place in her heart she believed she would, and why? *She still clung to his dark resident spirit.* Not the fascist, no, but Gricey as she'd known him when they were at the Watford Palace together, before all that. In truth what she clung to was not a man but an idea. Its fundamental proposition was this: there had to exist that which she could love without reservation and forever, and it was the habit of a lifetime for that object to be Charlie Grice.

When had he started to change? 1929. A very bad year. Hunger marches, street fights, police against the workers, no surprise there – and the government useless, quite unable to do a thing. That's when Oswald Mosley started to attract so much attention. By 1932 the BUF was in existence, and Gricey stopped talking about these matters to his Jewish wife. Ironic then, she thought, that it was into the body of *Franz Stein*—

Ah, but now Frank too was changing, thought Joan, and she didn't know why, *unless Gricey was turning him*. Yes, the dybbuk, she knew about all *that*, the demon in Frank's body, its sole entire purpose to do her harm. To not appear in the evening when he said he would, not once but *twice*! – and that first time with only a muttered apology when he did appear. She was not so foolish as to show disappointment or anger, oh no, that would do no good at all. No, what truly troubled her was that he should choose to abuse her like this, so soon. For barely had she given him her heart than he set about breaking it! Oh, she had been so very wrong about him. So it was all just an illusion, was it, just some piece of foolishness aroused by grief and with no foundation in the world? – or was it worse than that? She could hardly bear to think about it. Well, our hearts went out to her, yes they did.

It had been a bad night, the second time he failed to appear. The first night he had come, yes, at last, but very late. The second night he hadn't appeared at all. And desperate though she was, her mind writhing, oh, *serpentine* with suspicion, she believed that he was *sure* to come the night *after*, and tell her he'd had to look after his mother. But again – no sign of him. No note, nothing. She'd done what she'd promised herself she wouldn't do. She'd pulled a kitchen chair over to the cupboard, climbed on it and reached down the gin. She needed a little comfort from Uncle Alcohol tonight, she told herself, oh, and why not? Why not? Who could blame her?

It wasn't the only forbidden cupboard she went into that night. Came a moment about an hour and a half later she decided to go into Gricey's room. She was weaving and laughing a little, and crying too. She was clutching a tumbler in which a splash or two of neat gin was sloshing around as she made her way from the kitchen. It was hard to say what was in her mind exactly, for the balance of her mind was disturbed. It may have involved the decision to confront Gricey about Frank Stone, for although Gricey had spoken to her only twice, and she'd seen him only once, which was at the street meeting she'd attended – yes, she was sure of it now – she believed he would speak to her again if she talked to him *in the right way*. This is what some of us think anyway, those among us who have been through situations like Joan's. Where the ghost of a dead husband won't be still.

So she went into Gricey's room and turned the light on. She pulled closed the blackout curtains. She couldn't remember where she'd put the key of the wardrobe and – a curious thing – it was late one night some days earlier that she'd decided to hide it, thinking no good could come of continued exposure to its influence; the wardrobe's, that is. This was after she'd brought out a suit for Frank to try on. Gricey was displeased, she'd had

211

no doubt about that, so she'd locked the wardrobe and hidden the key and it took Uncle Alcohol to retrieve the memory, for she'd been in his company that night. She went into the bathroom, stood on the toilet seat and opened the little window. On the window ledge she found it.

Back in Gricey's room she unlocked the wardrobe door. Her hand was trembling. She was afraid. She stood very still for a few seconds. The night was deathly quiet. She had no idea what time it was. The light bulb flickered as she hauled open the doors of the wardrobe, and it felt to her as though she had opened the gates of hell but that was just dread, she told herself. She swayed a little and stood gazing into the wardrobe, holding on to the doors.

The clothes rail was less crowded than once it had been. Joan was familiar now with Gricey's displeasure and it intimidated her when she was sober, but she was not sober.

– Are you in there, dear?

If he was, he made no reply.

– I have to talk to you.

The silence was unbroken. The wardrobe had little clawed feet that raised it three inches above the floor. Joan placed her own foot inside it, clinging for stability to the doors. She was shod that night in black laced ankle boots with a low heel. She wore a long black skirt and had a large shawl over her head and shoulders. Her hair was pinned up but strands were drifting free and there was a wildness in her fine pale sculpted face, most particularly in her eyes, and she showed her teeth, a rare thing, we all commented on it. Somewhere in there a noise occurred but it may have been her foot on the wardrobe floor.

– Hello? Hello?

She laid a hand on her breast and then as though swept forward by an impulse of unknown origin, but probably from within herself, she reached into the wardrobe, and seizing a hook behind the rail, stepped *in* – and the doors at once banged shut behind her.

– Oh god, she cried out.

But no god heard her, only us. She would have screamed at any other time but she was not sober. It was utterly dark. It was just a draught, she told herself. Without turning around she bent her knee and pushed at one of the doors behind her with the sole of her boot. It didn't move so she tried the other door. It too was unyielding.

– Are you in here? she cried.

She heard a different noise now. The clothes on the rail were shaking on their hangers. For a few seconds it seemed to Joan that the entire wardrobe was shaking as the hangers, all wooden, began clanking against each other, and she was aware too of the rustle of agitated fabric. She turned around, bewildered now. There was a slit of light under the doors. She pushed with both hands but the doors still didn't open, so she stood up straight with the back of her neck against the rail and tried to keep her breathing under control.

– Gricey, stop this. Let me out. Let me out *now*.

The shaking and clanking died away and all was quite

still in the darkness. Then something touched her throat and she gave a small scream. It was very terrible for her to hear her own scream in that constricted space.

– I won't have this, Gricey, do you hear me!

Silence.

Then it touched her again, this time high up on the back of her thigh.

– What do you want? she shouted, slapping at it.

For a few seconds she lost control. There were fingers everywhere, touching her all over – she beat at herself, then tore the clothes off their hangers, and flung them about as though she could drive off whatever was in the locked wardrobe with her, which was of course only the clothes themselves, Gricey's clothes, but she was enraged now, shouting and cursing as she flapped about herself with a pair of trousers, then seizing a coat off its hanger and flinging it around, shouting: Fuck off, Gricey, leave me alone! *Let me out of this thing!*

And then she heard him. His voice was quite distinct. It cut through the rage and the panic and the gin, everything. She stood as though turned to stone as the voice faded, and it was Gricey's voice, of this she was in no doubt at all, and she should know.

– *Fucking hard-case East End Yids.*

Then with her renewed assault the doors were swinging open and banging against the sides of the wardrobe, and she staggered out of the shaking thing and into the freezing bedroom.

20

J OAN WENT TO Lupus Mews the next day, as
arranged. She'd taken some care with her appearance. It was a mark of the mettle of the woman that she
did not suffer a collapse or a breakdown after what had
happened. Rather her resolution, once tentative, became
strong and sure, and pure too, and it seemed fortuitous to
her that it now lay within her power to work against the
men Gricey had associated with in his last years. She was
in no doubt as to what she must do.

So after work she cycled down to Westminster Bridge,
Big Ben dim and silent in the dusk, then along the Embank-
ment and everywhere people going home, the streets
smoky and crowded, and despondent, the frowning men
and women in hats and heavy overcoats streaming over
the river, and on she went into Pimlico, until she reached
the ruins of Sutherland Terrace and its unstable walls,
empty black holes in them like lost teeth where once the

windows had been, and charred rafters in the wreckage above. She reached Julius' house at the corner of Lupus Mews. The window in the front room, Gustl's room, was bright against the gloom, and a figure stood within. Joan wheeled her bicycle up the path and leaned it against the railing. Climbing the steps, she banged the brass knocker. The door opened immediately.

– Hello love, said Auntie Gustl. You were being expected.

She led her into the front room where Joan's painting still stood on the easel. Joan paused before it. She barely recognised herself. Gustl didn't ask her what had happened. Joan sank into the wicker chair beside the fireplace. For a second she buried her face in her hands. Then she looked up.

– I'm ready, she said.

– I'll get Julius.

A little later they got in the Wolseley and Julius drove them to the quiet street in Chelsea where the Brompton Club occupied the ground floor. Julius and Gustl were silent in the car, and Joan remembered the voice of Gricey in the darkness of the shuddering wardrobe, and saw him again as she had during the street meeting, in the crowd, screaming, his arm lifted in the fascist salute and his face inflamed with hatred and rage. So much *rage*, would there never come an end to *rage*? It was another kind of grief she felt, and far worse, with what she thought of as this second death. Her sorrow now was for herself, that he hadn't allowed her to hold him in her memory as she would have liked to, but had left her with only a mask. She'd been thinking earlier of him telling stories in the saloon bar, doing his imitations of the great stage actors of their time. Oh, and with warm, laughing faces all around, and at a table nearby, the women, yes, we were there, with Joan among us taking quiet pleasure in her husband's talent to amuse. But all an act. The real man was *always elsewhere*. She saw that now, and so did we.

And the *elsewhere*, the place the real man was to be found? It was the Black House. It was the headquarters of the BUF, a grey, Gothic pile on Battersea Park Road that Mosley purchased with Italian money in August 1933. We shiver to think of it, it reminds us of a dark house, an empty theatre. He filled it with young Black-shirts, students of fascism, and older men with army backgrounds like Frederic Bacon, living together under military discipline and the club rooms ringing nightly with laughter and song. And who entertained them, these fierce young men for whom life had become worth living again? Gricey did. Gricey Grice entertained them. He told them stories, he sang them songs, he was even up for a soft-shoe shuffle with walking stick and straw boater should the situation require it. He pandered to their politics because he shared them. They loved him. He needed them. But never a word about Joan, of course.

Hilda Bacon opened the door and led them upstairs. Joan was stiff and unsmiling as she entered the drawing room and saw at once the portrait of Oswald Mosley. From their various perches fascists abruptly rose to their feet, like crows rising flapping from a branch. Many of them were in uniform that night, yes, some even in *full Nazi officer costume,* and they came forward to click their heels and she was chilled and at the same time fascinated to see these absurd Englishmen taking themselves so very seriously, each one bending to kiss her hand, each one muttering a few words of respect and admiration for her husband as though he were still alive and perhaps, she thought, they had to keep their heroes alive, so few had survived. But the whole thing was a masquerade, and Joan, a bit stunned now, murmured her thanks. She remained calm; Julius had told her what to expect. Perform the grieving widow, he'd said, and talk as little as possible. He stood at her left shoulder, Gustl on her right and slightly to the rear. When these extraordinary introductions were complete they *heiled* the picture of Mosley and Joan nodded her approval.

A silence fell. All eyes were upon her. How impressive she was tonight, tall and proud, serene, remote, oh, undeniably a most remarkable woman. Her voice was clear, steady, quiet. They strained to hear her.

– My husband would have wanted you to continue the struggle, she said. With all your vigour and resolve. He was proud of you all.

Julius had suggested it and it went down well. She then sat down. There was sustained applause. She saw Julius speaking in low tones to Frederic Bacon and she could detect no trace of suspicion or distrust in the other man. So it was working, she thought, and felt a fresh flicker of contempt for these idiotic characters all trumped up as though about to perform a light German military farce. In fact what they intended, what Mosley intended, was to resuscitate the fascist spirit, raise it from the dead – if ever it *could* die, thought Joan, for perhaps like Gricey it only slept. But it was beyond the imagination of any of them, she thought, that their hero Gricey could have been married to a Jew. If only they knew.

Frederic Bacon then said a few words about how Gricey had fallen like a good soldier. 'Fallen' at least was right, thought Joan, fallen down the back steps of Julius' house, about which event she was still in the dark, but more convinced than ever that he hadn't fallen at all. Pushed, rather. Their only martyr. And she knew who did the pushing. And now thought it the right thing.

How very honoured they were, Bacon then said, that Gricey's widow was with them now.

At that the clowns all clapped again and muttered their approval. Angry, brutal young men, vindictive with envy. Vain in their black tunics and breeches, their badges and armband swastikas, the visored caps and riding boots they could wear nowhere else. And a few of the older ones were there, Peter Ryder, not in uniform at least, and three or four other men who might have worked in a bank or a classroom, and two flushed ladies, sisters evidently, built on the same lines as Hilda Bacon and plainly aroused in the presence of so many young men alive with angry unclean passions born of failure, frustration and hate. Yes, and Frederic and Hilda Bacon, herself in the black blouse and belted skirt, him in a pale blue uniform – *Reichsmarschall und Frau* – the epitome, the sum of all the parts, gathering to themselves the various grudges of these misfits, and reflecting them back in the form of a wrong political idea to which these men might attach themselves and so acquire in their own eyes at least a spurious dignity, a sense of being lifted clear above their fellows.

But it was a frightful ordeal. She thought later she would rather spend all night in a locked wardrobe with Gricey's ghost than another minute in a drawing room full of inadequate Englishmen dressed up as Nazis. It rose up in her throat like bile – the curdled digest of something tainted, and consumed in error – and only with difficulty did she sustain her gravitas. These young men, oh, so very infatuated, drunk on myths of racial purity and martial glory, their imaginations sick, diseased—

– You are not impressed, Mrs Grice, Frederic Bacon murmured to her, as she stood by herself near the fireplace.

She turned to him.

– We are not impressive, I know that, he then said. We have not what the Germans had. No, we are an afterthought. It matters nothing, all this. A sideshow, at best. We try to ape what was once in its way quite magnificent, but it's laughable, is it not, Mrs Grice? But it is for them that I do it.

Joan was astonished by his candour. He lifted his glass to her and made a slight bow, a small ironic click of the heels, and moved away.

Later, coming away, she felt soiled, and asked Julius if they might stop somewhere for a cup of tea so she could wash her face and pull herself together. Not something stronger? This was Gustl's kindly suggestion. No, a cup of tea, she'd had far too much gin the night before, so they went into a little café where Joan sat for some moments covering her mouth with her hand as though frightened of coughing something up. Julius gazed at her in his lugubrious manner and told her he'd learned all he needed about the shipment from the publisher, and that Peter would do the rest.

– What shipment? said Joan.

So Julius then told her that a large shipment of fascist printed matter was to be delivered to the bookshop in the Bacons' house for distribution at the meeting in two weeks. It was his intention that these materials be burned unread. Joan was gratified that her visit to that loathsome house had done some good. The destruction of fascist literature was surely devoutly to be wished for.

21

VERA AT THIS time was of course subject to the anxiety every actress feels when approaching her first appearance in front of an audience in the role she's been rehearsing for weeks. But she had another, and far greater source of distress. It was this: that her father wouldn't see her work. He'd seen everything she'd been in. He'd been supportive as no one else had, in large part because he understood what she was doing. Invariably he told her she had astonished him, or that he'd found nuances of character heretofore unsuspected in her Nora, or whoever it might be. How was she to know if her Duchess was any good if Gricey wasn't there to tell her? Always he had told her what wasn't working, as well as what was. That mad idea she'd had as Cordelia to play the prison scene wearing a blindfold? Others had had their doubts and expressed them carefully. Not Gricey. Not until he attended a dress rehearsal did she understand why it was a bad idea.

– Dear girl, he'd said, if you don't give me your bloody eyes I can't tell what you're bloody feeling.

Grief swept through her whenever she contemplated performing without Daddy coming backstage after to give her the good news, for it was almost always good news. For two days she was sunk in despair. She was listless in rehearsal. The company was alarmed. Elizabeth Morton-Stanley was a woman with a headful of thunderstorm and it was Sidney who thought of asking Frank Stone to find out what was wrong. He spoke to him at the end of the corridor where the Madmen had their dressing room.

Frank Stone's hopes had at once been raised, when Sidney appeared at the door and asked for a private word. Was Antonio to be his? – but no.

– We'd like you to have a word with Vera, said Sidney, when they were out in the corridor and beyond earshot of the curious Madmen. She likes you, doesn't she?

A stagehand with an armful of electrical cable emerged from the door at the far end of the corridor, and Sidney at once laid a finger on Frank's lips.

– What sort of a word, Mr Temple? said Frank when the stagehand was gone.

– Calm her down, Frankie. Find out what's the matter. Reassure her, any way you can.

Frank was taken aback.

– I don't know, he said.

Sidney gazed at him. Frank was frowning.

– Elizabeth would take it as a personal favour.

The meaning of these words wasn't hard to read.

223

Frank was being offered something, or promised it, he didn't know what exactly although he guessed it was not unconnected to the role of Antonio. Frank allowed his ambition once more to take fire, well, he couldn't help it, and in a reckless surge of confidence he said: All right, Mr Temple, I'll do what I can.

– Good boy, purred Sidney.

He left Frank Stone kicking the dank brickwork in that gloomy corridor. Frank's brief elation died. He had no idea how he was supposed to proceed. He'd planned to go and see Joan that night. Now he would somehow have to contrive to see Vera instead. He kicked the wall again, then back to the dressing room he limped. How we laughed. Oh, he never failed to amuse us, that fellow.

In his bones Edgar Cartridge knew that Julius Glass and his alleged sister had infiltrated the movement so as to do it harm. That they had brought Gricey Grice's widow to Mr Bacon's house made no difference. He thought it likely that Joan Grice was no more a fascist than Julius Glass and his sister, and he voiced his suspicions later, when the meeting had broken up and Bacon sat conferring with his other closest lieutenants, Oakeshott and Rhinsfurt. *Kosher fascists,* he called them, spitting the words out. Jew power, bah.

– Kosher fascists, very good, said Bacon. You are a most perceptive man, Edgar. I should have known they wouldn't deceive you.

Edgar Cartridge went to the sideboard and splashed a measure of whisky into his glass. He was a small man of powerful build and a head that seemed too large, with a shock of blond hair that rose perpendicular from his broad, low brow. His was a squarish, sullen face, clean shaven and with a dimple in the middle of the fierce chin. He invariably wore a grey suit with a dark shirt, blue or black, and a pale grey tie, when he was among fascists. He had not been wearing a uniform that night, although he carried with him a cherished leather glove, once the property of the Leader. He moved with deliberation but his air of menace was softened by his pleasant voice. As a boy he'd been a promising chorister with a lovely soprano voice. The combination of a violent home, however, reversals in his early career in the wholesale textile business, for which he later blamed something he'd heard called 'the Anglo-Judaic plutocracy' – all very tedious – and a thick streak of ferocity in his nature, all had led him inexorably into the ranks of Mosley's movement. He'd entered the Black House as a teenager in 1934 and there he had flourished. During the war he'd gone to prison.

– You told him about the printed matter, he said.

Frederic Bacon shrugged, unconcerned.

– What can he do about it? He thinks I still trust him.

– He must be watched, said Victor Oakeshott.

He was one of the movement's intellectuals. A lanky, myopic man, shabby in his dress, ill-groomed, careless in personal hygiene, he was by occupation a lecturer in the same third-rate college in Paddington where Bacon taught Modern European History. Victor Oakeshott spoke fluent German and had once written a monograph on Schopenhauer, soon forgotten.

– You overestimate his capabilities.

– I think not, said Edgar Cartridge. We cannot have another meeting disrupted.

– He's right, said Hilda, sitting at the back of the room with a sleek white tomcat in her lap. She threw off the cat and went to the sideboard, where Edgar Cartridge poured her more gin.

– Perhaps.

– No, certainly, said Hilda Bacon. How can we recruit if we cannot be heard? You remember what the Leader told us.

– Yes dear, said Frederic Bacon, grimly, I remember what the Leader told us. The answer is more stewards, better equipped. This is your responsibility, Piet.

Piet Rhinsfurt was a short, flabby man with a bristly reddish moustache. There was something about his eyes. They were small and set close together, and shone with unnatural brightness. Some of us thought he used drugs. He certainly drank, and when he did his left eye wandered while the right one stayed put. Oddly, he worked in the film industry and, too, claimed to be the inventor of the razor-blade potato. Violence was his passion and fascism the means to that end. He had hinted more than once that he had thrashed a man to death in cold blood with a bicycle chain.

– There will be more stewards and I am weeding out the weaklings myself. You will not be disappointed, Mrs Bacon.

– I'm pleased to hear it, Piet, said Hilda, seating herself once more in a manner that was prim and feline at the same time. She invariably found herself aroused among the more dangerous of her husband's followers. Rumours of her susceptibilities were rife in these circles. She was once famously overheard speaking with some relish of her partiality for fascist dick. Quiet laughter here among the ladies of the Chorus.

There was no clear resolution other than that, come the next meeting, no hard-case East End Yid would get near the platform, and any who did would regret the day he'd been born.

Frank Stone waited near the stage door and when Vera emerged he asked her if she would like to go for a drink. These were the exact same words, he realised with some rue, he'd more than once spoken when it was Vera's mother he awaited at the stage door. Vera had never felt more alone. She was facing the challenge of carrying the lead in a difficult play in which her own performance would be rigorously scrutinised by the critics and others, who in her imagination had swollen into a howling multitude. No, she didn't want a drink.

– Cup of tea, then? said Frank Stone as he fell into step beside her.

The wind was brisk off the river and there was still some light in the day. Trees lashed about and ponderous grey clouds trampled across the sky like elephants. Vera stopped and turned to him, clutching her coat collar tight about her throat as the breeze snatched at her piled hair, and declared her heart's desire.

– Whelks, Frank, she said. I want whelks.

Twenty minutes later as the dusk was coming on they stood at an open-fronted tripe-and-eel shop in Borough Market. They saw before them marble slabs heaped with tripe, pigs' trotters, pigs' cheeks, and live, wriggling eels. Behind these counters loud cockney girls were selling the stuff to Londoners on their way home from work. The day was windy and the girls' hands were blue with cold despite the glowing brazier. Vera wanted a bag of whelks and Frank Stone purchased it, shouldering through to the front.

They stood shivering on the corner of the street, Vera gobbling whelks while leaning against a wall, and Frank smoking a desultory Woodbine. Around them men and women pushed against the wind towards the bus stop and the Tube. Darkness was falling from the air. Vera felt better. She licked her fingers and at last gave some attention to her companion.

– Now I want a glass of beer.

There was a pub nearby. It was just after six and they went into the public bar. It was not crowded. Vera was recognised and the landlord came round from behind the counter and showed them to a small table in the corner. Frank ordered two pints of bitter and had barely enough in his pocket to pay for them. Vera drained half of hers then dabbed at her whelky lips and sighed.

– What a fucking nightmare, she said.

– What is?

– Oh, everything, she said. We won't talk about it. What's up with you, First Madman?

– I'd sooner be Antonio.

She smiled at him rather archly. There were still a few shreds of whelk caught in her teeth. She picked at them, inspected them, then laid her fingers on Frank's cheek for a second. He thrilled to her touch.

– Maybe you will be.

– What do you mean?

– Oh nothing.

She heard the brief whisper of hunger in his voice and it reminded her of that which she wished to forget, the damn theatre and all its pressures and obligations, the compulsion always to *compete*, to *succeed* – could she never escape it? It would be better once they were on, she thought, and the notices were in, and they could just get on with it, flop or hit, who cared?

– Do you know my husband? she said suddenly.

Nobody in the pub was paying them any attention. She had been recognised, but London manners decreed she should be allowed to have her drink in peace like anyone else.

– I know who he is.

– Poor Julius.

Frank waited for more.

– I don't make his life very easy, you know. I'll tell you something I haven't told anybody else. You mustn't breathe a word.

– I won't.

– I sleep in the attic.

Frank Stone wasn't sure what to say.

– What, up at the top of the house?

– That's usually where they put the attic, Frank. I can't

bear to sleep with anyone when I'm in rehearsal, you see. But he's very good about it. He understands. Well, he knows actors, of course, but not every man would be so nice about it.

She drank off the last of her beer.

– You would, I think, she said. Be nice, I mean. Can I have another one?

Frank frowned as he groped about in the pocket of his overcoat, which had once been Gricey's, and which as he well knew was empty of cash of any kind.

– You're broke, darling, oh you poor thing! Here.

She went into her handbag and came up with a half-crown. When he returned from the bar she was peering at her face in the mirror of a small powder compact.

– I am a sight! You don't care, do you, Frank?

– Of course I don't, anyway you're not.

– What a sweetheart. Do you have a girl, Frank?

He shook his head. She didn't know! He sat there in her father's overcoat and she had no inkling of his true relations with her mother. Her earlier suspicions were forgotten. Gone clear out of her head. He'd been sure she knew. Then she looked at his coat. She took the lapel between her fingers. She leaned in and smelled the fabric. Her head was close to his chest and he sank his face into her hair. She sat back.

– Daddy's, she said, and her eyes at once filled with tears.

Again she groped about in her handbag, and produced a small handkerchief. Frank leaned over and touched her arm.

– Shall I take it off? he said.

She lifted her face and laughed and it was as though her laughter loosed the tears from her eyes for they suddenly overflowed and ran down her cheeks in two streams, and for a few seconds she glowed there with wet cheeks and eyes damp and gleaming.

– You fool, of course not. I like you wearing Daddy's clothes. It makes me feel he's still alive.

Christ almighty, thought Frank Stone.

– What is it?

– Nothing, it's just—

– What?

– Your mother said the same thing.

Vera stopped wiping the tears from her face and stared at him. Frank realised he'd given away far too much, and that in that moment a brilliant flashing intuitive insight had pierced to the very heart of his secret.

– Mummy said that?

He had the distinct certain feeling that the cat, oh, the cat—

We all saw it too, of course. We turned to each other, sadly shaking our heads, our laughter dying on our lips, and said in unison: It's out of the bag.

The cat was out of the bag.

Vera stared at Frank Stone and there could be no question about it. She remembered. She knew. If she hadn't before, she did now.

– Are you shagging my mum?

The colour rose in his cheeks. He was unable to speak.

231

He opened and closed his mouth like a trout. He was no good at lying. An actor who couldn't tell a lie!

– You are! You're shagging my mum!

A silence fell in the public bar as Vera's voice carried through the low murmuring conversations and quiet laughter of the early evening clientele. Vera slapped his face hard then flung her beer at his head. It happened so fast he had no time to react. The slap started a nosebleed and the beer caught him full in the face and went right up his nose, and into his hair too, and dripped from his chin as he choked and coughed and wiped at his eyes with his fingers and tried to speak but was unable to, and meanwhile blood was dripping out of his nose and Vera had risen to her feet with her own eyes blazing, seized her handbag, and crushed out her cigarette in the ashtray. She muttered a few obscenities, called him a *lecherous cunt* and stormed out.

The landlord came from behind the counter once more. He had a dish towel, which Frank accepted as the regulars turned to one another once more. Frank wiped beer, blood and snot off his face.

– Shagging her mum, are you, son? he said quietly.

With a damply strangled groan Frank managed to knock over his chair and stumble out into the street. It was now dark. He still had the dish towel. He walked blindly towards the river with the incoherent intention of throwing himself in.

Frank sat staring across the Thames to where the dome of St Paul's loomed pale in the gloom of early evening.

He would have to talk to Joan before Vera did. It might not help but he had to do it. He could smell the beer on him, it was in his hair and down his shirt, as was the blood. He set off east towards Tower Bridge. He flung the sodden dish towel into the river. He hadn't even the bus fare to Mile End for he'd given Vera back the change from the half-crown. It took him what seemed an eternity to get to Tower Bridge and then up to Aldgate and along Whitechapel. When he arrived at Joan's door he was chilled and he still stank of beer. She was not happy to see him. She brought him into the kitchen and relieved him of the coat.

– I'll have to sponge that down. It may have to go to the cleaners. What happened to you, Frank?

He told her all of it. She wasn't angry with him. Pragmatic, if anything. She had more serious matters on her mind.

– She was bound to find out some time, I suppose, what with you in Gricey's coat and all. And you walked all the way here from Southwark?

He told her he was broke.

She regarded him with concern. She was not amused, but nor did she feel in the least maternal towards him. She'd already arrived at the sad conclusion that he was not to be depended upon. She didn't ask him what he was doing in a pub in Southwark with Vera. When he tried to apologise she silenced him with a shake of the head. She was thinking about Vera, and whether she would now be having a little nervous collapse. It's what she usually did.

*

Earlier Joan had sat at that same kitchen table in a state of anxiety, such that she'd had recourse to the much-depleted bottle on the top shelf of the kitchen cupboard. An ordeal lay ahead. For not only was she to attend the street meeting in Hackney, she was to speak at it. This had first been proposed to her by Julius, and then by Hilda Bacon. Joan had listened to the woman with mounting dismay, but had learned to show nothing of her feelings to these people.

– I will have to think about it, Mrs Bacon. Public speaking is not a thing I've done much of.

– It will give the boys something to really cheer about, said Hilda Bacon. They need such a lot of bucking up these days.

They were in Joan's kitchen. Joan had been startled to hear the doorbell soon after getting home from work, and was frankly astonished to find the big blonde fascist on her doorstep. Ascending the stairs, she rapidly composed herself. She remembered Julius' advice: stay calm and say as little as possible.

– A cup of tea, Mrs Bacon? I've just put the kettle on.

– So this is where Gricey ate his dinner and laid his head, said Hilda Bacon, dreamily. It's a kind of shrine, you know, although very few of us ever saw it.

Joan, her back turned, was busy with the teapot. She thought, Gricey brought them *here?*

– Oh why is that? she said.

– May I smoke? Well, you must know. Such an inspiration he was to us all, especially during the war when the men were in prison. Such a comfort he was.

Joan turned to the table and saw through a cloud of cigarette smoke a cold woman with half-closed eyes and corn-yellow hair organised in a flawless chignon with an encircling plait. She smoked her cigarette, her face complacent and aquiline, and Joan detested her.

– Sugar, Mrs Bacon?

– I don't use it, Mrs Grice. I'll take mine black.

Joan sat down opposite this woman. Stay calm, she thought.

– What can I do for you, Mrs Bacon?

– You needn't say very much, dear. Frederic will write it for you. It's more the symbolism of the thing, if you know what I mean. The spirit of Gricey, still with us.

– Yes, I see.

– The fight goes on. Have you an ashtray?

– Of course. Biscuit?

– What a privilege it must have been.

Joan was on her feet getting ashtray and biscuits. She only had three left. She put them on a plate.

– What was a privilege, Mrs Bacon?

– To live with such a man. With all he had to do. His work and his beliefs. It isn't easy, with so much of the world against you. Gricey would say, think of the Führer, the early years. The wilderness years, he'd say. And see what he became. What he made of Germany.

Joan watched first one then another of her precious biscuits being dipped in black tea and rapidly devoured. She decided she would say nothing about Gricey whatsoever. They could think what they wanted. Hilda Bacon left soon after. An hour later Frank Stone had appeared at her door, sodden, covered in blood, and stinking of beer.

They are running Act IV. The Duchess is already in prison. Her twin brother the Duke visits her at night, in darkness, and offers his hand to be kissed. She brings it to her lips, then as torches appear she discovers that the hand is not his own, it is another man's hand, severed at the wrist. Barely is this horror absorbed than a curtain is drawn aside to reveal a *tableau mort*. The stage directions read: *Here is discovered behind a traverse the artificial figures of* ANTONIO *and his children, appearing as if they were dead.*

They are waxwork effigies but the Duchess cannot know this yet. Then in Act IV, scene ii she is visited by Madmen sent by the Duke. It is in this scene that Frank Stone as First Madman speaks the words: 'Doomsday not come yet?' The horror of the dead hand pales in light of what follows. It is a harrowing scene, and it is dominated by the Duchess. This is the scene in which they strangle her. It's not quick.

Vera was in a fine state of readiness. She'd slept well in her narrow bed in the attic and awoken prepared to sweep the gallant Duchess to her end with all the grandeur of spirit of a true tragic heroine. Wiping the sleep from her eyes and pushing her hands through her hair, she knew herself to possess just such a spirit, and she lay in her bath ready and eager to meet death with the name of her husband on her lips. She took the bus to work, contemplating her executioners entering her chamber with a present from her brothers. It is a shrouded coffin. She will say farewell to Cariola and forgive the men about to murder her. She will send a message to the Duke and the Cardinal, saying that this is the best she can hope for. A few seconds later she will kneel. *Come violent death,* she will say. *Serve for mandragora, to make me sleep./Go tell my brothers when I am laid out,/They then may feed in quiet.*

Vera was on top of it. They were close to opening night and over the weeks of rehearsal she had discovered a kind of narrative of feeling in this last scene, a movement from the sounds of approaching Madmen – *What hideous noise was that* – to her last breath, with Antonio's name on her lips. And then, on the very point of death: *Mercy.*

She knew it for the best death scene she was ever likely to play. It allowed for both terror *and* serenity. She had come to believe that she'd been preparing all her life to play it. She felt she possessed a charge of human passion like a fermenting spirit in a corked bottle which, once released, would inebriate the world. But to think this was to tempt fate, and no actor will dare entertain such thoughts for long. Nemesis will surely follow, and strike her down for pride and presumption, although – *although* – she did in her secret heart believe it would take the audience all of Act V to begin even to think of coming to terms with the death of this Duchess. With Elizabeth Morton-Stanley she'd hatched a scheme.

In the preceding scene, when she's given the dead man's hand to kiss, and servants come with torches, the Duchess cries: *Ha? Lights! – Oh horrible!* – then strides downstage centre – and flings the severed hand out into the horrified audience.

Genius.

Frank Stone stood in the wings with the other Madmen, and most of the rest of the cast, and none seemed able even to breathe as the scene was played. When it ended they broke into spontaneous applause. From the auditorium came the booming voice of Elizabeth Morton-Stanley – 'Splendid!' – and she lumbered up onto the stage, where she took Vera aside, the girl by this time drained and limp from the work she'd just done. Odd, thought Frank, to think this was the same girl who just last night had flown into a rage and called him a lecherous cunt. But then he thought, no, not odd, it was all in the same register of heightened dramatic tension. Thinking this he recognised an important precept about the craft of acting.

Elizabeth Morton-Stanley spoke in low tones to Vera for some minutes as she wiped the sweat from her face with a towel. Vera was grinning now, and as the director left her she laid a pudgy hand on Vera's bottom and patted it. Vera wandered upstage left, where the Madmen were waiting to know if they were needed again. Seeing Frank, she stopped. She placed her hands on her hips and cocked her head to one side. Frank gazed back at her with his eyebrows slightly lifted and his mouth a little open: expectant. She shook her head and walked off towards her dressing room.

– Someone's in the doghouse, said a Madman – it was

Willy Ogilvie – and they pushed him around a bit, asking what it was he'd done to upset the Divine One, as they called her. But Frank told them nothing, for he was still observing constant sanctuary for Vera's mother. Oh but Joan had made it clear to him she would rather he left her alone now. But first she had gone into her purse and put a pound note on the table.

– That's far too much, he'd said.

Joan didn't reply and Frank felt even more wretched than he did already, as though, being dismissed, he was now being paid off. He'd got to his feet and gone out of the flat and down the stairs and into Archibald Street, leaving the pound note where it was. Joan sank onto her chair, laid her arms on the table, laid her head on her arms, and wept.

Then she heard Gricey again.

It began with a crash. It brought her up from the table at once. It came from Gricey's room.

She flung open the door and the wardrobe was standing where it had always stood. But from inside it she heard him shouting, and he was in such a rage that at first she could make no sense of it.

– *Go hang yourselves all! you are idle shallow things. I am not of your element I am not of your element Sir Topas never was man more wronged* –

Malvolio!

– *good Sir Topas do not think I am mad: they have laid me here in hideous darkness. I am not mad Sir Topas I say to you this house is dark* –

These were Malvolio's lines, shouted from a dark chamber in Act IV, scene ii of *Twelfth Night* when at the connivance of Sir Toby Belch and others he has been declared insane and locked up, and Joan, oh, she was so very familiar with these lines –

– I say this house is as dark as ignorance though ignorance were as dark as hell and I say there was never man thus abused. I am no more mad than you are –

Joan sat down on the bed where she was all in shadow with just the light from the open kitchen door across the passage, and listened in silent wonder to her late husband shouting the lines of his last role until he fell silent. She didn't move. She sat staring at the wardrobe. Then came the voice again, now low, dreadful, full of threat.

– Madam you have done me wrong, notorious wrong –

And then silence again. Joan felt the hair on her neck begin to stir and a chill creep over her skin. Her lips turned white. As in a dream she couldn't seem to move. Then came a shrill voice, like a woman's voice, the shriek of a crone.

– He hath been most notoriously abused!

Then silence once more. The wardrobe grew still. The deathly coldness seemed to pass and all at once Joan realised she was alone in the bedroom and could move again. She rose to her feet unsteadily. Gulping for air she stumbled with her head down into the passage and shut the door behind her and locked it, then went into the kitchen and closed the kitchen door. She sat at the kitchen table and with trembling fingers poured herself a glass of gin. It was his voice. She didn't know who the woman was, probably it was himself imitating Olivia but unrecognisable in that last screechy voice, and with sinking heart she acknowledged at last that which she'd suspected for weeks but dared not properly fully confront.

– You're in the fucking wardrobe, she said aloud.

She lifted the glass shakily to her lips and drank, then turned towards the window. She repeated his words.

– *I say this house is as dark as ignorance though ignorance were as dark as hell.*

For a little while she sat with her hand over her mouth. Then she spoke again.

– You're in hell.

Gricey was in hell and Joan not much better off. She barely slept that night and what sleep she did get was crowded with nightmare. At one point she got out of bed and went down the passage to stand outside Gricey's room but it was silent in there, silent as the grave, she thought, as in her mind's eye the locked wardrobe became a great coffin stood on end, and trapped inside it an unquiet spirit in a hell of its own making, but no less a hell for that. Then she muttered the words: *you have come back to haunt me,* and she asked herself why, and at once discovered a whole raft of reasons, starting with Frank Stone and going all the way through to what she was planning to do at the street meeting. Thinking this she felt a distinct impulse stirring inside her, if impulse it could be called, and recognised it as an old familiar, a propensity or tendency in her which found expression in *blind resistance to the bully*; she didn't know how else to

241

describe it. She felt it now, in the middle of the night, standing there outside Gricey's room, and was on the point of going in and telling him so but decided instead to keep it to herself because she didn't want to get him started again. So she went back to bed and this time she slept because she wasn't frightened of him now.

Five miles away, across the silent sleeping city, Vera Grice was restless in the narrow bed at the top of her husband's house in Pimlico. She'd entered what she recognised as the impatient period which occurred in the days before the first dress rehearsal when the role has been learned and the character so thoroughly assimilated that any delay is fraught with the risk of loss of vital energy. With some roles she had known uncertainty until the moment she'd stepped onto the stage and only then with joyous relief discovered she knew what to do. Sometimes it didn't happen until the fourth or fifth or sixth perform-ance and sometimes, occasionally, it never happened, and craft alone got her through. But now with the Duch-ess she was impatient to step out of the wings and into the light and find herself at home and in control and in every fibre of her being so alert it was a kind of ecstasy, yes, act-ing was ecstasy when the work had been done, all the blind alleys gone down, all the wild risks taken, and she knew beyond a shadow of a doubt that, yes, she *had it*!

That moment had come three days earlier when she played the death scene and it was torture to have to wait and hold it inside of herself and not worry at it or lose any fraction of its trembling perfection. She wouldn't sleep properly until she'd started to play it, but actually she didn't need to sleep, not with this energy alive in her. If only Daddy were here to see her.

Gustl preferred to sleep in the front room downstairs when she wanted to wake up close to her work. She had made up a daybed, and liked to lie in the darkness beside a small electric fire with the smell of oil paint and turpentine in her nostrils. The street lamp on the pavement cast low light against the wall on which the leafless branches of the elm by the gate cast faint shadows, when stirred into movement by the wind. From time to time she heard a footstep pass along the mews. In the gloom stood her easel, and on it the stretchered canvas with her unfinished portrait of Joan. She was troubled about her friend. Julius had been so sure that Joan would be eager to seize the chance to strike at the fascists, in light of Gricey's betrayal, but Gustl glimpsed complexities in the thing, and was growing less confident of Joan's resolve. Gustl also suspected that there was serious trouble between Vera and Joan. She'd asked Vera earlier if she'd seen her mother and was surprised at the curtness of the response.

– I don't have time.

– Of course, said Gustl. On the stage it will be easier.

– I doubt it.

Vera had come in late from a technical rehearsal and was heating up last night's baked beans.

– Why such, dear?

Gustl sat down at the kitchen table.

– Oh not now, darling, said Vera, I'm knackered.

Gustl retired to the front room. She lay staring at the clear marble skin of the unsmiling woman on her canvas. The effect of her pallor was one of coldness and chill, a touch of ice in the shifting half-light drifting in above the shutters. She would have to talk to Julius in the morning. He was admirable. He would not be diverted from his path. He would not rest until those men and their cause were destroyed. But he expected too much of Joan. She wasn't as strong as he was, none of them were. She would talk to him in the morning. She fell into a restless sleep and dreamed of Joan, whose wintry image gazed blindly at her from the other side of the room.

Julius' sleep was not restless, nor was it disturbed by dreams. This was a man who'd lost a theatre and found his soul. He'd seen his theatre destroyed and from that loss had arisen a new clarity in his thinking; a rapid reordering of his moral priorities. There was nothing he could do about his theatre so he went back to work and invested carefully in other men's plays, and waited for the opportunity that he was sure would announce itself sooner or later. It came the day he saw the fascists shouting death and murder at Whitestone Pond, and watched as Karsh and his friends without hesitation knocked their heads together and overturned their platform. He had driven the car. It was exhilarating, not so much the danger of the thing as his certain understanding that he'd found the cause for which he'd been waiting. He would not be diverted from it now.

*

Frank Stone stood at the window of the garret off Seven Dials he shared with his mother and the boy, and sometimes with the cellist Gabor Szirtes. He played an air on his violin, as he looked out over the rooftops; it was a fragment of the *Liebestod*. He was beyond tears. It was his own weakness that had brought him this trouble. His mother lay murmuring in her sleep in the tiny room next door, the boy beside her. Frank at last turned and laid the violin down on the table. He stretched out on the couch and linked his fingers behind his head and stared at the ceiling, where a cheap yellow lampshade hung from a frayed cord. It put him in mind of a hanging he'd witnessed as a child.

22

FRANK HAS BEEN given another part to add to his First Madman. He is to play a courtier called Grisolan. He speaks only in scene iv of the last act, when he's on with the Cardinal and Count Malateste. He is to utter the immortal words: *'Twas a foul storm tonight.*

– *'Twas a <u>FOUL</u> storm tonight*, Frank says to his reflection in the mirror in the shared dressing room in the bowels of the theatre. He tries it again, this time with the emphasis shifted from *foul* to *tonight*.

– Want me to run your line with you? says Willy Ogilvie, who also plays Second Madman.

His companions are aware that Frank Stone's mood has darkened in recent days, and they suspect that Vera Grice is the reason. Frank will not speak of it. On one of his frequent nocturnal rambles he has wandered, again, into Pimlico – quite by chance? (we doubt it) and found a defaced synagogue, with nearby a bomb-damaged house under scaffolding, in a small barren park with children's swings in it hanging from a kind of gibbet. He feels confident that a hanged man would be discovered here not by a child but by a policeman, coming upon the body early in the morning, if the man did it at midnight. It would allow a modicum of bleak comfort, he reflected, to make an end of himself on the stroke of midnight. He decides the emphasis should revert to *foul*.

– '*Twas a* <u>FOUL</u> *storm tonight,* he says.

– '*Twas a foul* <u>STORM</u> *tonight?* says Willy Ogilvie. <u>'TWAS</u> *a foul storm tonight?*

The others join in, each with his own considered interpretation of the line.

– Oh fuck off the bloody lot of you.

Jasper Speke, the stage manager, now appears in the doorway.

– All right, girls, that's enough. Frankie, they want you. Harry's losing his voice and the boss is doing Act V.

Frank Stone brightens. Any chance to play Antonio is welcome, and although she's disembodied in this scene, only an offstage echo, it means working with Vera.

When he comes up through the wings she's sitting on a chair filing her fingernails and she doesn't look up. Frank steps onstage where Philip Herring, playing Delio, another courtier, awaits him. Oh, and look! – indistinct figures can faintly be detected in the front row centre of the gallery, high above the back stalls, and who can these shadowy ladies be? Yes, it's us! One of our rare outings to the theatre, and we're having a lovely time. Onstage meanwhile Sidney Temple is telling the actors they're running scene iii. This is Antonio's death scene. Frank knows it backwards. We're all ears.

– All right, Delio, let's get started. Yond's the Cardinal's window.

– *Yond's the Cardinal's window. This fortification/Grew from the ruins of an ancient abbey . . .*

The Gothic mood suits Frank nicely and with his first lines – *I do love these ancient ruins./We never tread upon them but we set/Our foot upon some reverend history* – he feels at home, at ease, on top of the thing, and they run the short scene through the echoes – Vera as the dead Duchess speaking offstage – and on into Antonio's freshening resolve: *I will not henceforth save myself by halves/Lose all, or nothing.*

When the scene ends Frank finds that, like Antonio, he has cheered himself up.

– Good work, everybody, says Sidney Temple. Half hour break then scene iv.

– Thank you, Miss Grice, says Frank as he passes her in the wings.

– Come here, she says.

His heart stops.

– Come *here!*

He stands before her.

– You are a lecherous cunt, she says, and his heart sinks.

– But there are worse things, she then says.

His heart exults.

– Although I can't think of one at this moment. What are you doing for lunch?

– Eating a sandwich, Miss Grice. What about you?

– Sharing your sandwich. Let's go to my dressing room.

As he follows her to her dressing room he catches the eye of Willy Ogilvie who's on his way to the stage door and off out down the pub. Willy makes a face as though to say, things looking up then, and Frank opens his eyes wide and flattens his lips, as though to say, I certainly bloody hope so.

Vera's dressing room is a spacious, furnished affair, a far cry from the constriction and squalor of the lower depths. She waves him towards an armchair heaped with clothing. She sits in front of her mirror. Frank sits on the edge of the armchair and pulls from the pocket of his overcoat a spam-and-onion sandwich on lard, in thick slices of grey bread, wrapped in newspaper.

– Very appetising, says Vera, watching him in the mirror.

– All I've got, says Frank.

She swings round in her chair.

– Those Daddy's trousers?

– I'm afraid so.

– And that's his shirt.

– Yes.

The sad fact of the matter is that all Frank Stone's clothes now are items from Gricey's wardrobe as donated by Joan. Having once tasted these pleasures he finds he can't go back to cheap shabby fabrics and threadbare cuffs and patched elbows and the rest.

– What am I to do with you?

– What do you mean?

– You're about the best damn actor in this company and you haven't got anything to say.

Frank Stone cannot believe his ears.

– Who do you want to play?

– Antonio?

– Don't be stupid.

He thinks fast. Grisolan has only three lines. Count Malateste, however—

– Malateste.

Poor Willy Ogilvie, but Frank has no time for sentiment now.

– I'll see what I can do, says Vera.

She tosses her script at him.

– Have a look at it, she says.

Frank gazes at her, his face a frowning smudgy thing of hope and gratitude.

– Give me that bloody sandwich.

So as Frank goes through Malateste's lines in the last two scenes, Vera devours the revolting sandwich, all the while staring at him. When he gets to the end she makes a suggestion. Frank begins to nod his head.

– She won't like it.

– She'll like it. Sidney will make her like it. OK, bugger off, learn it if you can, you've got ten minutes. Oh sorry, I seem to have eaten all your lunch.

He leaves Vera's dressing room like an Elizabethan courtier, unwilling to turn his back on the Divine One for even a second.

*

Willy Ogilvie was not well pleased when the actors came together after lunch to run scenes iv and v and Sidney Temple told them that he and Frank Stone were changing places. *Cunt,* he whispered.

– Nothing to do with me.

– I had thirteen lines now I have three.

– Sorry, Willy.

– You owe me ten lines.

Sidney Temple was clapping his hands.

– Positions, everybody. You'll be on book, will you, Willy?

– Yes, Mr Temple.

– Frank?

– I think I know it, Mr Temple.

– Oh do you? All right, Cardinal, ready?

And they were off. In the first seconds of scene iv poor Willy Ogilvie has to speak the line he'd earlier uttered in mockery.

– *'Twas a foul storm* <u>TONIGHT</u>.

The director speaks: Stress on *foul,* I think, Mr Ogilvie.

RODERIGO: *The Lord Ferdinand's chamber shook
like an osier.*

MALATESTE: *'Twas nothing but pure kindness in the
devil/To rack his own child.*

The joke is enjoyed in the stalls, where director and assistant are sitting; also by us ladies up in the gallery. A little later Bosola stabs Antonio in the dark, in error, fatally wounding him.

– Good. Last scene. Cardinal! shouts the director. Are you with us?

– With you, drawls David Jekyll, and enters, *with a book*. Coming onstage *with a book* is a convention that suggests melancholy. Hamlet comes on *with a book* in the second scene of his own Act II. And melancholy the Cardinal should be: Bosola tells him he has come to kill him. The Cardinal panics; then *Enter, above*, PESCARA, MALATESTE, RODERIGO, GRISOLAN. It's almost finished now. The Cardinal is further wounded and Bosola suffers a death bite to the throat from Duke Ferdinand, who suffers from lycanthropy and believes he's a wolf. Then the Duke in turn is killed by the dying Bosola. So with four corpses on the stage, the four Courtiers who have watched from the gallery above now enter. It is given to Count Malateste to say the words: *Oh sad disaster.*

It was about these words that Vera had made her suggestion to Frank earlier. *Oh sad disaster,* he says now, but he says it not tragically, no, but instead – sardonically. There is again laughter, and Elizabeth Morton-Stanley buries her head in her hands. Sidney says nothing. Then the director's head comes up. She hears in that laughter what Sidney had been trying to explain to her earlier: the laughter is edgy, it is hollow, almost, for of course it is *no sad disaster at all* to lose villains like Duke Ferdinand and his brother the Cardinal. There is no ridicule here, no joyous trivialising revel in the excess of the thing; rather, the arousal of laughter does exactly what Sidney had suggested it would: it heightens the horror. Elizabeth

Morton-Stanley clamps her hand on Sidney's slender gouty knee and nods, and they watch the resolution, the arrival of Delio with Antonio's son.

The director is satisfied. She heaves herself up, using Sidney's knee as a kind of fulcrum to gain purchase, and heads for the stage. Frank Stone turns towards the wings, and the Divine One is still there, leaning against a wall backstage, ankles crossed, in baggy slacks, a tight sweater and a headscarf. Her arms are folded under her breasts, and her eyes are hooded, half closed, against the smoke from the roll-up hanging from her lips. She lifts her hand and touches her index finger to the top of her thumb to make a little circle, an O.

23

IT WAS WITH a sadness verging on pathos that Edgar Cartridge divested himself of his uniform in his bedroom at night. For a blessed hour or sometimes two he has stood at attention, saluted, marched back and forth across the floor, lain on his bed staring at the ceiling, his right hand in a black leather glove held aloft where he can admire it. But there was a Saturday night, once, when he'd got home from the pub and put on his uniform, and come clattering downstairs in it like the young Hero of the Blackshirts he knew himself to be. And oh, it was a fine thing in the midnight hour to sit with his boots up on the kitchen table, and a glass of whisky to hand, his mother and his little brother asleep upstairs, and himself not wanted at the abattoir in the morning. A fine thing.

He'd started to sing the Horst Wessel song – and woken his mother. She came downstairs in her nightie, in her curlers.

– Oh Edgar, you've been drinking. But don't you look nice in your uniform.

Edgar attempted to rise smartly from the table and salute his mother but somehow the chair fell down and he stumbled over it.

– Oh you fool, you'll wake your brother.

It was too late. His brother Hughie Cartridge aged fifteen was already awake, and he appeared now in the kitchen door in his dressing gown and slippers. He was amused to see Edgar clearly drunk and dressed up as a fascist.

– Where did you get the costume, Edgar?

– You shut your mouth.

– You go back to bed, son, said Mrs Cartridge. Your brother's not well.

– He's pissed, said Hughie.

Edgar did not have a strong head for alcohol. The whisky had done for him. He lifted his fist but Hughie laughed.

– *Sieg heil,* is it, Edgar?

– Hughie! said his mother.

In the morning Edgar remembered only that he'd been laughed at and that he'd spilt whisky on his uniform. But what he didn't forget was the pleasure it gave him to wear it outside his bedroom, to come clattering downstairs in it, to sit with his boots on the kitchen table like the fine young Blackshirt he knew himself to be. He was the future, was he not?

It was one night a few weeks later that a sober Edgar Cartridge slipped out of the little terraced house on Inkerman Street, Hackney, in full blackshirt under his overcoat.

He made his way to the Regent's Canal. It was late, nobody about. A towpath ran along the canal under the gasworks, with the moonlight gleaming on its oily skin. It was there he took off his overcoat and laid it on a bench.

He then marched up and down in the bitter chill of the night, and tasted again the simple joy of playing the part of the young fascist he'd been before the war. Back and forth he marched, a happy man. He yearned for applause – and he got it. Two girls a bit the worse for drink were crossing a bridge over the canal. They'd been in town, a pub in Soho. Now they paused, and leaned on the parapet to watch Edgar marching about in his uniform. They were soon helpless with laughter. They fell about, clutching each other. They clapped their hands and cheered, and Edgar had the good grace to come to attention and salute them. Right arm at eye level, rigid from the shoulder, hand straight and heels together, as he'd been taught; thinking, bloody tarts. Then he put his coat on and made his way home, the girls' laughter growing faint in the night, then dying away. He encountered nobody else. He got into the house and upstairs to his room without incident. He stood before his mirror, panting, exhilarated. He slept soundly that night. It was a performance that deserved to be repeated. He only wished he didn't have to do it by himself.

We're not sure exactly when it was that Joan once more unlocked the doors of Gricey's great wardrobe. But we believe it was towards the end of March, a Sunday morning, yes, late March or early April. There had been a thaw, but with it had come flooding. Much distress in rural parts of the country, and after the brief flare of optimism as the cold fingers of winter seemed to loose their grip, now came the ghastly sodden aftermath, rising waters flooding homes and drowning livestock, crops ruined, banks broken in great rivers, these new hardships wearing the face not of ice but of water. So, a damp clear Sunday morning, church bells chiming in St Clement's, and Joan unlocked the wardrobe door and allowed light to flood into the great coffin where Gricey's mouldering spiritual residue lay.

There was a trunk in there. She worked steadily, garments emerging, each to be inspected, inventoried, laid out on the bed in one of various piles. All of good quality. Extraordinary how much was in there. He had thrown nothing away.

She went back to the kitchen to have a sit down and a cup of tea and review her list. Did she suspect even then that there was an odd *incompletion*, something hidden, an absence; that which ought to be accounted for but was not? So many memories, she may have been deaf to the small voice that told her to look further, or deeper, but whether she heard it or not, when she went back, and pulled out the empty trunk, only then did she see a brown suitcase pushed into the far back corner of the wardrobe.

She'd been warmed by what she'd found in Gricey's trunk, and his iniquitous duplicity, only lately discovered, could not spoil it, nor could the memory of the recent rage of his trapped, damned spirit. The nights she'd been on his arm as they moved through the world of the London theatre, yes, the first nights, the dinners, the parties, so many parties at which she'd stood at his side among their friends as he talked, and talked, and talked—

Then later, back at the flat, as he got undressed, as he unbuttoned his shirt, removed the collar stud and the cufflinks, set them down on the dressing table. Slipped his braces off his shoulders and stood in his white vest with the braces hanging at his thighs, lit only by the glow from Joan's bedside lamp. He was lean, hard. He'd kept himself trim. He took exercise, he watched what he ate, so no fat on Charlie Grice as he sat on the end of the bed, unlacing his shoes and kicking them off, and then his suspendered socks. Again he stood at the end of the bed, his eyes still upon her, and unbuttoned his trousers, which fell to the floor. He stepped out of them. He hung them over a chair. He was at the side of the bed now, in his underwear, and he slipped in between the sheets. Joan turned towards him.

– Turn off the light, love, she whispers.

Turn off the light. But now there was the suitcase. It was scuffed and faded, with two buckled straps and brass studs along the seams. It was locked. She took it into the kitchen and put it on the table. With a small pair of scissors and her heavy shears, the steel ones with the long pointed blades, very sharp indeed, she unpicked the stitching, prised loose the studs and snipped the seam. She sat at the table and stared at the unbound suitcase. Then she stood up and lifted it open. It was as she expected. Every fascist has a uniform somewhere in his wardrobe.

24

WHATEVER THE PLAY, whoever's in the cast, it *will* have its opening night, and it *will* be a night to remember, if only with chagrin. The 1947 production of *The Duchess of Malfi*, by John Webster, starring Vera Grice, Harry Catermole, Edmund Colefax and David Jekyll, directed by Elizabeth Morton-Stanley, and produced by Julius Glass and Partners, at the New Apollo Theatre on the Charing Cross Road, was no exception. For Joan, it was a night which, in her anticipation of it, had little of the old glamour and excitement she'd felt when Vera last opened in a play, when Gricey was still alive. Was it *As You Like It?* Surely not. It seemed an age. Could so much really have changed in a winter? But what a winter. The discoveries she'd made in the wake of Gricey's death, and now, just the last in what seemed an endless string of nightmares, the uniform in the suitcase. She'd lifted out the folded shirt and breeches, the belt, the boots and the cap, carried them from the kitchen and into his bedroom and laid them on the bed as she had laid out his other clothes. They were all of a piece. The sum of his parts.

She had unbuttoned her blouse, and then her skirt, then she had kicked off her shoes and shuffled out of her slip until she stood before the mirror on the back of the door, in her corset and underwear only. She stood with one arm at her side, the other clutching her gathered hair to the back of her skull, mindful, painfully so, of what had changed since first she'd stood naked before her husband, when with delicate fingers he'd spread the hair from her face, held it as she did now, gathered behind her head, and called her his Venus de Mile End. No, she was a hard, thin woman now, a long winter of grief and poor diet had seen to that. There was no flesh on her hips or thighs, and the bicycle had seen to *that;* she was more boy than woman, she thought: gaunt. She lifted the black shirt, shook it out and, tentative now, eyes still on the mirror on the back of the door, inserted an arm in a sleeve—

Frank Stone was at this time preoccupied with Count Malateste. He'd thought at first he had only thirteen lines, forgetting the eight in Act III. Willy Ogilvie also has more lines than he first thought: in Act I, in his new role, that of Grisolan, he has three. True, they are not *expansive* lines, and will not significantly add to Willy's lustre. The first he shares with Roderigo in scene i: *Ha ha ha!* A little later he says: *They are, my lord.* And in scene ii: *I shall, instantly.* Willy is not much assuaged, and in the shallows of his heart has resolved to have his revenge on Frank Stone.

Frank has been greatly encouraged by Vera telling him he is the best actor in the company, and by the success of his *Oh sad disaster*. He is determined that his Malateste will not go unnoticed. Alterations have been made to the costume for which Willy was first fitted. Frank is pleased with it. There is black silk in the tunic, also in the floppy cap, and he's decided to make his face a thing of ghostly pallor, with black around the eyes and lips. Malateste will thus, he believes, be both a count at the court and something more: a pale figure unmoved by the tragedies that befall the House of Malfi and those it supports. He will at the same time be both a player in the drama, and a commentator upon it. His will be the voice of what he believes to be the black humour of irony that colours this sustained piece of horror.

It is in the assumed posture of lofty, sneering disdain, then, that he leaves the theatre after the second dress rehearsal, his first time playing the character of Count Malateste. Nobody has suggested that his black-and-white make-up is overdone, and when he returns to his mirror afterwards he wipes much of it off but not all. In fact from his make-up box he gets out the black pencil and touches in his lips and eyes, leaving enough pallor high on the cheeks and brow to suggest the shadow, merely, of the persona that is becoming more himself than himself in these fraught last days. He has not far to go to reach the alley off Seven Dials and the two small rooms he shares with Rosza and the boy, but he cannot go home yet. He is

261

too full of the work. His brain is on fire. Like Vera, he is impatient for an audience.

He thinks of Vera now. When at last they're in performance he will see more of her, but to think of Vera is to think of her mother. Frank Stone is not altogether without conscience. He is clear enough to know that he bears responsibility for the hurt she has suffered, and that he's made it worse by failing to go to her. He tells himself this is a difficult time for him but he's lying and he knows it.

He stands among the lights of Cambridge Circus pondering the enormity of his cruelty to a woman who took him in when he felt himself friendless. He succeeds then in delivering to himself a small shock of moral dismay. Without properly realising it, he has turned his steps towards Piccadilly Circus, and the Beaumont, where Joan of course runs the wardrobe. It's only nine in the evening. The play will be in progress, he thinks, unaware that it came down ten days earlier and the theatre is dark. So Frank Stone, fierce now in his determination to make amends to the woman he's wronged, turns his steps again, this time towards Mile End.

Joan is still in Gricey's uniform. She hasn't troubled to make herself a hot supper. She could have done. She has an egg. She has half a loaf. She even has a pat of butter although it might have gone off by now. Instead she opens a tin of corned beef and spoons a little into the cat's bowl, and then forks out a mouthful for herself. She washes it down with a teacup of gin. Dear Uncle Comfort has come down from the top shelf and lives behind the dinner plates now. Joan sits at the kitchen table gazing at the night through the window by the stove. It is always at about this time that she drifts across the passage and unlocks the door of Gricey's room, just to be sure, of – what? – she can't rightly say. That he hasn't returned, she supposes. She turns the light on. It sheds but a dimness on a room containing a bed with its mattress rolled up, and piled on the exposed springs the cardboard boxes she has filled with shoes and hats, and in the trunk the clothes that remain, wrapped in tissue paper and mothballed.

Across the few bare boards, against the wall opposite, stands the wardrobe with its doors wide open as though in welcome to the unwary; as though to say, *we have nothing to hide.*

Joan has brought her kitchen chair with her. She sets it down between bed and wardrobe where she can stare into what she's now come to think of as his coffin, and to indulge feelings that grow more confused and, inevitably, more maudlin with every teacup of gin. A moment will arrive when she'll start to address the wardrobe. But when she hears a familiar cry from the street below, that moment has not yet arrived.

She goes to the window. It's him. That wretched man. And then she thinks: *he's back.* She turns off the light and stands at the window and her face is deep in shadow now, for the lamp at the top of the street is the sole source of light. Frank Stone gazes up at her and can see almost nothing for she is like a jade statue, all in black, the fascist black, still and silent behind the dark window, and he

263

calls again. He can't know the struggle that's occurring in this woman's heart, nor the havoc he is causing her, even now. She cannot open the door to him. Frank Stone can't see the tears coursing down her cheeks, but he opens his arms, and with his pale upturned face, eyes blackened and lips like coal, he implores her to let him in, but she turns her head away.

> But, soft! What light through yonder window breaks?
> It is my lady, O, it is my love.
> O, that she knew she were!

But no light through yonder window breaks tonight, and Frank stands there for a while then turns away and walks off towards St Clement's and the cemetery.

Ten minutes later the front door is flung open and the distraught Joan runs out into the street, still in Gricey's fascist black, looking about wildly, this way and that. But there is no one in sight. The street is deserted.

Later she folded the uniform and put it back in the suitcase, as it had been before. She had further need of Uncle's comfort. What she would do with the suitcase she didn't yet know, but that it had to go, about this there could be no question. Steadied by gin she was horribly fascinated by what had occurred, by how she had felt herself shiver into nothing, and the sheer panic that then ensued. Is that what happened to Gricey, she thought, that he tried the thing on, and was lost?

See her now on her black bicycle, a quiet London

Sunday morning as she pedals with sedate purpose towards the docks, and down to Wapping Stairs she comes, high in the saddle, yes, and determined, with her face to the wind off the river. Strapped to the rack behind the saddle is the suitcase. She turns down by the warehouses, what few are still standing. She is alert for a quiet place where she can dispose of the damn thing unobserved. She doesn't have far to go. A lonely stretch of river wall and some pebbled strand beyond, she thinks, lifting her head to smell the air, large clouds scudding high in the sky, the wind freshening as she dismounts by the wall and lowers the kickstand. She unfastens the suitcase and carries it to the slimy, weedy steps cut into the stones of the old river wall. The Thames is high today, roiling and bucking in great tumult as new waters come streaming in from the melting snows of Gloucestershire and Berkshire and Surrey and the rest.

She descends a few steps to where the river surges against the stones, then all at once she lifts the suitcase in both hands high over her head. Thinking this is the last of him, surely, she hesitates – then hurls it with all her strength and out it sails on the wind, the lid tumbling open, garments drifting out like so many black flags, flapping and turning, then settling briefly on the river before being swept away. The suitcase bobs on the swells then sinks from sight. A seagull nearby lifts screaming from the river and shears away in the breeze.

A sudden fit of shivering seizes Joan and she turns and climbs back up to the cobbled alley between the warehouses. Then she's on her bicycle and away.

*

Meanwhile, in Pimlico, Julius and Gustl are having a serious discussion about Joan. In German. They are in his study. Gustl is upright in the armchair and her pale eyes are on her friend as she points a finger at him. She's told him she's worried Joan isn't strong enough for what he wants her to do: speak at a public meeting, in a voice not her own but that of a fascist. Or the wife of a fascist – the *widow* of a fascist. She's only skin and bones, she says, *Haut und Knochen!* Julius tells her that Joan is one of the strongest women he knows. Gustl remains unconvinced. She hopes he's right.

– *Ich hoffe du hast Recht, Julius.*

He says he is.

– *Ich habe Recht, nicht wahr.*

Gustl was no materialist. She was German. Deep strains of Germanic thought and feeling coursed through her allegedly impure veins. She'd read Kant and Schiller as a child, she believed in the progressive ideals of Romanticism, and at times, when she was a very young woman, had thought she walked in beauty like the night. Then had come the doctrine of the Superior Man and his illimitable Will. The destruction of the institutions soon followed, then more destruction, and worse, a dizzying spiral, horror piled upon horror, and there had to be a better way, she thought, but barely had she started to articulate the alternative than the gates were closing and she was trapped in the city of her birth, which wished now only to destroy her. She no longer understood what had happened to Germany.

Gustl doesn't say this, but now she thinks that while Julius believes he knows Joan's strength, he doesn't see her as she, Gustl, does. He didn't survive two years a step ahead of the Gestapo. He didn't have to fear that every person who helped him might be an informer, eager to betray him so as to secure their own safety. Oh, and she'd made mistakes, and every one of them almost cost her her life. When she stayed with a family, always the father came to her in the night, and she couldn't say no. In the daylight, on some streets, she would tear off her star. Other streets she'd slip into a doorway and stitch it back on again. Would she have trusted the grieving Joan, when Joan behaved not with her usual steady iron control, but with recklessness, with hysteria—? No she would not.

– *Ich habe Recht, nicht wahr,* said Julius again.

Gustl said nothing.

Later she lies on her bed unable to sleep. It wasn't so strange, that winter, to see one's neighbours grow thin, thinner even than they were in the war years, these sad Londoners. But Gustl has observed a more marked difference in Joan, and it's not the effects of short rations only, but a sort of *wasting.* And there are other changes, at times a kind of darting quickness in her movements, a feverish quality, and a new light in her eyes, a fixedness of stare. She's drinking, thinks Gustl, and failing to eat properly, as much as anyone can eat properly these days. This is no ordinary grief, she thinks, although she is all too aware that grief can wear a thousand faces, and last as long as it has to. But something else is happening to

Joan and she's never seen it before. Would she trust her with what it is they're asking her to do? At this time, no, she would not.

Oh but it was late. The house was quiet now. Vera was exhausted and had gone up to the attic. Julius too had retired. In her scarlet dressing gown Gustl quietly descended the dark stairs to her studio. She turned on the light and sat before the unfinished portrait on her easel. She stares at the face of her friend, and at last she sees the ghost. *Sie war besessen*. Haunted.

In the morning Vera arose early and came downstairs as calm as Julius had ever seen her. For this he had been hoping, and seeing it now, was greatly relieved.

– Sit down, my darling, let me give you breakfast. Will you eat an egg? I have kippers.

Vera gazed at her husband with tender eyes. It was so very curious when it happened, thought Julius. He would never understand her. She came to him where he stood at the stove in his apron and put her arms around him, pressing herself close to him and kissing his neck.

– You are so good to me.

– I am so proud of you.

– You might not be.

Julius laid his hands on her cheeks. He told her that yes, he would be. She embraced him.

– This will soon be over, she whispered.

She meant that she would come down from the attic.

– I know, said Julius.

Later she gathered the cards she'd written to the other

members of the cast, and the presents she would distribute when she got to the theatre, and packed them in a large shopping bag. She had a bath in the little clawfoot bathtub in the attic, then got dressed in a sweater and slacks, and performed her few superstition rituals for First Night. In the hall downstairs she got her coat from the cupboard. Gustl came out of her studio.

– Are you off now, love?

– I might as well.

– *Du wirst heute Abend glänzend sein!* I just know it.

The two women kissed. Julius appeared from the back of the house. There was nothing really to say. They would be in her dressing room afterwards, where Vera had left her nice frock, and then all go out to dinner. Julius didn't say, 'to celebrate', nothing but bad luck would come of that. He took her out to the street while Gustl stood in the open front door. Along came a cab and Julius hailed it. He saw Vera into the back of the cab then handed her the shopping bag with the cards and the presents. He stepped onto the pavement and the cab drove off. Julius turned towards the house and he and Gustl went in together. Both were affected by the calm courage Vera displayed, both thinking of what it was that young woman had to accomplish in the next hours.

The cab driver knew who his passenger was and where she was going without Vera having to say a word. When they reached the theatre he got out and opened the door for her.

– All good luck tonight, Miss Grice, he said.

Vera was gracious. She thanked him and made her

way round to the stage door, where William Pettifer, who'd looked after that door for half a century, greeted her warmly.

– Who's in, Bill? said Vera.

– You're the first, miss.

She stepped into the theatre.

25

VERA SITS IN her dressing room listless and alone, and missing her father. When Gricey was present it all *mattered*, somehow. It became a proper, genuine theatrical event. She remembered coming to this same theatre as a young girl to see him in the Scottish play, and going back-stage afterwards with her mother, and being allowed a small glass of champagne, her very first. And Gricey at his mirror, wiping his face clean, the room full of her parents' friends, and bottles and cards everywhere, laughter—

Her reverie is shattered by her dresser's noisy arrival. Vera turns to her and prepares to begin the business. She changes into her dressing gown and then out comes her toolbox, the Leichner sticks, the powders, the kohl, and all thoughts of her father have dispersed for there is so much to be done. Actors will soon stop by with cards and gifts and good wishes, and the theatre like a living organism will gather its various energies and move

271

towards the moment when the audience settles and the lights go down.

Already at the front of house the doors have been opened and the first members of this first-night audience have divested themselves of their coats and hats and made their way to one of the several theatre bars where over cocktails and champagne they murmur what they remember of the play, and the last time they saw Vera Grice onstage, but whatever topic of conversation arises, all are conscious of the fierce anticipation that will always attend a first night in a big West End theatre. The bars begin to fill and, slowly at first, then more quickly, the volume of talk increases, and the volume of smoke with it, while behind the curtain Jasper Speke hovers over the props table, a dresser rushes along a corridor clutching a wig, and an actor realises he remembers not a single one of his lines, *not one,* while a carpenter replaces a broken banister in the courtiers' gallery that might otherwise give way in the last scene of the play.

Joan is accompanied to the theatre by Julius and Gustl. They have picked her up in the Wolseley, and from Mile End come into the West End by way of Aldgate and the Strand. Julius is of course in evening dress and wearing his white silk scarf. Gustl is in her best frock, the green velvet with the parrot, also an old silver fur with broad shoulders, on which she has spent an hour with a hair-brush, and the dark felt hat with the two feathers that reminds her of the Tyrol. Joan is in black.

It did not occur to her not to wear black. She is not conscious of any funereal association, and if asked about it might have said she was attending the performance of a tragedy, but nobody asks. The car makes its slow way to the New Apollo, Julius handling the big Wolseley with aplomb, a cigar between his teeth, and Gustl beside him, who turns to speak to Joan, all in black in the back like an orphan child or a maiden aunt – oh, a figure of pathos, surely, and we were all affected, some of us even experienced *foreboding*, yes, a touch of dread. Stepping down amid the milling, curious crowd, she sees her daughter's name in lights over the marquee. She thinks how Gricey would have stood there in the street, gazing up at it, drawing the attention of others to it, and for a second or two she becomes emotional. He'd have wiped a speck of a tear from his eye, she thinks, then he'd have taken her arm, and into the foyer they'd come, himself once more in character: old Gricey.

But this night she had not Gricey's arm but Julius', and on her other arm dear Gustl, and it was just as well, for how else would she have got through the next minutes? It was all a blur of faces, of kisses, of greetings, snatches of talk, bright lights, smoke and laughter. She'd entered such foyers on nights no different from this one a thousand times before. And yet she was dismayed, and a little frightened, distracted and unable to focus, unable to cope with an eruption of disturbing memories.

Gustl knew her friend was in distress. She guided her through the throng as though she were blind, to a small banquette at the back of the foyer where they could sit removed from the rest.

– Are you all right? she whispered.

– I need a drink, dear, said Joan.

Gustl saw a waiter and they each took a cocktail.

– I don't know what's come over me. That's better.

– Such a crowd, said Gustl as she waved her hand in front of her face. *Es ist sehr heiß, wir hätten unsere Fächer mitbringen sollen.*

– English, dear.

– Very hot. We should need fans. It will be more cold inside.

– I doubt it, said Joan.

She made rather short work of her cocktail. She laid her hand on Gustl's arm.

– One more of those, dear, please, and I'll be fine.

So Gustl got her another one.

Then Julius joined them and suggested they take their seats. Rising from the banquette Joan was unsteady. Julius and Gustl understood the strain she was feeling, so they thought. First time without Gricey.

Julius had requested seats not in the front stalls but halfway down the house in the middle of the row. Without mishap they found their seats and settled in, Joan sitting between her two friends. She was then able to look around the auditorium and see who was present and what they were wearing. In fact this crowd was showing some elegance. The women's hats were certainly improving. Others were having a look round too, and Joan, being the mother of the leading lady, and known to many of those present, was a figure of some interest. Few of them had seen her since Gricey's funeral in January, and some were shocked by her appearance. The gauntness of her face, and oh, to be in deep mourning still, on this of all nights, a night which surely belonged to Vera. And not a few wondered, if she was unable for her daughter's sake to set aside her grief, at least for this one night, why she had come at all, for this was not how it was done. The brave face, the gay smile, the lifted chin, this is how show people faced misfortune and tragedy, and hadn't they all been doing exactly that for years now? The show *had* to go on. But Joan Grice, still beautiful, but thin, stone-faced, more pale than ever and dressed as though for the crematorium, no, this was not the spirit, this was not it at all.

The auditorium doors have closed. The theatre imperceptibly darkens. The audience is at once quiet. Then comes that long moment when the lights at last die away – the curtain is about to rise – the tension is palpable, both out front and backstage too. A last cough is heard. Jasper Speke glances at his people. Actors stand in readiness in the wings.

Joan has become absorbed in a memory. She is in an air-raid shelter in the crypt of a church, it is December 1940, one of those nights of noise and fire and danger, and a pervasive sense of physical vulnerability. People feel very close to death at such times, during nights like this, and are afraid of dying and afraid to show they are afraid. Suddenly there is the most tremendous blast – it makes a vacuum in her ears, and when the dust has settled she discovers a child, a small girl, lying before her on the flagstone floor of the crypt. She is very still, this child, in her buttoned coat, and her eyes are open. She is unscathed but for a slight pink puffiness in her cheeks.

But she is dead. The blast has burst her little lungs. Somewhere her mother is screaming.

Lifting her head, blinking at the memory of the dead child, and the screaming mother, it's then Joan sees him – he's here! She's outraged. Rising to her feet in the darkened auditorium, and with her arm outstretched and trembling, she points a finger at a figure at the end of the front row stalls even as an usher melts into the gloom near the exit beyond.

– Gricey! she cries.

There is a murmuring all around her.

– Oh what do you *want*, Gricey? Why *now?*

Her voice is loud in the silent theatre and none can miss the tremor of hysteria in it. Another second of silence. Jasper Speke barks a quiet command – *Hold the rag!* – and the curtain does not rise. The house lights come up. The murmuring swells as those in the front stalls crane around to see who it is who's shouting – is it part of the play? – and the back stalls all lean forward, and Joan stands there in the middle of the row staring at someone only she can see, both arms outstretched now, palms open, imploring him like a bereft lover—

Actors in the wings peer at each other in perplexity while ushers come swiftly down the aisle. Then Gustl is helping Joan, confused, but becoming aware that she has been shouting in a dark theatre, and unsure why, and eager in her distress to leave at once. She stumbles with her head down, shuddering, towards the exit, Gustl beside her, taking her arm, and the ushers in close attendance.

The lights again go down, and now at last the curtain rises. The courtier, Delio, speaks the first line of the play, as later in the evening he will speak the last.

– You are welcome to your country, dear Antonio –

Even as the words ring out clear and strong, Gustl helps Joan from the auditorium. The company manager hovers but Gustl waves him away. She mutters at Joan, but in German.

– What?

– I think you've seen a ghost, *Liebste*.

Into the bar they go, and sit on the same banquette as before.

– Is that what happened? Joan whispers.

– You grieve for him and you have not finished.

– I haven't started.

Gustl sees the truth in this.

– I can't go back in there.

– What shall we do, love?

Joan again turns to face her friend and, taking Gustl's hands in her own, tells her that she, Gustl, has to see the play even if she, Joan, does not. Gustl won't hear of it. She suggests they go back to Julius' house but oh no, Joan wants to go home. Gustl insists on coming with her.

Out on the Charing Cross Road it's raining. They have no umbrella. It's a few minutes before they see a taxi. Joan climbs in and before Gustl can stop her she slams the door. Gustl is tapping at the window, but Joan sits staring straight ahead, telling the cabbie to drive on, leaving Gustl in her damp fur with no choice but to go back into the theatre.

*

The play is, after all, and despite the curious incident at the start, a success. A dark thing, but these are dark times. A world has been overturned but there is a promise of renewal, of political hope, of a continuing collective life, and Elizabeth Morton-Stanley has seen to it that this comes through with volume and clarity. With the appearance of Antonio's son in the last moments a flame of *hope* is lit in the Court of Malfi, and it's shared by all those in the theatre who've survived the war years and emerged in one piece. Then, too, it is exhilarating theatre, and on this they are all agreed, for the cast is superb, in particular Vera Grice.

Yes, our Vera. She dominates the drama when she's onstage, and her absence from the stage only sharpens the audience's eagerness to see her again. She is by turns playful, seductive, haughty and tender, and fearless in the face of death: the terror is there, as Vera had realised, but so is serenity. She is a lover, a mother, a tragic sister to a twin brother bent on her destruction. She is impatient of authority, most pointedly the authority of those who would tell her who to love. She is a war hero to an audience weary of war.

When hope has gone they see in her a kind of courage the idea of which they've lived with since September 1939 but been unwilling to call as such, for that's not the British way. But here, now, on a London stage, in a play written more than three hundred years earlier, by an Englishman, they see it on display, and in the inarticulate depths of their weary souls they exult. What other country in Europe has stood firm against the Nazis?

What other has given not an inch, collaborated not at all, been never occupied, has fought on to the bitter end and from the ruins emerged victorious? The Duchess of Malfi is the defiant antagonist of a demented megalomaniac with absolute power over life and death. In her they see themselves.

They rise to their feet as one when the play is over and they bring the actors back out, not once, not twice but time and again, and there might have been more had they not all been so eager to get a glass in their hands and tell each other what they thought of it. None who was there that night will forget Vera Grice, damp, exhausted, exhilarated, her black hair tumbling over the diaphanous white gown in which she was murdered in Act IV, holding the hands of Harry Catermole on her right, and Ed Colefax on her left, and each of them clutching the next one's hand, the actors in a line that stretches from one side of the stage all the way to the other, and a second rank behind them. They look to Vera for the bow and as her head drops, so do theirs.

Later, in Vera's dressing room, the mood is giddy. The place is crowded. Elizabeth Morton-Stanley dispenses glasses of champagne and on her face there's an expression rarely seen before even by Sidney Temple, who has been crying. Julius and Gustl stand together at the far end of the dressing room enjoying Vera in her glory and determined that she know nothing yet of her mother's wild lament. As for Frank Stone, he is similarly committed to silence in this matter. His guilt about Joan is the mere shadow of a blemish on what is, for him, otherwise a night of accomplishment, for his Malateste was warmly received, in particular his *Oh sad disaster*.

Later still this glorious night, in Congreve's Grill in Covent Garden, Vera asks Julius where her mother is and he tells her that she's tired and sends her love, and will speak to her in the morning. It is a big, happy table, and the restaurant had risen to its collective feet when the company first swept in. Vera is oddly calm, and Julius, watching her, sees something in his wife that he hasn't seen before, a mood, an attitude, signalled in her temperate demeanour amid the raucous good cheer of the actors around her, and he believes that for the first time she is taking responsibility for her genius. Frank Stone sees it and never forgets it. He will in his own time know it too.

When Gustl rings the doorbell in Archibald Street the next morning, Joan comes down to let her in. The question she wants answered at once is whether or not Vera knows.

– No, says Gustl, she does not.

– Thank Christ for that.

She leads her friend upstairs and into the kitchen. Now she wants to know how it went, for she hasn't been out for the newspapers. Gustl tells her how many curtain calls they had and Joan's hands fly to her mouth.

– It can't be—

– *Sieben,* she says, showing seven fingers.

Joan sinks onto her chair.

– Then it's going to be all right.

– Now you have to tell me, love, says Gustl, what happened last night.

Joan busies herself with the kettle. Gustl, who has seen the ghost behind Joan's eyes, now wonders why her discovery of Gricey's involvement with the fascists did not destroy her illusions, why it didn't expose him to her as someone other than the man she'd loved all those years, and not the man whose spirit, in the wild delusion of her grief, she'd tried so very hard to sustain in the world. Why did the whole rickety structure not fall down? Why the *haunting?*

Ah, but in the end, Gustl then thought, watching her friend make the tea, and catching the odour of grief, oh, such a very desperate grief – we smelled it, didn't we, ladies? – Gustl thought: what did it matter, in the end? Couldn't she love a fascist? Many women loved a fascist. She herself had loved a fascist once, briefly, in 1937. Who is to tell us who we can love? Which is what *The Duchess* is all about, in the end.

She left Joan an hour later, troubled that what seemed most to concern Joan now was Vera finding out what happened in the theatre, what she'd done.

– She will think I'm mad.

– *Für einige Zeit macht der Tod Wahnsinnige aus uns allen.*

– English! Dear god, Auntie!

– Death makes us all for a time mad, said Gustl.

They'd sat across the kitchen table and Joan had then seized her friend's hands and told her it changed nothing, that she would come to the meeting, she would speak from the platform; they must go on. Gustl was surprised.

This she hadn't been expecting. She didn't understand why their conversation had produced this sudden insistence on keeping her promise to Julius and speaking at the meeting, but was glad of it all the same.

Vera in fact did hear a whisper about there being a disturbance in the theatre on the first night. She paid no attention to it. But three days later her dresser let slip the truth, saying she hoped her mother was feeling better.
– What?
Vera was half naked in front of her mirror. She was made up for the stage. A stocking cap was pinned tightly to her skull in preparation for the wig. The dresser was lacing up her corset, and she at once realised that Vera didn't know.
– What do you mean, feeling better, Janet?
Then out it had to come.

Frank Stone had tried to make his peace with Willy Ogilvie but Willy was not to be placated. It had not escaped him that Frank was receiving favourable mentions in the glowing notices the play received. Willy knew that he could have done what Frank was doing with Malateste, and he resented it. Such grievances can bite deep into the tender tissue of an actor's heart. But Frank, he had no worries now. For they remembered his Malvolio, those whose job it was to be aware of such things, and now they saw him make something fresh of Count Malateste. An actor to keep your eye on, they said. And backstage too there was a new respect, and most gratifying was the warmth he felt coming from Vera. Until Friday.

On Friday in her dressing room Vera heard that her mother had almost ruined the first curtain. After the show she sent for Frank, and when her visitors had left she told him to stay. She asked him what he knew about her mother on opening night and Frank pretended to know nothing. Vera was at once angry. She told him not to treat her like an idiot and to please just answer the question.

Frank was sitting as usual on the edge of the armchair with his hands clasped between his knees. His feet were wide apart and his head was hanging. She was cleaning her face and watching him in her mirror. Now she turned in her chair and faced him. She'd put a sweater on over the gown she wore to be strangled in. The theatre was very cold after the show.

– The question is, *Frank,* why did my mum start shouting before the first show?

– I don't know.

– Try.

– I think she's angry with your father.

– Why? My father's dead.

– I think that's why.

Frank was groping in the dark here, but then so was Vera. She had to agree he was probably right. But she hadn't finished with him.

– You haven't helped matters, have you?

Frank deserved this, he knew.

– My father was barely in his grave!

– He was cremated.

– She's almost old enough to be your mother.

– I know.

– So why did you do it?

– It just happened. These things happen, Vera. A man, a woman—

Vera stood up and went behind the screen at the far end of the dressing room to change. Her voice, when it came, was disembodied, although as she got out of her gown Frank could see parts of her actual body in the mirror.

– What are you going to do now?

– Nothing! I'm sorry it happened at all.

– Not good enough, Frank.

She emerged from behind the screen buttoning her blouse over her brassiere and Frank didn't turn away.

– I want you to comfort her, she said.

Frank didn't know what to say.

– That's what she needs and who else is going to do it?

– What about you?

– Don't be so fucking daft, she needs a man. Anyway I'm busy right now if you hadn't noticed.

Frank didn't like to say that he was busy too. He agreed to go and see Joan and comfort her.

– You'll have to tell me what happens. Everything.

– Yes, Vera.

– All right. Is the pub still open?

– We might get a quick one in.

– Come on then.

26

IT HAPPENED DURING what they called the graveyard
scene in Act V. Antonio and Delio were under the
walls of the ruins of an ancient abbey. The stage was
dark, the atmosphere distinctly eerie, for the Duchess,
who unknown to Antonio has already been murdered,
will be heard as an echo. Antonio at one point says: *Echo,
I will not talk with thee/For thou art a dead thing*.

And comes the Echo: *Thou art a dead thing*.

Antonio, unnerved, turns away, takes a few steps – takes
one too many – and falls off the stage. He lands in the
orchestra pit and almost destroys the bassoon. The curtain descends on the graveyard scene and the house lights
come up.

There is a rapid conference backstage. Harry Catermole can put no weight on the leg, so Frank will cover
Antonio and be stabbed in the next scene by Bosola, who
tells him as he lies dying that his wife the Duchess and

two of their children have been murdered. Frank makes a last speech and a few seconds later his body is carried out to the accompaniment of a funeral march from the percussion section of the orchestra with much bass drum. A deep solemn silence in the auditorium.

In the last scene Willy Ogilvie takes over Count Malateste, and Grisolan is played by an unemployed Madman. Frank, standing in the wings, hears Willy imitate his *Oh sad disaster,* but misses the sardonic languor that he himself perfected, and the laughter is uncertain. It hardly matters. The play ends with the arrival of Antonio's son. The audience rises to its feet, delirious.

Meanwhile backstage a doctor has been called in. It doesn't look good. Frank Stone is among the cast members clustered in the door of Harry's dressing room. Harry himself is seated with his hose off and the bare leg stretched across a chair. Swelling is already apparent. The doctor turns to the company manager and tells him that this man will be off for several weeks. He's lucky not to have broken it.

A kind of groan is heard from the actors in the doorway. There are expressions of condolence. Harry turns to them and speaks in tragic cadences.

– I told them it was too dark, he cries, but did they listen?

But the indignation soon fades. There's nothing to be done. A couple of actors glance at Frank, who sadly shakes his head, but inwardly he's exulting. The rest of them know it. They'd be the same.

*

If only Gricey were going to die. But Gricey would never die, of this Joan grew more certain every day she heard him in the wardrobe, and she heard him in the wardrobe often now. How he must have hated her, this was what she thought, and not for the first time. This was the intolerable thought. This was what broke her heart, and thinking it she would have to sit down, or lie down on the couch, or her bed, and the sobs would rack her body until she was exhausted. Then she'd get up and go about her tasks, and ask herself how much longer she could carry this burden, the knowledge that whatever it was she'd done to Gricey, all unknowing, it had aroused such hatred in him. Poor Joan, it never occurred to her that it had nothing to do with her. He hated her because he could. He'd have hated anyone. It was the fascist way.

She attended *The Duchess of Malfi* for the second time. She pretended to be an old woman. She was bent and gaunt with her mittened fingers clasping the upturned collar at her throat. She took her seat in the gallery, and when the house lights went down her eyes darted about the auditorium, but no, Gricey wasn't present, or not yet. She watched her daughter with real pleasure, and sadness, and anxiety, and she clapped with enthusiasm at the end of each act.

It was not until Antonio suffered his unscheduled accident in the orchestra pit that she became alarmed. She had grown sensitive to the untoward. She had begun to think there were no accidents now. The discovery of his fascist pin was just the start of it. Now she recognised Frank Stone coming on, saw him replace the other man, the injured one. She watched him coldly as he took up the part of Antonio, and was at first bitter to think that he would now play the husband of Vera, as once he'd played her father, that is, when he took Gricey's role as Malvolio.

She didn't go round to see Vera afterwards. Instead she slipped away and rode home through the dark streets with less composure than once she'd shown in the saddle, careless in the handling of the large bicycle such that she drew the attention of two policemen, but was not apprehended. Furiously she pedalled through the East End then past the cemetery, and St Clement's, and into Archibald Street where she rattled over the wet cobbles to her own front door. She swiftly unlocked it then wheeled her bicycle in, and left it on its side in the hallway under the stairs.

She was soon in her kitchen and before she'd even taken her coat off she'd got the bottle out of the cupboard, and only after strong fortification did she feel able to go into Gricey's room and kick the hated wardrobe, and shout at it a few times, but he wasn't to be roused tonight, being elsewhere, as she supposed, and with something like triumph in her voice she wished him bad dreams then turned off the light and locked the door and returned to the kitchen.

Frank had promised Vera he would visit her mother, and the following morning he did. She was surprised to see him; shocked, even.

– Mr Stone? she said when she opened the front door. What are you doing here? Never mind, come in, it's raining.

For days it had been raining. Frank did not own an umbrella but he did have a decent raincoat, courtesy of Gricey, also his black fedora. In he came, and it was only with some effort of will that he did not at once tell her his good news. She knew it already, of course.

Joan set off up the stairs, Frank following. He'd pushed the hat to the back of his head, in what he considered a slightly raffish manner, as befitted his mood, and unbuttoned the overcoat so it flapped about his legs. There had been times, and not so long before, when he'd had eyes only for the sleek swells and curves of Joan's hips and bum, a glimpse of long pale fingers on the banister, and the rather severe chignon which clung to her white swan's neck, just a few stray wisps escaping, so that by the time they'd ascended the staircase to the first-floor landing, more had risen—

But this was not the case today. Frank had come to make amends. He'd been rehearsing his speech on the bus. He felt sure it would be well received. He would then go back to Vera and tell her that he had done what she'd asked him to.

– You want a cup of tea, I suppose.

He didn't immediately recognise her tone of voice. He knew her tender mood, he knew her affectionate, maternal mood, and he'd felt, too, the quiet pushing whispery intensity that this most private of women had shown him in the darkness of her bed. He'd known her tearful, and he'd known the dry humour in which she indulged when she indulged in dry gin. But this offer of a cup of tea he didn't recognise.

289

– Mrs Grice, I came to tell you—

– Oh you can spare me all that, Mr Stone, I don't have the time for it, frankly. I don't require you to apologise. I imagine my daughter put you up to it, did she?

– She thought you might be—

– Angry. Oh yes. Oh yes, Mr Stone – *Frank* – *Francis* – I *am* angry. I am *very angry indeed*.

She turned from the stove and stared at the actor seated at her kitchen table. His mouth fell open. He did not know what to say. In fact he was for the first time glimpsing what he would later come to think of as a woman in the first stages of a nervous breakdown of some kind, and a stray thought passed through his mind, he knew not where it came from, that we are all born mad and some of us remain so – it hardly matters, it only goes to show that on seeing Joan in her kitchen that morning, the idea of madness suggested itself, and he was bewildered.

– Are you angry with me?

Joan sank laughing onto a kitchen chair.

– You poor dear fool. No, *Franz*, I'm not angry with *you*.

– Then who?

But she had grown weary of him. He spoke in tongues.

– I won't give you a cup of tea. I would like you to leave.

– But Joan—

She stood up and leaning forward, with her hands spread across the table, she stared at him with fierce hatred and as she did so, she groped for the breadboard, which was at the end of the table, and then as her fingers

290

closed on the bread knife Frank Stone knew beyond a shadow of a doubt that he was being threatened, and felt himself to be at risk, for she frightened him now. He was never sure precisely what happened after that, for his next memory is of standing in the middle of Archibald Street in the rain, then walking rapidly in the direction of the cemetery and the bus stop. He'd left his hat behind.

Frank was quiet in the theatre that night. He'd moved his things into the dressing room Harry had been sharing with Ed Colefax, and now he sat at his mirror, distracted. Only when Jasper called the half did he rouse himself and begin to get ready for the evening performance. He would not tell Vera about his strange encounter with her mother. He didn't know what to say about it.

He knew what to say on the stage of the New Apollo Theatre, however. From his first entrance he was a warmly passionate Antonio, dedicated only to the welfare of the woman he adored. Never had he and Vera acted in front of an audience together, and it escaped the notice of nobody familiar with the production, as it had been played with Harry Catermole, that the temperature was raised a number of degrees. However, to those of us who know about such things, Frank's performance, while spirited, lacked discipline; and Vera thought so too.

Julius Glass meanwhile was a distracted man but not to the extent of forgetting for a moment his wife's triumph in the theatre. He was just as pleased to know that his investment in the production was proving sound, for the advances were good. It was Gustl who mentioned to him the power of the onstage chemistry.

– Julius, she said, darkly, they are liking each other.

They were in the circle bar at the interval, a few nights after Frank took over, the Saturday night in fact. They had come in to see how Harry's cover was getting on. But Julius was never troubled by what his wife did onstage.

27

S HE AWOKE WITH a start. It was a wet morning, that Sunday, the day of the street meeting, and Joan had had a restless night. She'd dreamed about Gricey again, and she knew now where he was hiding. Oh *stupid* woman, she told herself – you should have realised he'd do this! But it hadn't occurred to her. It was very bad. She had to go over there and confront him, tell him to *leave Vera alone*. But not yet. She sat at her sewing machine and worked on a length of parachute silk that had come into her possession. She was making a pair of slacks for Vera. Oh, that girl – she didn't even *know* the danger she was in. Silk slacks weren't enough but they were something. Joan had no need of a pattern, she just went at the silk with the long draper's shears. She knew Vera liked them baggy so she was adding panels down the seams; you'd have to for silk, anyway. She would use a sharp needle and silk thread, and how lovely they'd be on Vera, and what a nice swishing, scroopy sound they'd make when her thighs rubbed together. Odd not to have the austerity rules any more, she thought, what with limits on how many pleats you could have, how many buttons and so on. Not now. Now she could do what she liked with Vera's slacks, and how nice they'd feel next to the skin because nylon was so clammy, and so much harder to stitch. Silk was slippery but if she only wore them in the bedroom it wouldn't matter. No, you had to have silk.

So ran Joan's restless, anxious, distracted thoughts as she sewed Vera's silk slacks for the bedroom, and the danger grew every moment more real to her. It was a while since she'd made clothes for her daughter, and now it gave her a strange, uneasy comfort. Later she would dye them in the kitchen sink. Old tea leaves in muslin bags, they'd come up lovely—

Then all at once she grew impatient, for there was something that had to be done and she couldn't put it off a second longer. She flung the slacks aside, abruptly left the sewing room and got her coat and hat on. Soon she was on her bicycle. A light rain was falling. It was ten thirty in the morning when she arrived at the house in Lupus Mews. Gustl came to the door.

– Hello *Liebste,* I did not know you were so early coming. Julius is I think not ready.

– No no, I must just go up to Vera's room.

They were in the hallway and Gustl was trying to get Joan's wet coat and hat off her but Joan wouldn't let her, in too big a hurry she was. Gustl told her that Vera now slept, not in the attic, but with her husband.

Then Joan was climbing up through the house in her wet coat, up the stairs to the attic, where she stood in the doorway of the small room with the slanted ceiling and the old beams and the dormer window. The floorboards were bare but for a raffia rug by the bed. The bed had been stripped. There was a wardrobe in there now, an old black thing pushed up against the wall across from the bed, one door hanging open. But Joan had no interest in this wardrobe, it was the space under the rafters she wanted. She crossed the floor and lifted the latch. She peered into the darkness and knew at once she was right: morbid spiritual residue. She could smell it.

– I'm coming in *now*, she said, and with lowered head she entered.

She pulled the door closed behind her. She was in there for some time. When she came downstairs again she looked exhausted. She would say nothing of what she'd been doing upstairs, and soon after, with Gustl and Julius, she left for Hackney.

Actors don't usually work on a Sunday but Vera wants to do more with the wooing scene. Only once during rehearsal had Frank Stone stood in as Antonio, so he'd missed all the work she and Harry had done. Vera realises that's why he comes in too strong too soon. He peaks when she puts her ring on his trembling finger, and then has nowhere to go in the last three pages, which involve kisses, a hasty marriage, then exit. Vera wants the audience to know that these two will *explode* if they can't get into a bedroom *now*.

So she asks Frank to come round to Lupus Mews to work on the scene. Julius and Gustl will be out on Sunday afternoon, and they'll have the house to themselves. It takes Frank about half a second to say yes to this suggestion. When he appears Vera brings him into the kitchen, where her script lies open on the table, middle of Act I, scene i. Frank tells her he was in the wings watching Harry every night, when he wasn't onstage himself.

– I'm trying to give you everything he did, he says.

– No, says Vera, not what I want at all, Frank. He was like a block of wood and from you I want more.

– More what?

– Feeling, you fool. Fucking electricity, Frank.

Frank finds it hard at times not to laugh when Vera is cross with him.

– I need you *dirty*. But not immediately. Do you see?

She takes his hand and draws it towards her groin. Her eyes never leave his face. He almost touches her, then all at once she pushes him away! She then draws his hand in once more, still closer to her body now – shallow breaths, tongue on her lip, mouth open, eyes on his face – then away again – dropping his hand only when she sees he understands.

– Dirty, he says.

– Yes, darling.

They're standing in the kitchen, him having struggled out of his coat, and her padding back and forth in her plimsolls, leggings and big grey jersey, with her hair up in a leaky bun.

– So let's start with Cariola going behind the arras.

You enter, I say: I sent for you. Sit down; take pen and ink and write.

She looks up. Frank sits down. Yes, he says, and picks up a pen and makes as if to write. Off they go. Frank soon grasps the movement and feeling of the scene the way Vera wants it – that is, the push and pull of sexual electricity as the current shifts and surges between them. On the third run-through it begins to feel like a dance, and to those watching them – that would be us, of course – they do seem to be dancing, and if at first it had been a minuet, it soon becomes a quickening waltz, as formality vanishes and the scene impels them ever closer together, until at last they stand panting in the kitchen, damp with the effort and delighted with themselves and each other.

It's then they hear voices in the hall.

Vera throws open the kitchen door and cries out. At the end of the hall a tall man covered in blood leans groaning against the front door. He's clinging to Julius' shoulder. With his other hand he presses a bloody hand-kerchief to his face. He and Julius now lurch towards the kitchen, Julius holding up this injured man who's unable, it's now clear, to put any weight on one leg. Frank is there at once, and he and Julius between them somehow get him into the kitchen, and onto a chair, where he lays his head on the table, wheezing in pain.

– Some entrance, darling, says Vera, gazing at the bloody man in their kitchen. She knows him, of course, this is Peter Ryder, who now lifts his head off the table and asks her if she's got a cigarette. Vera's already on the telephone. She tells him that what he needs isn't a bloody cigarette, it's a bloody doctor.

When a doctor's been summoned, and Frank has poured everyone a whisky, Julius tells them what happened. He stares at the floor through much of the account. Many more people had showed up than anyone had anticipated. There were a lot of fascists, and a lot of people who hated fascists, and then another crowd who thought it was all a bit of theatre, a bit of a lark. But there was tension in the air all right, said Julius. The sun came out very late in the afternoon, he said, and the light was strange after the rain, with the dusk coming on, a ghostly sort of damply drizzled half-light, really, with some kind of a rainbow in the west, off towards Hampstead, but not much of one, more an excuse for a rainbow, really—

Julius faltered; he paused. Still staring at the floor he lifted his eyebrows, as though in some slight surprise. Peter Ryder threw back his whisky, pushed his glass across the table and asked for another one. He smoked, groaning.

– Where's that bloody doctor? Vera said, and went off down the hall to see if he was in the mews. When she returned Julius continued.

– Then that idiot appeared, he said.

– What idiot?

– Edgar Cartridge. He came in the van. He was wearing the uniform.

– Oh Christ, that's against the law—!

– He should have been arrested. They should have got

him straight out of there. It set something off in her, made her furious, I don't know what. The boots, the belt—

– Set something off in who?

Julius gazed at Vera for a second or two, with a terrible *pity*, so it seemed to us.

– Your mother.

– What did she do, Julius? *Julius?*

– She had a pair of scissors.

– Oh Christ, no—

– In her handbag. The long sharp ones for cutting material.

– Oh Jesus, no, don't tell me!

Vera's hands flew to her face.

– She was standing by the stage, she was waiting to go on, she was going to talk to the crowd but I could see she was in a bad way—

Vera was on her feet now and Julius was growing tearful.

– I don't know, darling, she was, oh, she was demented, and I'd just stepped away for a second and Gustl was with her when Edgar Cartridge appeared all in blackshirt and he gave her a bit of a shock—

– I can't bear this!

– I mean he jostled her, she stumbled and then when – well, she got the shears out of her bag and she just *stabbed* him.

– No.

– Just like that. Pulled them out of her bag and stuck him in the stomach, it was all so quick and poor Gustl, she had no chance to stop her—

Julius sat down. Vera was standing at the sink staring at him.

– She *stabbed* him? But—

Frank stared at Julius with his mouth open. Peter Ryder had his elbows on the table and his face in his hands. Julius gazed at his wife with the tears now streaming down his cheeks.

28

RIDLEY ROAD IS a busy market street in Hackney. It runs into Dalston Lane at one end and Kingsland High Street at the other. At the Kingsland end it opens out into a square that could hold five thousand, and that Sunday afternoon, when Charlie Grice's widow was to speak from the stage, the fascists were there early to secure their pitch. Frederic Bacon expected trouble and he'd brought in a lot of young toughs, Mosley boys mostly, BUF street soldiers who still had uniforms in their wardrobes, which by law they were now forbidden to wear. There'd be a big crowd so they planned to distribute their *literature,* but just that morning a problem had arisen: there *was* no *literature.* There was no printed matter at all! It had been shifted out of the warehouse at dead of night, and gone up in flames on a lonely bomb site in Dulwich. That was Karsh's work, for which he'd relied on Julius' intelligence, much of it supplied by Peter Ryder.

Two dozen of Karsh's hardest men were selected for the assault on the platform, with thirty more in support. They would come to the meeting in groups of five, and after Joan had done her piece they would attack the platform in wedges. None of them was happy about it. They all had a bad feeling about it, although, since she'd arrived, Joan was now strangely calm. But that was just dread, or so Gustl thought.

Julius left the car in Hackney and they walked in from Sandringham Road. Hundreds were already in the square when they arrived. The fascists around the platform were silent, spooked. They looked over at the uniformed police lined up along the shopfronts. Fascists and coppers, they were as edgy as each other. All the shouting came from the crowd.

Later that day, in the house in Lupus Mews, you could hear a pin drop. Julius was paralysed by the heaving gravitational mass of the monstrous tragic event he'd witnessed. Vera was impatient.

– Then what happened, Julius, for Christ's sake!

He looked up, blinking and smeared a hand across his face.

– He was vomiting blood.

Each of them in their own mind saw the astonished fascist, down on his knees beside the platform, clutching his stomach and choking.

– We had a doctor but there wasn't much he could do . . .

Julius drifted off again.

– Word got round fast, he said. The police were moving people away. Nobody felt like fighting, or giving speeches—

– Where was my mum?

Julius gazed at his wife.

– In the back of a police car.

– Was there an ambulance?

– Oh yes.

– Where is she now?

– At the nick. Stoke Newington.

– I want to see her, Julius.

– Yes, of course.

The police station was on the High Street and as they approached in the Wolseley, Julius and Vera, with Frank in the back, they saw remnants of the crowd hanging around outside the pubs, still somehow caught up in the horror of this thing that had happened earlier. There'd never been a death before. Did it mean the end of it? There were rocks and bricks and overturned dustbins in the street. Gustl was in the police station waiting for them. There were tearful cries of desolation when they found her there, but they weren't allowed to see Joan. The desk sergeant told them to wait. It was after eight at night by this time, and reporters were around, but they wouldn't speak to the press, not yet. Peter Ryder had been taken to Casualty to have his injuries seen to. Worst of it, he'd taken a deep cut the length of his face from a razored potato.

They sat on hard chairs in an ill-lit waiting room. It was cold. Vera at least had her fur coat. The sergeant brought them cups of tea. They heard shouts from the street and could only think that fascists were still wandering around out there. Time dragged. The desk sergeant told them nothing. Vera imagined her mother sitting in a bare room with bars on the window, and she couldn't hold back a cry. Julius at once put his arm around her and she sobbed into his chest as he stroked her head.

At midnight they were told that Vera and Julius could go down to the cells. They were met in the narrow stairwell by a bearded man in a black suit who introduced himself as Dr Strathclyde and told them he was a psychiatrist.

– Doctor—

– Yes?

He was impatient. It was late.

– What's wrong with her?

– Delusional insanity. She's psychotic. I don't want her any more agitated—

Then there's a cry from below. Vera pushes past him—

– than she is already—

She rushes blindly down the stairs. She screams and it echoes through those dank police cells and up the stairwell. She is standing in the doorway of her mother's cell with her hands lifted to her face. Julius joins her. In the cell he sees Joan Grice splayed sideways, recumbent, on a wooden bench pushed up against the wall. One arm is hanging limp to the stone floor, fingers trailing. Her hair is unkempt, her eyes are open, as is her coat, and so is the front of her blouse, with several buttons undone, and on the inside of her left breast is what looks like a small silver coin around which blood is pooling and staining the material and dripping onto the floor. Her hat lies upside down nearby.

The doctor pushes past them into the cell. He goes down on one knee and with thumb and forefinger touches the silver coin. It is the head of a hatpin. He does not withdraw it: to do so would surely kill her, that is, if she's not dead already. The hatpin has penetrated the pericardial membrane of her heart and is acting as a plug, and he doesn't know how far it's gone in. He lightly slaps her cheek but Joan's eyes don't close. They remain fixed, staring, ghastly.

– Can you hear me, Mrs Grice?

He bends over her and lays his ear against her breast, with his fingers on her wrist. A few seconds pass. Then he straightens up and turns to Julius and Vera.

29

SHE DIDN'T HAVE a large funeral in Golders Green, as Gricey did. She wouldn't have liked that. She didn't want a service in a synagogue either, but that's what Vera wanted. And she knew the one she wanted, it was that modest place of worship in the deserted park near Lupus Mews where she and Joan had walked together more than once that winter, and where Vera had told her mother about the creeping man she'd seen at the bottom of the garden. The synagogue had since been whitewashed by unknown benefactors, so it was no longer defaced by swastikas or other fascist insignia.

It was a small domed structure with a Romanesque arch over the front doors. Inside, a few benches with a central aisle between them were placed parallel to the side walls, which were unadorned. On the eastern wall stood the sanctuary ark, concealed by a curtain. The floor was of cold grey fieldstone. The Jewish congregation in Pimlico was never large, and preferred these days to worship in one of the grander West London synagogues. It was in one of those that Julius had found a rabbi willing to conduct Joan's funeral service. The building seated no more than sixty, but less than half that number attended. The day was damp and there was mist in the trees. The sky was grey. The funeral was scheduled for four o'clock on a Sunday afternoon.

It was not a long service. Julius spoke for a few minutes. Gustl of course was there, it was she who'd sat up in the front room in Lupus Mews and prepared the body for the hearse. She and Vera had ridden with Julius in the Wolseley, and were met at the synagogue by the rabbi, also by Frank Stone and his mother. Also present were Esther and Eunice from the costume shop of the Beaumont, and others from the London theatre world. Mabel Hatch was there, Hattie Waterstone, Ed Colefax. Jimmy Urquhart. Sir John sent flowers, as did Delphie Dix. And two more, from a different world: Karsh was there, grey-faced, solemn, his patchy hair scraped flat with grease and his pale eyes opaque, almost milky. He and Joan had become close friends towards the end of her life.

Beside him with a livid scar the length of his sallow face sat Peter Ryder. Also present, a Hungarian in a green tweed overcoat, there to pay his respects and give comfort: Gabor Szirtes, the cellist.

Joan was in a simple pine box. It was a closed coffin, and when it came time, six men including Julius and Frank, and Peter Ryder, and Karsh, lifted it easily onto their shoulders and brought it through the cold mist into the overgrown cemetery behind the synagogue. A few flowers had struggled to life since the snow melted, a snowdrop, a crocus, but there was little foliage in the old elms that hung over the gravestones in the fading light.

A curious exchange had occurred earlier. As the family entered the synagogue, Julius had murmured to Vera, who leaned on his arm, her head veiled and lowered, oh, and her spirit a good deal less bold and stoic than it had been for her father's funeral three months earlier – *and why a synagogue?*

Vera didn't look up, and her answer was barely audible.

– Show Daddy what's what.

Vera crouched to scoop up a handful of soil from the heap at the head of the grave. Still not a tear, not a sound. Near the wall there was some shuffling among the strangers who had gathered there. Vera all at once flung the soil onto the coffin then rose to her feet, and stumbling a little, with a loud sob fell into the arms of her husband.

Gustl then stepped up and threw in a handful of soil, and after her came Frank Stone, and then his mother, who never had the chance to bury her own husband, or hear Kaddish said over his grave. Karsh came forward and so did Peter Ryder, as Vera had asked them to, and they too threw soil onto the coffin. The murmuring of the rabbi continued throughout, and then they were done. The family and their friends moved away from the grave, towards the synagogue and the cars.

Over by the wall, beneath the trees, by ones and twos

the others left the cemetery and were swallowed in the gathering gloom. Only one remained. A minute passed, then two. The place was empty, deserted. No workman had yet appeared to fill in the new-dug grave. He was a boy, the one who was left, and now he emerged from the deeper shadows under the trees into the last of the misty afternoon. But wait – we know him! We know him. He's the brother, he's Hughie, he's the little brother of the dead fascist, Edgar Cartridge! And look, he's approaching the grave. His hand is on the lapel of his raincoat, and now he stands at the edge of Joan's grave and from his lapel he unpins a badge. He tosses it into the grave, where it lands among the small heaps of soil on the coffin.

Now we can see it – and it's *that* badge, the one that caused all the trouble, Edgar had one, Gricey had one, they all did. White lightning on blue, and now it's in Joan's grave, flung down there in scorn and anger – and oh, poor Joan, that she should have to see that! Oh, we despair of them, don't we, ladies, and none of us more so than Joan herself! Well, she's with us now, isn't she? Of course she is. We tell her it's finished, it's all over, but what do we know? We're just the ladies of the Chorus.

The boy stands there a moment longer, and then with some deliberation he leans over – and he spits into the open grave. What a dirty little bugger he is. Gazing down now at what he's done, he wipes his mouth with the back of his hand as though he's some sort of a hero. Silly cunt. Then for some moments he doesn't move. Just stands there. He turns, at last, to our not inconsiderable relief, and walks off through the deserted cemetery. His manner is sombre, funereal. He holds his right arm by his side, oddly, the hand in a black leather glove now, with the fingers pointing straight down, in a rigid vertical salute.

that, Harriet! I also learned a lot about how Malvolio might be played from John Lithgow, by way of Neil Bartlett, who also taught me all about understudies.

Thanks so much, Neil.

Courtesy of Peter Carey at Hunter College, my reality instructor, and through him the Hertog Fellowship, I've had an annual supply of very smart, resourceful research assistants. Brian Harkin, Jack Austin, Danny Lorberbaum and Josh Krigman, thank you all very much. And belated big thanks to my good friend Lynne Tillman, particularly for her warm support and clear insight during my writing of *Constance*.

I'd like also to acknowledge a great debt to Morris Beckman's fascinating book *The 43 Group: Battling with Mosley's Blackshirts*, published by The History Press of Stroud, UK. It opened the door.

And Jocasta Hamilton! – who edited this novel with tact and taste and consummate skill, and to whom I'm very grateful *indeed*. You've made me a better writer.

But my greatest thanks of course go to my wife Maria Aitken, a creature of the theatre from the age of four. She answered my questions at all hours of the day and night and without her, yet again, my work would be a thin thing indeed: as would my life.

Patrick McGrath
New York
March 2017

314

Acknowledgements

First I must thank Nancy Hamann, who is Costume Director at the Huntington Theatre in Boston. For many months she answered my questions, and always with great warmth and expertise. She also gave me an extensive guided tour of her own department, which was hugely helpful. Diana Toman, with good humour and much subtle shading of meaning, gave me all the German I required to voice my brave refugee painter, Gustl Herzfeld. Gustl's work as described in these pages was inspired by the paintings of Marie-Louise von Motesiczky, who fled the Nazis in 1938 and later settled in Hampstead. Numerous actors and directors gave me a hand, among them Julie Legrand, Giles Havergal, Jefferson Mays, Dame Susan Lyons and Edward Hibbert, all of whom I'd like to thank. I plundered a very good and useful essay about playing the lead in *The Duchess of Malfi*, written by my friend Harriet Walter, so ta very much for